The Forever Girl

ALEXANDER McCALL SMITH

The Forever Girl

Polygon

THIS BOOK IS FOR
NEIL AND JUDY SWAN

First published in Great Britain in 2014 by
Polygon, an imprint of Birlinn Ltd
West Newington House
10 Newington Road
Edinburgh
EH9 1QS

www.polygonbooks.co.uk

ISBN 978-1-84697-229-4

British Library Cataloguing-in-Publication Data
A catalogue record for this book is available on
request from the British Library

Typeset by Studio Monachino
Printed and bound in Australia by Griffin Press

Part One

I

I have often wondered about the proposition that for each of us there is one great love in our lives, and one only. Even if that is not true – and experience tells most of us it is not – there are those, in legend at least, who believe there is only one person in this world whom they will ever love with all their heart. Tristan persisted in his love of Isolde in spite of everything; Orpheus would not have risked the Underworld, one imagines, for anyone but Eurydice. Such stories are touching, but the cynic might be forgiven for saying: yes, but what if the person you love does not reciprocate? What if Isolde had found somebody she preferred to Tristan, or Eurydice had been indifferent to Orpheus?

The wise thing to do in cases of unreturned affection is to look elsewhere – you cannot force another to love you – and to choose somebody else. In matters of the heart, though, as in all human affairs, few of us behave in a sensible way. We can do without love, of course, and claim it does not really play a major part in our lives. We may do that, but we still hope. Indifferent to all the evidence, hope has a way of surviving every discouragement, every setback or reversal; hope sustains us, enables us to believe we will find the person we have wanted all along.

Sometimes, of course, that is exactly what happens.

This story started when the two people involved were children. It began on a small island in the Caribbean, continued in Scotland, and in Australia, and came to a head in Singapore. It took place over sixteen years, beginning as one of those intense friendships of childhood and becoming, in time, something quite different. This is the story of that passion. It is a love story, and like most love stories it involves more than just two people, for every love has within it the echoes of other loves. Our story is often our parents' story, told again, and with less variation than we might like to think. The mistakes, as often as not, are exactly the same mistakes our parents made, as human mistakes so regularly are.

The Caribbean island in question is an unusual place. Grand Cayman is still a British territory, by choice of its people rather than by imposition, one of the odd corners that survive from the monstrous shadow that Victoria cast over more than half the world. Today it is very much in the sphere of American influence – Florida is only a few hundred miles away, and the cruise ships that drop anchor off George Town usually fly the flag of the United States, or are American ships under some other flag of convenience. But the sort of money that the Cayman Islands attract comes from nowhere; has no nationality, no characteristic smell.

Grand Cayman is not much to look at, either on the map, where it is a pin-prick in the expanse of blue to the south of Cuba and the west of Jamaica, or in reality, where it is a coral-reefed island barely twenty miles long and a couple of miles in width. With smallness come some advantages, amongst them a degree of immunity to the hurricanes that roar through the Caribbean each year. Jamaica is a large and tempting target for these winds, and is hit quite regularly. There is no justice in the storms that flatten the houses of the poor in places like Kingston or Port Antonio, wood and tin constructions so much more vulnerable than the bricks and mortar of the better-off. Grand Cayman, being relatively minuscule, is usually missed, although every few decades the trajectory of a hurricane takes it straight across the island. Because there are no natural salients, much of the land is inundated by the resultant storm surge. People may lose their every possession to the wind – cars, fences, furniture and fridges, animals too, can all be swept out to sea and never seen again; boats end up in trees; palm trees bend double and are broken with as much ease as one might snap a pencil or the stem of a garden plant.

Grand Cayman is not fertile. The soil, white and sandy, is not much use for growing crops, and indeed the land, if left to its own devices, would quickly revert to mangrove swamp. Yet people have occupied the island for several centuries, and scratched a living there. The original inhabitants were turtle-hunters. They were later joined by various pirates and wanderers for whom a life far away from the prying eye of officialdom was attractive. There were fishermen, too, as this was long before over-fishing was an issue, and the reef brought abundant marine life.

Then, in the second half of the twentieth century, it occurred to a small group of people that Grand Cayman could become an off-shore financial centre. As a British territory it was stable, relatively incorrupt (by the standards of Central America and the shakier parts of the Caribbean), and its banks would enjoy the tutelage of the City of London. Unlike some other states that might have nursed similar ambitions, Grand Cayman was an entirely safe place to store money.

"Sort out the mosquitoes," they said. "Build a longer runway. The money will flow in. You'll see. Cayman will take off." Cayman, rather than the Cayman Islands, is what people who live there call the place – an affectionate shortening, with the emphasis on the *man* rather than the *cay*.

Banks and investors agreed, and George Town became the home of a large expatriate community, a few who came as tax exiles, but most of them hard-working and conscientious accountants or trust managers. The locals watched with mixed feelings. They were reluctant to give up their quiet and rather sleepy way of life but found it difficult to resist the prosperity the new arrivals brought. And they liked, too, the high prices they could get for their previously worthless acres. A tiny white-board home by the sea, nothing special, could now be sold for a price that could keep one in comfort for the rest of one's life. For most, the temptation was just too great; an easy life was now within grasp for many Caymanians, as Jamaicans could be brought in to do the manual labour, to serve in the restaurants frequented by the visitors from the cruise ships, to look after the bankers' children. A privileged few were given *status*, as they called it, and were allowed to live permanently on the islands, these being the ones who were really needed, or, in some cases, who knew the right people – the people who could ease the passage of their residence petitions. Others had to return to the places from which they came, which were usually poorer, more dangerous, and more tormented by mosquitoes.

Most children do not choose their own name, but she did. She was born Sally, and was called that as a baby, but at about the age of four, having heard the name in a story, she chose to be called Clover. At first her parents treated this indulgently, believing that after a day or two of being Clover she would revert to being Sally. Children got strange notions into their heads; her mother had read somewhere of a child who had decided for almost a complete week that he was a dog and had insisted on being fed from a bowl on the floor. But Clover refused to go back to being Sally, and the name stuck.

Clover's father, David, was an accountant who had been born and brought up in Scotland. After university he had started his professional training in London, in the offices of one of the large international accountancy firms. He was particularly able – he saw figures as if they were a landscape, instinctively understanding their topography – and this led to his being marked out as a high flier. In his first year after qualification, he was offered a spell of six months in the firm's office in New York, an opportunity he seized enthusiastically. He joined a squash club and it was there, in the course of a mixed tournament, that he met the woman he was to marry.

This woman was called Amanda. Her parents were both psychiatrists, who ran a joint practice on the Upper East Side. Amanda invited David back to her parents' apartment after she had been seeing him for a month. They liked him, but she could tell that they were anxious about her seeing somebody who might take her away from New York. She was an only child, and she was the centre of their world. This young man, this accountant, was likely to be sent back to London, would want to take Amanda with him, and they would be left in New York. They put a brave face on it and said nothing about their fears; shortly before David's six months were up, though, Amanda told her parents that they wanted to become engaged. Her mother wept at the news, although in private.

The internal machinations of the accounting firm came to the rescue. Rather than returning to London, David was to be sent to Grand Cayman, where the firm was expanding its office. This was only three hours' flight from New York – through Miami – and would therefore be less of a separation. Amanda's parents were mollified.

They left New York and settled into a temporary apartment in George Town, arranged for them by the firm. A few months later they found a new house near an inlet called Smith's Cove, not much more than a mile from town. They moved in a week or two before their wedding, which took place in a small church round the corner. They chose this church because it was the closest one to them. It was largely frequented by Jamaicans, who provided an ebullient choir for the occasion, greatly impressing the friends who had travelled down from New York for the ceremony.

Fourteen months later, Clover was born. Amanda sent a photograph to her mother in New York: *Here's your lovely grandchild. Look at her eyes. Just look at them. She's so beautiful – already! At two days!*

"Fond parents," said Amanda's father.

His wife studied the photograph. "No," she said. "She's right."

"Five days ago," he mused. "Born on a Thursday."

"Has far to go ..."

He frowned. "Far to go?"

She explained. "The song. You remember it ... Wednesday's child is full of woe; Thursday's child has far to go ..."

"That doesn't mean anything much."

She shrugged; she had always felt that her husband lacked imagination; so many men did, she thought. "Perhaps that she'll have to travel far to get what she wants. Travel far – or wait a long time, maybe."

He laughed at the idea of paying any attention to such things. "You'll be talking about her star sign next. Superstitious behaviour. I have to deal with that all the time with my patients."

"I don't take it seriously," she said. "You're too literal. These things are fun – that's all."

He smiled at her. "Sometimes."

"Sometimes what?"

"Sometimes fun. Sometimes not."

2

The new parents employed a Jamaican nurse for their child. There was plenty of money for something like this – there is no income tax on Grand Cayman and the salaries are generous. David was already having the prospect of a partnership within three or four years dangled in front of him, something that would have taken at least a decade elsewhere. On the island there was nothing much to spend money on, and employing domestic staff at least mopped up some of the cash. In fact, they were both slightly embarrassed by the amount of money they had. As a Scot, David was frugal in his instincts and disliked the flaunting of wealth; Amanda shared this. She had come from a milieu where displays of wealth were not unusual, but she had never felt comfortable about that. It struck her that by employing this Jamaican woman they would be recycling money that would otherwise simply sit in an account somewhere.

More seasoned residents of the island laughed at this. "Of course you have staff – why not? Half the year it's too hot to do anything yourself, anyway. Don't think twice about it."

Their advertisement in the *Cayman Compass* drew two replies. One was from a Honduran woman who scowled through the interview, which did not last long.

"Resentment," confided David. "That's the way it goes. What are we in her eyes? Rich. Privileged. Maybe we won't find anybody …"

"Can we blame her?"

David shrugged. "Probably not. But can you have somebody who hates you in the house?"

The following day they interviewed a Jamaican woman called

Margaret. She asked a few questions about the job and then looked about the room. "I don't see no baby," she said. "I want to see the baby."

They took her into the room where Clover was lying asleep in her cot. The air conditioner was whirring, but there was that characteristic smell of a nursery – that drowsy, milky smell of an infant.

"Lord, just look at her!" said Margaret. "The little angel."

She stepped forward and bent over the cot. The child, now aware of her presence, struggled up through layers of sleep to open her eyes.

"Little darling!" exclaimed Margaret, reaching forward to pick her up.

"She's still sleepy," said Amanda. "Maybe …"

But Margaret had her in her arms now and was planting kisses on her brow. David glanced at Amanda, who smiled weakly.

He turned to Margaret. "When can you start?"

"Right now," she said. "I start right now."

They had not asked Margaret anything about her circumstances at the interview – such as it was – and it was only a few days later that she told them about herself.

"I was born in Port Antonio," she said. "My mother worked in a hotel, and she worked hard, hard; always working, I tell you. Always. There were four of us – me, my brother and two sisters. My brother's legs didn't work too well and he started to get mixed up with people who dealt in drugs and he went the way they all go. My older sister was twenty then. She worked in an office in town – a good job, and she did it well because she had learned shorthand and everything and never forgot anything. Then one day she just didn't come home. No letter, no message, no nothing, and we sat there and wondered what to think. Nobody saw her, nobody heard from her – just nothing. Then they found her three days later. She was run over, thrown off the road into the bush, I tell you, and the person who did it just drive off – just drive off like that – and say nothing. How can a person do something like that to another person – run over them like they were a dog or something? I think of her every day, I can't help it – every day and wonder why the Lord let that happen. I know he has his reasons, but sometimes it's hard for us to work out what they are.

"Then somebody said to me that I could come to Cayman with her. This woman she was a sort of aunt to me, and she arranged it with some people at the church, she did. I came over and met my husband, who's Caymanian, one hundred per cent. He is a very good man who fixes government fridges. He says that I don't have to work, but I say that I don't want to sit in the house all day and wait for him to come back from fixing fridges. So that's why I've taken this job, you see. That's why."

Amanda listened to this and thought about how suffering could be compressed into a few simple words: *Then one day she just didn't come home* ... But so could happiness: *a good man who fixes fridges* ...

There was a second child, Billy, who arrived after a complicated pregnancy. Amanda went to Miami on the last day the airline would let her fly, and then stayed until they induced labour. Margaret came with David and Clover to pick her up at the airport. She covered the new infant with kisses, just as she had done with Clover.

"He's going to be very strong," she said. "You can tell it straight away with a boy child, you know. You look at him and you say: this one is going to be very strong and handsome."

Amanda laughed. "Surely you can't. Not yet. You can hope for that, but you can't tell."

Margaret shook her head. "But I can. I can always tell."

She was full of such information. She could predict when a storm was coming. "You watch the birds, you see. The birds – they know because they feel it in their feathers. So you watch them – they tell you when a storm is on the way. Every time." And she could tell whether a fish was infected with ciguatera by a simple test she had learned from Jamaicans who claimed it never let them down. "You have to watch those reef fish," she explained. "If they have the illness and you eat them then you get really sick. But you know who can tell whether the fish is sick? Ants. You put the fish down on the ground and you watch the ants. If the fish is clean, they're all over it – if it's got ciguatera, then they walk all the way round that fish, just like this, on their toes – they won't touch it, those ants: they know. They've got sensitive noses. You try it. You'll see."

Amanda said to David: "It could have been very different for Margaret."

"What could?"

"Life. Everything. If she had had the chance of an education."

He was silent. "It's not too late. She could go to night school. There are courses."

Amanda thought this was unlikely. "She works here all day. And then there's Eddie to look after, and those dogs they have."

"It's her life. That's what she wants."

She did not think so. "Do you think people actually want their lives? Or do you think they just accept them? They take the life they're given, I think. Or most of them do."

He had been looking at a sheaf of papers – figures, of course – and he put them aside. "We *are* getting philosophical, aren't we?"

They were sitting outside, by the pool. The water reflected the sky, a shimmer of light blue. She said: "Well, these things are important. Otherwise ..."

"Yes?"

"Otherwise we go through life not really knowing what we want, or what we mean. That's not enough."

"No?"

She realised that she had never talked to him about these things, and now that they were doing so, she suddenly saw that he had nothing to say about such questions. It was an extraordinary moment, and one that later she would identify as the precise point at which she fell out of love with him.

He picked up his papers. A paper clip that had been keeping them together had slipped out of position, and now he manoeuvred it back. "Margaret?" he said.

"What about her?"

"Will she have children of her own?"

She did not answer him at first, and he shot her an interested glance.

"No?" he said. "Has she spoken to you?"

She had, having done so one afternoon, but only after extracting a promise that she would tell nobody. There had been shame, and tears. Two ectopic pregnancies had put paid to her hopes of a family. One of them had almost killed her, such had been the loss of blood. The other had been detected earlier and had been quietly dealt with.

He pressed her to answer. "Well?"

"Yes. I said I wouldn't discuss it."

"Even with me?"

She looked at him. The thought of what she had just felt – the sudden and unexpected insight that had come to her – appalled her. It was just as a loss of faith must be for a priest; that moment when he realises that he no longer believes in God and that everything he has done up to that point – his whole life, really – has been based on something that is not there; the loss, the waste of time, the self-denial, now all for nothing. Was this what happened in a marriage? She had been fond of him – she had imagined that she had loved him – but now, quite suddenly and without any provoking incident, it was as if he were a stranger to her – a familiar stranger, yes, but a stranger nonetheless.

She closed her eyes. She had suddenly seen him as an outsider might see him – as a tall, well-built man who was used to having everything his way, because people who looked like him often had that experience. But he might also be seen as a rather unexciting man, a man of habit, interested in figures and money and not much else. She felt dizzy at the thought of … of what? Years of emptiness ahead? Clover was eight now, and Billy was four. Fifteen years?

She answered his question. "I promised her I wouldn't mention it to anyone, but I assume that she didn't intend you not to know."

He agreed. "People think that spouses know everything. And they usually do, don't they? People don't keep things from their spouse."

She thought there might have been a note of criticism in what he said, even of reproach, but he was smiling at her. And she was asking herself at that moment whether she would ever sleep with another man, while staying with David. If she would, then who would it be?

"No," she said. "I mean yes. I mean they don't. She probably thinks you know."

He tucked the papers into a folder. "Poor woman. She loves kids so much and she can't ... Unfair, isn't it?"

There was an old sea-grape tree beside the pool and a breeze, cool from the sea, was making the leaves move; just a little. She noticed the shadow of the leaves on the ground shifting, and then returning to where it was before. George Collins. If anyone, it would be with him.

She felt a surge of self-disgust, and found herself blushing. She turned away lest he should notice, but he was getting up from his reclining chair and had begun to walk over towards the pool.

"I'm going to have a dip," he said. "It's getting uncomfortable. I hate this heat."

He took off his shirt; he was already wearing swimming trunks. He slipped out of his sandals and plunged into the pool. The splash of the water was as in that Hockney painting, she thought; as white against the blue, as surprised and as sudden as that.

3

George and Alice Collins had little to do with the rest of the expatriates. This was not because they were stand-offish or thought themselves a cut above the others – it was more a case of having different interests. He was a doctor, but unlike most doctors on the island he was not interested in building up a lucrative private practice. He ran a clinic that was mostly used by Jamaicans and Hondurans who had no, or very little, insurance and were not eligible for the government scheme. He was also something of a naturalist and had published a check-list of Caribbean flora and a small book on the ecology of the reef. His wife, Alice, was an artist whose watercolours of Cayman plants had been used on a set of the island's postage stamps. They were polite enough to the money people when they met them on social occasions – inevitably, in a small community, everybody eventually encounters everybody else – but they did not really like them. They had a particular distaste for hedge fund managers whom George regarded as little better than licensed gamblers. These hedge fund managers would probably not have cared about that assessment had they noticed it, which they did not. Money obscured everything else for them: the heat, the sea, the economic life of ordinary people. They did not care about the disapproval of others: wealth, and a lot of it, can be a powerful protector against the resentment of others. Alice shared George's view of hedge fund managers, but her dislikes were even broader: she had a low opinion of just about everybody on the island, with the exception of one or two acquaintances, of whom Amanda was one: the locals for being lazy and materialistic, the expatriates for being energetic and materialistic, and the rest for being uninterested in anything that interested her. She did not want to be there; she wanted to be in London or New York, or even Sydney – where there were art galleries and conversations, and things happened; instead of which, she said, I am here, on this strip of coral in the middle of nowhere with these people I don't really like. It was a mistake, she told herself, ever to come to the Caribbean in the first place. She had been attracted to it by family associations and by the sunsets; but you could not live on either of these, she decided, not if you had ambitions of any sort. *I shall die without ever having a proper exhibition – one that counts – of my work. Nobody will remember me.*

The Collins house was about half a mile away from David and Amanda's house, and reached by a short section of unpaved track. It could be glimpsed from the road that joined George Town to Bodden Town, but only just: George's enthusiasm for the native plants of the Caribbean had resulted in a rioting shrubbery that concealed most of the house from view. Inside the house the style was not so much the *faux* Caribbean style that was popular in many other expatriate homes, but real island décor. George had met Alice in Barbados, where he had gone for a medical conference when he was working in the hospital on Grand Cayman. He had invited her to visit him in the Caymans, and she had done so. They had become engaged and shortly afterwards she left Barbados to join him in George Town, where they had set up their first home together. Much of their furniture came from a plantation house that had belonged to an aunt of hers who had lived there for thirty years and built up a collection of old pieces. Alice was Australian; she had gone to visit the aunt after she had finished her training as a teacher in Melbourne, and had stayed longer than she intended. The aunt, who had been childless, had been delighted to discover a niece whose company she enjoyed. She had persuaded her to stay and had arranged a job for her in a local school. Two years later, though, she had died of a heart attack and had left the house and all its contents to Alice. These had included a slave bell, of which Alice was ashamed, that was stored out of sight in a cupboard. She had almost thrown it away, consigning that reminder of the hated past to oblivion, but had realised that we cannot rid ourselves so easily of the wrongs our ancestors wrought.

They had one son, a boy, who was a month older than Clover. He was called James, after George's own father, who had been a professor of medicine in one of the London teaching hospitals. Alice and Amanda had met when they were pregnant, when they both attended a class run in a school hall in George Town by a natural childbirth enthusiast. Amanda already knew that she was not a candidate for a natural delivery, but she listened with interest to accounts of birthing pools and other alternatives, knowing, of course, that what lay ahead for her was the sterile glare of a specialist obstetric unit in Miami.

Friendships forged at such classes, like those made by parents waiting at the school gate, can last, and Alice and Amanda continued to see one another after the birth of their children. George had a small sailing boat, and had once or twice taken David out in it, although David did not like swells – he had a propensity to sea-sickness – and they did not go far. From time to time Amanda and Alice played singles against one another at the tennis club, but it was often too hot for that unless one got up early and played as dawn came up over the island.

It was not a very close friendship, but it did mean that Clover and James knew of one another's existence from the time that each of them first began to be aware of other children. And in due course, they had both been enrolled at the small school, the Cayman Prep, favoured by expatriate families. The intake that year was an unusually large one, and so they were not in the same class, but if for any reason Amanda or Alice could not collect her child at the end of the school day, a ride home with the other parent was guaranteed. Or sometimes Margaret, who drove a rust-coloured jeep that had seen better days, would collect both of them and treat them, to their great delight, to an illicit ice-cream on the way home.

Boys often play more readily with other boys, but James was different. He was happy in the company of other boys, but he seemed to be equally content to play with girls, and in particular with Clover. He found her undemanding even if she followed him about the house, watching him with wide eyes, ready to do his bidding in whatever new game he devised for them. When they had just turned nine, David, who fancied himself as a carpenter, made them a tree-house, supported between two palm trees in the back garden and reached by a rope ladder tied at one end to the base of the tree-house and at the other to two pegs driven into the ground. They spent hours in this leafy hide-out, picnicking on sandwiches or looking out of a telescope that James had carted up the rope ladder. It was a powerful instrument, originally bought by David when he thought he might take up amateur astronomy, but never really used. The stars, he found out, were too far away to be of any real interest, and once you had looked at the moon and its craters there was little else to see.

But James found that with the telescope pointed out of the side window of the tree-house, he could see into the windows of nearby houses across the generously sized yards and gardens. Palm trees and sprays of bougainvillea could get in the way, obscuring the view in some directions, but there was still plenty to look at. He found a small notebook and drew columns in it headed *House*, *People*, and *Things Seen*.

"Why?" asked Clover, as he showed her this notebook and its first few entries.

"Because we need to keep watch," he said. "There might be spies, you know. We'd see them from up here."

She nodded. "And if we saw them? What then?"

"We'll have the evidence," he said, pointing to the notebook. "We could show it to the police, and then they could arrest them and shoot them."

Clover looked doubtful. "They don't shoot people in Cayman," she said. "Not even the Governor is allowed to shoot people."

"They're allowed to shoot spies," James countered.

She adjusted the telescope so that it was pointing out of the window and then she leaned forward to peer through it.

"I can see into the Arthur house," she said. "There's a man standing in the kitchen talking on the telephone."

"I'll note that down," said James. "He could be a spy."

"He isn't. It's Mr Arthur – Teddy's father."

"Spies often pretend to be ordinary people," said James. "Even Teddy might not know that his father's a spy."

She wanted to please him and so she kept the records assiduously. The Arthur family was watched closely, even if no real evidence of spying was obtained. They talked on the telephone a lot, however, and that could be suspicious.

"Spies speak on the telephone to headquarters," James explained. "They're always on the phone."

She had no interest in spies and their doings; the games she preferred involved re-enacted domesticity, or arranging shells in patterns, or writing plays that would then be performed, in costume, for family and neighbours – including the Arthurs, if they could be prised away from their spying activities. He went along with all this, to an extent, because he was fair-minded and understood that boys had to do the things that girls wanted occasionally, if girls were to do the things that boys wanted.

Their friendship survived battles over little things – arguments and spats that led to telephone calls of apology or the occasional note *I hate you so much*, always rescinded by a note the next morning saying *I don't really hate you – not really. Sorry.*

"She's your girlfriend, isn't she?" taunted one of James's classmates, a boy called Tom Ebanks, whose father was a notoriously corrupt businessman.

"No. She's just a friend."

Tom Ebanks smirked. "She lets you kiss her? You put your tongue in her mouth – like this – and wiggle it all around?"

"I told you: she's my friend."

"You're going to make her pregnant? You know what that is? You know how to do that?"

He lashed out at the other boy, and cut him above his right eye. There was blood, and there were threats from Tom Ebanks's friends, but it put a stop to the talk. He did not care if they thought she was his girlfriend. There was nothing wrong with having a girlfriend, not that that was what she was anyway. She was just like any of the boys, really – a friend. She had always been there; it was as simple as that; she was a sister, of a sort, although had she been his real sister he would not have got on so well with her, he thought: he knew boys, quite a few of them, who ignored their sisters or found them irritating. He liked Clover, and told her that. "You're my best friend, you know. Or at least I think you are."

She had responded warmly. "And you're mine too."

They looked at one another and held each other's gaze until he turned away and talked about something else.

4

Amanda was surprised. The fact that she had fallen out of love with David seemed to make little difference to her day-to-day life. That would not have been the case, she told herself, if affection had been transformed into something stronger, into actual antipathy. But she could not dislike David, who was a kind and equably tempered man. It was not his fault; he had done nothing to bring this about – it had simply happened. She knew women who disliked their husbands, who went so far as to say that they found them unbearable. There was a woman at the tennis club, Vanessa, who was like that; she had drunk too much at the Big Tennis Party, as they called their annual reception for new members, and had spoken indiscreetly to Amanda.

"I just can't stand him, you know," she had said. "I find him physically repulsive – actually repulsive. Can you imagine what that's like? Can you? When he puts his hands on me?"

Amanda had looked away. She wanted to say that you should never talk about the marriage bed, but she could not find the words. *That's private* would have done, of course, but it sounded so disapproving.

"I'll tell you," went on Vanessa, sipping at her gin and tonic, and lowering her voice. "I have to close my eyes and imagine that I'm with somebody else. It's the only way." She paused. "Have you ever done that?"

The other woman was looking at Amanda with interest, as if the question she had asked was entirely innocuous – an enquiry as to whether one had ever read a particular book.

Amanda shook her head. But I have, she thought.

"That's the only way I can bear to sleep with him," Vanessa

said. "I decide who it's going to be and then I think of him." She paused. "You'd be surprised to find out some of the men I've slept with. In my mind, of course. I've been *very* socially successful."

Amanda looked up at the sky. It was evening, and they were standing outside; most of the guests were on the patio. The sky was clear; white stars against dark velvet. "Have you thought of leaving him?"

Vanessa laughed. "Look at these people." She gestured to the other guests. One saw the gesture and waved; Vanessa smiled back. "Every one of the women – I can't speak for the men – but every one of those women would probably leave their husbands if it weren't for one thing."

"I don't think …"

"No, I'm telling you. It's true." The gin and tonic was almost finished now; just ice was left. "Money. It's money that keeps them. It's always been like that."

"Not any more, surely. Women have options now. Careers. You don't have to stay with a man you can't stand."

"No," said Vanessa. "You're wrong. You have to stay, because you can't do otherwise. What does this tennis club cost? What does it cost to buy a house here? Two million dollars for something vaguely habitable. Where do women get that money when it's men who've got the jobs?" She looked to Amanda for an answer. "Well?"

"It's not that bad."

"No, it *is* bad. It's very bad."

The conversation had left her feeling depressed, because of its sheer hopelessness. She wondered if Vanessa was at a further point on a road upon which she herself had now embarked. If that were true, she decided, she would leave well before she reached that stage. And she could: there were her parents back in New York – she could go back to them right now and they would accept her. She could take the children, and bring them up as Americans rather than as typical expatriate children living in a place where they did not belong and where they would never be sure exactly who they were. There were plenty of children like that in places like Grand Cayman or Dubai and all those other cities where expatriates led their detached, privileged lives, knowing that their hosts merely tolerated them, never loved them or accepted them.

But then she thought: she had no difficulty living with David. She did not dislike him; he did not annoy her in the way he ate his breakfast cereal or in the things he said. He could be amusing; he could say witty things that brought what she thought of as guilt-free laughter – there was never a victim in any of his stories. He did not embarrass her with philistine comments or reactionary views, as another friend's husband did. And she thought, too, that as well as there being no reason to leave, there was a very good reason to stay, and that was so that the children could have two parents. If the cost of that would be her remaining with a man she did not love, then that was not a great price to pay.

"That poor woman," said Margaret one morning. "She's going to lose a leg."

"What woman?" asked Amanda. Margaret was one of those people who made the assumption that you knew all their friends and acquaintances.

They were standing in the kitchen, where Margaret was cooking one of her Jamaican stews. The stew was bubbling on the cooker, giving off a rich, earthy smell.

"She works in that house on the corner. The big one. She's worked there a long time, but they don't treat her right."

The story could be assembled through the asking of the right questions, but it could take time.

"Who doesn't treat her right? Her employers?"

"Yes, the people in that house. They make her work all the time and then she gets sick and they say it's got nothing to do with them. She twists her leg at their place, you see, and they still say it's got nothing to do with them. Some people say nothing is to do with them – nothing at all. At their own place too."

"I see …"

"So now the leg is fixed by that useless doctor. He kills more people than he saves, that one. The Honduran one. All those Honduras people go to him when they get sick because he says he was a big man back in Honduras and they believe him. You know how they are. They believe things you and I would laugh at – the Hondurans believe them. They cross themselves and so on, and believe all the lies that people tell them. No questions asked."

She elicited the story slowly. A Honduran maid – a woman in her early fifties – had slipped at the poolside in the house of a wealthy expatriate couple. They were French tax exiles, easily able to afford for their maid to see a reputable doctor, but had washed their hands of the matter. They had warned her about wet patches at the edge of the pool, and now she had injured herself. It was her fault, not theirs.

The maid had consulted a cheap Honduran doctor who was not licensed to practise in the Cayman Islands, but who did so nonetheless in the back of his shipping chandlery. Now infection had set in in the bone and progressed to the point that the public hospital was offering an amputation. There was an ulcer, too, that needed dressing.

The leg could be saved, Margaret said, but it would be expensive. "You could ask Dr Collins," she said. "He's a good man. He could do something."

"Has he seen her?" Amanda asked.

Margaret shook her head. "She's too frightened to go and see him. Money, you see. Doctors charge a lot of money just for you to sit in their waiting room."

"He isn't like that."

"No, so they say. But this woman is too frightened to go."

There was an expectant silence.

"All right," said Amanda. "I'll take her."

It was not onerous. And she realised that she wanted to see him. She had never been into his clinic – the run-down building past the shops at South Sound – but she had seen the badly painted sign that said *Dr Collins, Patient's at Back*. She knew that he was not responsible for the apostrophe; that was the fault of the sign-writer, and she knew, too, that it remained there because the doctor was too tactful to have it corrected. The sign-writer was one of his patients and always asked him, with pride, if he was happy with his work. "Of course I am, Wallis," the doctor said. "I wouldn't change a word of it." That had been told her by Alice.

Margaret arranged for her to pick up the Honduran woman, Bella. She did so one evening, waiting at the end of the drive while the maid, who was using crutches, limped towards her.

"My leg's bad," she said, as she got into the car. "Swollen. Bad inside. I'm sorry. It smells bad too. I can't help that."

She caught her breath. There was an odour – slightly sweet,

but sinister too; the smell of physical corruption, of infection. She wondered how this could go untreated in a place of expensive cars and air conditioning. But it did, of course; illness and infection survived in the interstices even where there was money and the things that money bought. All they needed was human flesh, oxygen, and indifference; or hardness of heart, perhaps.

She reached out and put a hand on the maid's forearm. "I don't mind. I can't even notice it."

The maid looked at her. "You're very kind."

Amanda thought: am I? Or would anybody do this; surely anybody would?

She drove carefully. The road from the town centre was busy, and the traffic was slow in the late afternoon heat. She tried to make conversation, but Bella seemed to be unwilling to speak, and they completed the journey in silence.

The clinic was simple. In a waiting room furnished with plastic chairs, a woman sat at a desk with several grey filing cabinets behind her. There was a notice-board on which government circulars about immunisation had been pinned untidily. A slow-turning ceiling fan disturbed the air sufficiently to flutter the end of the larger circulars. There was a low table with ancient magazines stacked on it – old copies of the *National Geographic* and, curiously, a magazine called *Majesty* that specialised in articles about the British royal family. A younger member of that family looked out from the cover. *Exclusive*, claimed a caption to the picture. *We tell you what he really feels about history and duty.*

Amanda spoke to the woman at the desk. She had phoned her earlier on and made the appointment, and this had been followed by a conversation with George; now there was a form to be filled in. She offered this to Bella, who recoiled from it, out of ancient, instinctive habit. And that must be how you felt if you had always been at the bottom of the heap, thought Amanda. Every form, every manifestation of authority, came from above, was a potential threat.

"I'll fill it in for her," she said, glancing at the receptionist to forestall any objection.

But there was none. "That's fine," said the woman. "As long as we have her name and date of birth."

They sat on adjoining chairs. She smiled at Bella. "It'll be all right."

"They said at the hospital …"

She stopped her. "Never mind what they said. We'll see what Dr Collins says. All right?"

Bella nodded miserably. Then she seemed to brighten. "You've got those two children, M'am."

"Not M'am. Amanda."

"Same as me. Two. Boy and a girl. You have that Clover? I've seen her. Pretty girl."

"Thank you. Yours?"

"They're with their grandmother in Puerto Cortes. In Honduras."

"You must miss them."

"Yes. Every day. Specially now."

A consequence of the expatriate life, Amanda thought – or of another variety of it.

The door behind the receptionist's desk opened. A woman came out – a young woman, tall, with the light-olive complexion of some of the Cayman Islanders. She turned and shook the doctor's hand before walking out, eyes averted from Amanda and Bella.

"Mrs Rosales?"

He nodded to Amanda; they had spoken on the phone about Bella when he had agreed to see her.

Bella looked anxiously at Amanda. "You must come too."

Amanda caught George's eye. "If she wants you in, that's fine," he said. "That's all right, Mrs Rosales. She can come in with you."

They went into the doctor's office. The receptionist had preceded them and was fitting a fresh white sheet to the examination couch. Amanda felt what she always felt in such places: the accoutrements reminded her of mortality. The couch, the indignity of the stirrups, the smell of antiseptic, the gleam of medical instruments: all of these underlined the seriousness of our plight. Human life, individually and collectively, hung by a biological thread.

Bella lay on the couch, wincing as she stretched out her damaged leg. Amanda stood back. She wanted to look away, but found her gaze drawn back to the sight of George removing the dressing. His touch looked gentle; he stopped for a moment when Bella gave a grimace of pain.

"I'm not surprised," he said. "This is very nasty."

The wound made by the ulcer was yellow. She had not expected that. She had expected red.

He probed gently with an instrument. She noticed the watch he was wearing, a square watch of a sort the advertisers claimed as *thirties retro*. She noticed that the belt he was wearing had been incorrectly threaded, missing a loop at the back. She thought of him dressing for work in the morning; dressing for his encounters with his patients, dressing for whatever the day brought him – the breaking of bad news, the stories of physical discomfort and pain; while David dressed for his meetings, his daily stint in the engine room of money. She looked at the back of his neck; at his shoulders.

Suddenly Bella reached out a hand towards her. She had been on the other side of the room, only a few feet away, but crossed over immediately and took the extended hand. She saw that there were tears in the Honduran woman's eyes.

George turned away from Bella and addressed Amanda. "She needs proper hospital treatment. Intravenous antibiotics at the very least. There might need to be some surgical excision of tissue. They'll need to get the infection under control."

She whispered. "There's no insurance. They won't send her off-island."

He shook his head. "There are some good people in Kingston. Medical missionaries from Florida. They have a first-class surgeon who knows all about these infections. I've used them before. If we can get her to them." He looked down at Bella and laid his hand on hers, the hand being held by Amanda. The three of them were holding hands now.

"I'll pay the fare. It isn't much."

"Good. That's nice of you. They'll take care of the rest."

He let go of Bella's hand and turned to the receptionist. "Can you put on a clean dressing, please, Annie?"

He drew Amanda aside. "Why has this been allowed to get to this point? Was there nobody?"

She shook her head. "The employers washed their hands of it. You probably know them. That French couple on the corner."

He raised his eyes. "They're very wealthy."

"Of course they are."

He sighed. "You said that it happened at work? In the house?"

"She slipped at work."

He asked whether she couldn't get a lawyer. "There are enough of them. This place is crawling with lawyers."

"They work for the banks."

"Of course. They work for the banks."

After the dressing had been changed, George helped Bella off the couch. He explained that he would try to make an appointment for her to see somebody tomorrow who would make arrangements for her to go to a hospital in Jamaica. Bella said nothing, but nodded her assent.

"A drink?" said George, as he showed Amanda out.

She felt her heart leap. "Why not? After I've taken Mrs Rosales home."

"Yes. The Grand Old House?" he suggested. "An hour's time? Six-thirty?"

"I haven't been there for ages."

The Grand Old House was a restaurant and bar on the shore near Smith's Cove. At night you could sit out at the front and watch the lights of boats on the water. The staff tipped food into a circle of light they created in the water and large grey fish swam in to snap up the morsels in the shallows.

She thought about the invitation as she drove home. She should call David, perhaps, and tell him, and something would have to be done about the children. They were with Margaret, at her house, and they could stay there, perhaps, until she came home. Margaret fed them pizzas and other unhealthy foods; they loved eating there.

No, she would not call David. He had said he was likely to be delayed at the office because somebody had come in from London and there was an important meeting about one of the trusts they administered. He might not be back until ten, or even later.

Back at the house, after dropping off Bella, she had a quick swim in the pool to cool off. Then she washed her hair and chose something that she could wear to the Grand Old House. She chose it with care; with the fingers of excitement already tapping at the door, insistent, unmistakable.

5

They had decided to investigate more closely what was happening at the Arthur house. The onset of cooler weather in December meant that Mr Arthur, who normally worked in an air-conditioned study, had opened his windows. The house was built in the West Indian style – both Mr Arthur and his wife came from Barbados – and had wide doors and windows under the broad sloping eaves of a veranda. If the windows of Mr Arthur's study were closed to allow the air conditioners to function, then they could not see what was going on within, even with the telescope. But with the windows open and a light switched on inside, then they were afforded a perfect view of Mr Arthur, framed by the window, at work at his desk.

"What does he do?" asked James. "He just sits there and phones. Is it all spying?"

"Teddy says that he sells ships. I asked him, and that's what he says his father does."

James looked doubtful. "Where are all the ships? In his yard?"

She agreed that it was an unlikely story. "That's probably what he's told Teddy," she said. "Because he'll be ashamed to tell his own son he's a spy. Spies don't like their family to know."

"Yes," said James. "You can't trust your own family not to tell other people."

One afternoon, they saw a man come into the study. Clover was at the telescope, but yielded her place to James. "Look," she said. "Somebody's come to see him."

James crouched at the telescope.

"What's happening now?" she asked.

"There's a piece of paper," said James. "Mr Arthur is giving it to the man. The man's handing it back to him."

"And now?"

He hesitated. "Now he's ... Look. You just look. He's burning it. He's set fire to the paper."

She resumed her place at the telescope. The instrument had shifted, but a small movement brought it back to focus on the lighted window, and she saw a man's hand holding a piece of blackened paper, then dropping it.

"Burning the evidence," she said.

"The codes," James said. "Burning the codes."

They stared at each other in silence, awed by the importance of what they had just seen.

"We're going to have to do something," James said at last.

"Such as?"

She waited for his reply.

"I think we need more evidence," he said. "We need to take photographs."

She asked how they would do that.

"We go and see Teddy. Then we take photographs while we're there."

"Teddy doesn't like us," she pointed out. "He'll wonder why we're there."

That was not an insurmountable problem in James's view. They would make overtures to Teddy – they would invite him to their tree-house, even ask him to join in their counter-espionage activities.

"But it's his own dad," objected Clover. "He's not going to like that."

"We start off by watching our own parents," he said. "That'll show him we're not just picking on him. We'll say that we have to watch everybody – with no exception. We'll say that his dad is probably innocent, but we need to prove that he's innocent."

"That'll work," she said.

He took the leadership in these matters. It was her tree-house and her telescope, but he was the leader in these games. It had never been discussed, but that was the way that things were ordered. And this was to be the case always; she would always be the one in waiting, the one hoping for recognition, for some sign from him.

She looked at him; something quite different had crossed her mind. "Have you ever heard of blood brothers?"

The question did not seem to interest him. He shrugged.

"Well, have you?" she pressed.

"Maybe. It's stupid."

She frowned. "I don't think it's stupid. You mix your blood. That makes you blood brothers. Lots of people do it."

He shook his head. He was still avoiding her gaze. "They don't." He paused. "Name one person who's done it. Name them."

"Lance Bodden. He's a blood brother with Lucas Jones. He told me. He said they both cut themselves and then put the blood together. In the palm of their hands. He said there was lots of blood."

"You can get things from that," he said. "You get the other guy's germs. There are lots of germs in blood. It's full of germs, especially if you're Lucas Jones. He's dirty."

She did not think there was much of a risk. "Blood's clean. It's spit that's full of germs. You don't mix your spit."

"I wouldn't be a blood brother anyway," he said. "Not me."

She hesitated. "We could be blood brothers – you and me."

Now he looked at her incredulously. "You're joking."

"No, I'm not. We could be blood brothers. Not with lots of blood – just a little. We could use a pin – pins don't hurt as much as knives."

This was greeted with a laugh. "But you're a girl, Clover. We can't be brothers. You have to be a boy to be brothers."

She blushed. "Girls and boys are not all that different."

He shook his head. "They are."

Her disappointment showed. "They can be friends. Best friends even."

He rose to his feet. "I have to go. Sorry."

"Because of what I said? Because you don't want to be blood brothers?"

"Not that. I've got to go home – that's all."

He began to climb down the ladder. From above she watched him. She liked the shape of his head. She liked his hair, which was dark blond and a bit bristly up at the top. Boys' hair seemed different, but she could not put her finger on the reason why it seemed different. Could you tell if it was just a single hair you were looking at? Could you tell under a microscope?

He reached the bottom of the ladder and looked up at her. He smiled. She loved his smile too. She loved the way his cheeks dimpled when he smiled. She loved him. It was a strange feeling – a feeling of anticipation, of excitement. It started in her stomach, she thought, and then worked its way up. She slipped her hand under her T-shirt and felt her heart. You fell in love in your heart, she had heard, but she was not sure how you could tell. Could you feel your pulse and count it? Was that how you knew?

Teddy was keen.

"Yes," he said. "I've often thought that people round here are hiding something."

"There you are," said James. "So what we have to do is just make sure that everybody round us is okay. We check up on them first, and then we move on to other people. We'll find out soon enough who's a spy and who isn't."

"Good idea," said Teddy. He looked puzzled. "How do you do it?"

"You watch," Clover explained. "Spies give themselves away eventually. You note where they go. You have to keep records, you see. And you take photographs. I've got a camera."

"Me too," said Teddy. "For my last birthday. It has this lens that makes things closer …"

"Zoom lens," said James knowingly. "Good."

"And then we can load them onto the computer and print them," said Teddy. "I know how to do that."

"We can begin with your dad," said James casually. "Just for practice."

Teddy shook his head. "No. Why begin with him? Why not begin with yours?"

James glanced at Clover.

"All right," she said. "We don't have to start with your dad, Teddy. We can start with mine. Or even my mum. My dad's out at the office most of the time. We can start with my mum."

"Doing what?" asked Teddy.

Clover put a finger to her lips in a gesture of complicity. "Observation."

6

He was there when she reached the bar, which is the way she wanted it to be. If she had arrived at the Grand Old House first then she would have had to sit there, in public, looking awkward. George Town was still an intimate, village-like place – at least for those who lived there – and somebody might have come up to her, some friend or acquaintance, and asked her where David was. This way at least she could avoid that, although she realised that this meeting might not be as discreet as she might wish. People talked; a few months previously at a tennis club social she had herself commented on seeing a friend with another man. It could have been innocent, of course, and probably was, but she had spoken to somebody about it. Not that she had much time for gossip, but when there was so little else to talk about … And in due course she, and everybody else who had speculated on the break-up of that marriage, had been proved right.

She should have said no. She could have said that she had to get back to the children – they had always provided a complete excuse for turning down unwanted invitations. Or she could have suggested that he called at the house for a drink later on, and she could then have telephoned David asking him whether he could get back in time because George Collins was dropping in. And David would have told her to explain to George about his meeting and that would have been her off the hook – able to entertain another man at the house in complete propriety. But she did not do this, and now here she was at the Grand Old House meeting him without the knowledge of her husband.

She tried to suppress her misgivings. Men and women could be friends these days without threatening their marriages. Men and women worked together, collaborated on projects, served on committees with one another. Young people even shared rooms together when they travelled, without a whiff of sex. It was natural – and healthy. It was absurd to suggest that people should somehow keep one another at arm's length in all other contexts simply because their partners might see such friends as a threat. The days of closed, possessive marriages were over; women were no longer their husbands' chattels, to be guarded jealously against others.

That was a rationalisation, though, and she was honest enough to admit it to herself. She wanted to see George Collins because he interested her – it was as simple as that. She thought, with shame, of how different it would have been if it were David she was meeting for a drink; she would have felt nothing. Now something had awakened within her – she had almost forgotten what it was like, but now she knew once more.

He was sitting some distance away from the bar, at a table overlooking the sea. When he saw her come in, he simply nodded, although he rose to his feet as she approached the table. He smiled at her as she sat down.

"It's been a hellish day," he said. "And alcohol helps. I know it shouldn't, but it does."

She made a gesture of acceptance. "I'm sure you don't overdo it. But I suppose, being a doctor ..."

He completed the sentence. "Makes no difference. None at all. Doctors are as weak as the rest of humanity. The only difference is that we know how all the parts work, and we know what the odds are." He paused. "Or I used to know them. You'd be surprised at how much the average doctor has forgotten."

She laughed. Talking to him was pleasant – so easy. "But

everybody forgets what they learned. I learned a lot about art when I was a student. I could rattle off the names of painters and knew how they influenced one another. Nowadays, I've forgotten everybody's dates."

He went off to order her a drink at the bar. While he was away she looked around the room, as naturally as she could. There was nobody she knew. She relaxed.

They raised their glasses to one another.

"Thank you," he said. "Thanks for coming at virtually no notice. I thought that you'd have the children to look after."

"They're with the maid. They love going to her house. She spoils them."

He nodded. "Jamaican?"

"Yes."

"They love children. They ..." He stopped himself. "Or does that sound patronising?"

She thought it did not. "It's true. It's not patronising in the slightest. Complimentary, I'd have thought. Italians love children too."

"Yes," he said. "Yes, but ... white people can't really say anything about black people, can they? Because of the past. Because of the fact that we stole so much from them. Their freedom. Their lives. Everything."

"You didn't. I didn't."

He looked into his glass. "Our grandparents did."

"I thought it was a bit before that. How long do people have to say sorry?"

He thought for a few moments before answering. "A bit longer, I'd say." He paused. "After all, what colour are the people living in the large houses and what colour are the people who look after their gardens? What colour are the maids? What does that tell us?"

She thought: yes, you're right. And then she thought: David would never say that. Never. That was the difference.

"We had a Jamaican lady working for us," he said. "She was with us until a year or so ago. She was substitute grandmother. The kids still miss her."

"They would."

There was a brief moment of silence. He took a sip of his drink. "That poor woman …"

"Bella?"

"Mrs Rosales."

"Yes, Bella."

He looked up at the ceiling. "It makes my blood boil."

She waited for him to continue.

"I assume that her employers know what's what. I assume that somebody told them what she needed."

"I believe they did. I only heard about it from Margaret – the woman who helps me. She implied that they just couldn't be bothered."

He shook his head in disbelief. "It could be too late, you know. She may have to lose the leg anyway."

"Well, at least you'll have tried. This person in Kingston – who is he?"

"He's a general surgeon – an increasingly rare breed. He does anything and everything. He used to be in one of the big hospitals in Miami but he retired early and went off to this clinic in Kingston. They're Lutherans, I believe. Missionaries. People like that still exist."

"Do you think he'll be able to help?"

He nodded. "I phoned him just before I came here. He says that he'll see her tomorrow. We took the liberty of booking her on the Cayman Airways flight first thing. I've got my nurse to go round and let her know."

She told him that she would reimburse him for the flight, and he thanked her. "It's not all that uncommon, you know," he said.

"Infections like that?"

"Yes. But I meant it's not uncommon for people to let their domestic workers fend for themselves. I see those people every day of the week. Filipina maids, any number of Jamaicans, Haitians – the lot."

She said that she had heard about the way he helped. "It's very good of you …"

He brushed aside the praise. "I have to do it. It's my job. I'm a doctor. I'm not a hero or anything like that. That's not the way it is, you know. You just do what you were trained to do – same as anybody."

She watched him. She could tell that he was uncomfortable talking about his work, and she decided to change the subject. Although they had known one another for years, she knew very little about him. She knew that he was British, that Alice was Australian, and that they kept to themselves much of the time. Apart from that, she knew nothing. She asked him the obvious question – the one that expatriates asked each other incessantly. How did you end up here?

He smiled. "The question of questions. Everybody asks it, don't they? It's as if they can hardly believe that anybody would make a conscious, freely made choice to come to this place."

"Well, it's what we all think about, isn't it?"

He agreed. "I suppose it is. In so far as we have any curiosity about our fellow islanders. I'm not sure if I find myself wanting to know about some of them." He hesitated. "Does that sound snobbish?"

"It depends on which ones you're thinking of."

"The rich ones," he said. "I find their shallowness distasteful. And they worship money."

"Then it doesn't sound at all snobbish. And anyway, we all know why they're here. It's the others who are interesting – the people who've come from somewhere else for other reasons. Not just because they're avoiding tax."

He looked doubtful. "Are there many of those?"

"Some people come for straightforward jobs. David did." She felt that she had to defend her husband, who was not as obsessed with money as many of the others were. He was interested in *figures*, and there was a difference.

He was quick to agree. "Of course. I wasn't talking about people like David."

She decided to be direct. "So how did you end up here?"

He shrugged. "Ignorance."

"Of what?"

"Of what I was coming to. You know, when I saw the advertisement in the *British Medical Journal*, the ad that brought me here, I had to go off and look the Caymans up in the atlas – I had no idea where they were. I thought they were somewhere in the South Pacific, you know. I thought they were somewhere down near Samoa. That shows how much I knew."

"So you took a job?"

"Yes. I had just finished my hospital training in London. I was offered the chance to go on to a surgical job, also in London, but somehow I felt that to do that would be just too obvious. All too predictable. So I looked in the back pages of the BMJ and saw an advertisement from the Caymans government. It was for a one-year job in the hospital – somebody had gone off to have a baby and there was a one-year position. I thought: why not?"

"And so you came out here?"

"Yes. I came to do a job, which I did, and then I met Alice. My job at the hospital came to an end but I applied for a permit to do general practice and I got it. The rest is history, as they say."

She smiled at the expression. *The rest is history.* That meant things that happened – everything that happened. The moss. The acquisitions. Children. Inertia. Love. Despair.

She looked about her. A group of four people – two couples – had come into the bar and had taken their places at a table on the other side of the room. They were locals – wealthy Caymanians who had what David called *that look* about them. They did not carry their wealth lightly. She thought she might have seen one of the women before somewhere, but she could not be sure. People like that kept to themselves, to their own circles; they disliked the expatriates, only tolerating them because they were useful to them; they needed the banks, and trusts, and law firms because without them all they had were mangrove swamps, some beaches, and a reef.

George had said something to her that she had missed while being distracted by the newcomers.

"Sorry," she said. "I wasn't paying attention."

"I said: how long are you and David going to stay?"

She sipped at the drink he had bought her: a gin and tonic in which the ice was melting fast. She shrugged. "Until he retires. Which will be … heaven knows. Another twenty years? Fifteen?" She put down her glass. "And you?"

"I'd leave tomorrow."

She was surprised, and her surprise showed.

"Are you shocked?" he asked.

"No, not really. It's just that I thought you were so … so settled here. I've always imagined that you and Alice are happy."

For a moment he said nothing. She saw him look out of the window, past the line of white sand on which the hotel lights shone, into the darkness beyond, which was the sea. Then he said, "I only stay because these people – my patients – depend on me. It's an odd thing. I could say to them that I was packing up and leaving, but somehow I can't bring myself to do it. Some of them actually rely on me, you know, and that wouldn't be easy. So if you said to me: here's your freedom, I'd go tomorrow. Anywhere. Anywhere bigger than here. Australia. The States. Canada. Anywhere that's the opposite of a ring of coral and some sand in the middle of the Caribbean."

She stared at him. "You're unhappy?" She had not intended to say it, but the words slipped out.

"Not unhappy in the sense of being miserable. I get along, I suppose. Maybe I should just say that I'd like to be leading another life. But then, plenty of people might say that about their lives."

She looked at his hands. She thought they were shaking. No, perhaps not.

"And Alice?" she said.

He looked back at her. "She's not too unhappy," he said. "She doesn't like this place very much – she's bored with it. But in her case, there's something else that is far more important. You see, Alice is completely in love with me. Completely. Not as most wives are with their husbands – they're friends, they rub along together out of habit and convenience. With her, it's something quite unlike that. She lives for me. I'm her reason. I'm her ... well, I suppose I'm her life."

She whispered now. Nobody could hear them, but the intimacy of the conversation dictated a whisper. "And you? How do you feel?"

He shook his head. "I'm sorry. I wish I could give you a different answer, but I can't. I don't dislike her, but I'm not in love with her. Not like that."

"Like me," she said.

For a moment he did not react, and she wondered whether he had heard. In a way, she hoped that he had not. She should never have said that. It was a denial of her marriage. It was an appalling thing to say. David had done nothing to deserve it – but then Alice had done nothing either. They were both victims.

Then he spoke. "I see," he said. 'That's two of us, then. Trapped."

7

David came home from the office at nine-thirty that night, which was two hours after Amanda had returned from the Grand Old House. She had collected the children from Margaret's care and settled them in their rooms. They were full of pizza and popcorn washed down, she suspected, with coloured and sweetened liquids. But they were tired too: Clover had played basketball with Margaret's niece and Billy had exhausted himself in various energetic games with the dogs. They took no time to drift off, and were both asleep by the time she went down the corridor to check up on them. She liked to stand in the doorway and watch her children as they slept, her gaze lingering on the faces she loved so much. That evening she stood for longer than usual, thinking of the stakes in the game she had started. One ill-thought-out, impulsive act could threaten so much: in flirting with adultery she had thrown her children's futures onto the gaming table, but it was not too late. She would stop it right there, before anything else happened. All she had done was to sit and talk with another man, a doctor to whom she had delivered a patient, who had suggested a drink at the end of a difficult day. That was all. There had been no discreet assignation on the beach; no furtive meeting in a car; they had not so much as touched one another. And nobody had seen them anyway.

She turned out the children's lights and made her way back into the kitchen. She would have to eat alone; David had left a message on the answering machine that they would be getting something sent in to eat at the meeting; there was a restaurant in town that dispatched Thai food in containers to the office when required, at any time of day or night. She would have something simple – scrambled eggs and toast, or spaghetti bolognese: the adult equivalent of nursery food. Then she would have an early night and be asleep by the time he came back.

She ate her simple meal quickly. The night was hot and in spite of the air conditioning her clothes seemed to be sticking to her. She got up from the table, not bothering to clear her plate away – Margaret could do that in the morning. She went outside, out of the chilled cocoon of the house into the hot embrace of the night. It was like stepping into a warming oven: the heat folded about her, penetrated her clothing, made the stone flags under her feet feel like smouldering coals. She stepped onto the lawn; the grass was cool underfoot, but prickly. She walked across it to the pool and looked into the water. A light came on automatically when it grew dark, and so the pool had already been lit for several hours, although there was nobody there to appreciate the cool dappling effect on the water.

She looked into the water, which was clear of leaves, as the pool-man had come earlier that day. He took an inordinate pride in his work, spending hours ensuring that every last leaf, every blade of grass or twig that blew into the water was carefully removed. "It must look like the empty sky," he said. "Just blue. Nothing else."

She sat down at the edge of the pool, immersing the calves of her legs in the water. With the day's heat behind it, the water was barely cooler than the surrounding atmosphere, and provided little relief. Swimming now would be like bathing in the air itself.

She sat there for twenty minutes or so, before she arose and crossed to the far side of the garden. Beyond the hedge of purple bougainvillea, she could make out the window of Mr Arthur's study. The lights were blazing out, and she saw Gerry Arthur himself standing with his back to the window. She stood still and watched. He was moving his arms around, as if conducting a piece of music.

She stepped forward. The sound of a choir drifted out into the night. *Carmina Burana* – she recognised it immediately. *O Fortuna!* Mr Arthur raised his hands and brought them down decisively, to bring them up again sharply. She smiled as she watched him, and then turned away.

She went back to the pool and took her clothes off, flinging them carelessly onto one of the poolside chairs. The air was soft on her, and now there was the faintest of breezes, touching her skin as a blown feather might, almost imperceptibly. She stepped into the pool and launched herself into the water. She thought again of the Hockney paintings of the boys in the swimming pool, brown under the blue water. She ducked her head below the surface and propelled herself towards the far side of the pool. She thought of George. She imagined that he was here with her, swimming beside her. She turned in the water, half-expecting to see him. He would be naked, as she was. He would be tanned brown, like Hockney's California boys, and youthful. He would be beautiful.

She surfaced. She had shocked herself. *I am swimming by myself. I'm married. I have children. I have a husband.*

When David returned she was still in the pool. He saw her from the kitchen and he called out to her from the window before he came out to join her. He had a beer with him that he drank straight from the bottle. He raised it to her in greeting.

"They settled their differences," he said. "I thought it was going to be acrimonious, but it wasn't. The lawyers were disappointed, of course. They were hoping that the whole thing would end up in litigation." He paused. He had suddenly noticed she was naked. "Skinny dipping?"

She moved to the end of the pool, where she could sit, half lie, on one of the lower concrete steps.

"It was so hot."

He fingered at the collar of his shirt. "Yes. Steaming."

He took a swig of his beer.

She said, "The kids ate at Margaret's tonight. She filled them up with pizza. Do you know how many calories there are in an eighteen-inch pizza?"

"A couple of thousand. Too many, anyway. And heaps of sodium. And what do you call those fats? Saturated?"

"I wish she'd give them something healthy," she said. "Vegetables. Soup. That sort of thing."

"Oh well," he began, and then continued, "Why did they eat there?"

"Because I was late back. I took Mrs Rosales to have her leg looked at. I told you, didn't I? Margaret spoke to me." She had mentioned something to him, but could not recall exactly what she had said.

He took another swig of beer. "Took her to the hospital?"

"No." She tried to sound casual. "I took her to see George Collins. He takes people like that. He takes anybody who hasn't got insurance."

"When?" he asked.

"When what?"

"When did you take her?"

"Late afternoon."

He moved his chair forward and slipped out of his shoes and

socks. He put his feet into the water, not far from her. "And then?" he asked.

She moved her hands through the water, like little underwater ailerons, playing. The movement made ripples, which in turn cast shadows on the bottom of the pool, little lines, like the contour lines on a chart. She was not sure whether his question was a casual one; whether he was merely expressing polite interest, or whether he really wanted to know. So she said nothing, concentrating on the movement of her hands, feeling the water flow through the separated fingers like a torrent through a sluice. Water could be used in massage; the French went in for that, she thought: they had themselves sprayed with powerful jets of seawater. It was meant to do something for you; provoked sluggish blood into movement, perhaps. Thalassotherapy.

He repeated the question. "And then?"

She looked up at him, and saw that he was not really looking at her, but was staring up at the moving leaves of the large sea-grape tree. The breeze, hardly noticeable below, seemed stronger among the highest branches of the tree.

"And then what?" She needed time to think.

He looked down and met her eyes. His expression was impassive. "And then what did you do? After you'd taken what's-her-name …"

"Mrs Rosales," she said quickly, seeing her opportunity. "Bella Rosales. I think she prefers Bella. She's Honduran – the usual story – children over there being looked after by grandmother. Her leg …"

"Yes," he said. "But your day – what happened afterwards?"

"I came home," she said. It was not a lie, she told herself, as she had come home – eventually.

"But you didn't go to fetch the kids?"

She frowned. Why would he ask that?

"I did. Later. I let them eat at Margaret's."

"I see." He paused. His beer was almost finished now, and he tilted the bottle back to drain the last few drops. "You didn't go anywhere else?"

She felt her heart beating wildly within her. She had been seen. Somebody had said something.

"No." This time the lie was unequivocal.

He turned round. "I'm going in. I'm tired."

There was nothing in his tone of voice to give away what he was thinking.

"David …"

"Yes?"

She looked at him. She would tell him. She would say that she had forgotten. She had been invited by George to have a drink because he had had a wretched day and needed to talk to somebody. But she could not. It was too late. He would never believe her if she said she had forgotten the events of a few hours before. And he did not look suspicious or offended; he did not look like a man who had just established that his wife was lying to him.

"Why don't you join me in here? The water's just right. And Tommy did the pool today. It's perfect."

He hesitated.

"Why not?" He always slept better if he had a swim just before going to bed. It was something to do with inner core temperature; if it was lowered, sleep came more easily.

He took off his clothes; she was aware of his familiar body. He joined her. He put his arm about her shoulder, wet flesh against wet flesh.

8

"Why the tennis courts?"

Teddy had wanted to know. It would take twenty minutes to ride there on their bicycles, and the Saturday morning was already heating up.

"You can die of thirst," he said. "You know that? You can die of thirst if you ride for a long time in the heat. My cousin had a friend who died of de-something …"

"Dehydration," said Clover. "And don't be stupid. Nobody dies of dehydration these days. It's like being eaten by a lion. It's one of things that used to happen, but don't happen any more."

Teddy looked indignant. "He did. He did die from dehydration. You can see it on his gravestone at West Bay. I promise you."

Clover smiled. "So it says *died of dehydration*, does it? Gravestones never say things like that. They just say *dead*. That's all they say. Then they give the date you were born and the date you died, and maybe something about Jesus and God. That's all."

Teddy looked sullen. "I'm not a liar."

She was conciliatory, and had intercepted a warning look from James. "Maybe he died a bit from dehydration. Maybe there were other things. You can die from two things, you know. Sometimes as many as three things."

"You get bitten by a snake and then a lion eats you on the way to hospital," suggested James. "That's two. You might also get rabies from the lion."

They thought about this. "Anyway," said Clover decisively. "I'll take a water bottle with me and if you get thirsty on the way you can have a drink. We have to go there, you see."

"Why?"

She explained carefully, enunciating each word for Teddy's complete understanding. "Because that's where they all are on Saturday morning. They have this tennis league, you see. All of them."

"Not my mum and dad."

"No," she said. "Not yours. But for the moment we're only watching my mum, remember. She's there, and all her friends. We can watch them. There's a really good place for us to hide – it's a big hedge and nobody would see us in there. Or we can climb one of those big trees and look down on the tennis club. They wouldn't see us there either."

"There might be iguanas," said Teddy. The island was populated by fecund iguanas that feasted on the leaves of trees.

"That's another thing that could kill you," offered James. "If an iguana bites you in the right place, you can die. Not everybody knows it, but it's true."

"Nonsense," said Clover. "You're frightening Teddy."

Amanda sat on the veranda of the tennis club. It was cool there under the broad-bladed ceiling fans; there was shade and there were languid currents of air, while outside under the sun the members of a foursome exerted themselves. There were shouts of exasperation, of self-excoriation; somebody's game was not up to scratch. *I'm sorry, partner. I don't know what's happened to my game. Never mind, never mind.*

She had completed her own game of doubles and had played well, pushing their team a step or two up the club league tables. She was pleased; lessons with the club coach were paying off, as David had said they would. Money well spent, he said.

She was holding a glass of lime soda in which a chunk of ice cracked like a tiny iceberg. She was thinking of the day ahead: Billy was with Margaret on an outing to the dolphin park. She disapproved of the capture of dolphins and did not want to go, but he had set his heart on it. Everybody at school had been; everybody else had been allowed to go, and so Margaret had volunteered. Clover was up to something with James; off on her bicycle somewhere. That, at least, was the benefit of living on a small island; they were safe to wander; they had a degree of freedom that city children could only dream of. In New York there had been Central Park, but it had only been visited under the eyes of parents; there had been skating at the Rockefeller Center; there had been blissful summer weeks at a camp in Vermont. But there had been no individual expeditions to the corner store; no aimless wandering down the street; no outings without watchful adults. At least not until the teenage years, when things changed, even if the world suddenly became less exciting than it had been before.

She would go back to the house and shower before going to the supermarket to stock up with provisions for the weekend. After that … She kept a diary near the telephone and she envisaged the page for today. There was something at six-thirty – one of those invitations that pointedly did not include dinner. She remembered the name of the hosts: the Hills. They were white Jamaicans who had got out when most of their fellow white Jamaicans had left, cold-shouldered out of the only country they knew, fleeing from the growing violence and lawlessness. There had been a diaspora – some had gone to the United States and Britain; others took the shorter step to the Caymans, where the climate was the same and political conditions kinder. They also fitted in better there: the Caymanians understood them and they understood the Caymanians. The other expatriates – the Australians, the Americans, the British – were not sure how to take them. Here were people who seemed to have a lot in common with them but spoke with a West Indian lilt in their voice, who had been in the Caribbean for six or more generations. They were different.

There would be the Hills' drinks party and then a cooling swim at home, followed by a movie that David would go to sleep in front of; and then the day would end. Another Saturday, like all the other Saturdays.

She watched the players on the court. It was getting too hot to play, really, even in December, and they were all slowing down, hardly bothering to run for the ball. Easy returns were missed because it was just too much effort to exert oneself sufficiently. The score wandered aimlessly.

"Far too hot for tennis, isn't it?"

She looked round. George was standing behind her. He was dressed in a pair of khaki chinos and a blue T-shirt. She realised that she had never seen him in casual attire and had pictured him only in his more formal working clothes.

She laughed. "I played earlier. I'm glad I did."

He drew up a chair and sat down. As he did so, she glanced along the veranda to see who else was there. There was a woman she knew she would see at the Hills' later that day – she was very close to their hosts, a fellow Jamaican exile. There was that teacher from the prep school, the man who taught art, she thought, or was it gymnastics? She did not know the others, although she had seen them at the club before. Nobody seemed to be paying any attention to her, or to George.

"I didn't know you played," she said. She had never seen him at the tennis club before.

He was holding his car keys and he fiddled with these as he replied. "I don't. I was driving past. I noticed your car."

She caught her breath. It was not accidental; he had sought her out.

He waited for a moment before continuing. "So I thought I'd drop by. I was going somewhere else."

"Yes?"

"I sold the yacht and bought an old powerboat. It's seen better days, but it goes. I don't know if you'd heard."

She shook her head. "No."

"I thought maybe James had mentioned something to Clover. He's terribly proud of it." He slipped the keys into his pocket. "They seem to spend a lot of time together, those two."

"They're very friendly. There's a bit of hero-worship going on, I think."

He smiled broadly. "Oh? Him or her?"

"Girl worships boy, I think."

"Childhood friendships," he said. "They might not find it so easy when they hit adolescence. Friendship becomes more complicated then."

"Your boat …"

"Is nothing special. I can't afford anything expensive. And it's not a sailing boat like the one David and I went out in. It's a knockabout old cruiser with an outboard that's seen better days. It can get out to the reef and back, but that's about it."

She said that she thought that this was all one needed. "Where else is there to go?" she asked.

"Precisely."

"Those great big monsters …"

"Gin palaces."

"Yes. Why do people need them?"

He smiled. "They can go to Cuba. Or to Jamaica. But it's really all about extensions to oneself, to one's ego. Those are *look at me* boats." He paused. "I was just heading over there. To the boat. Why not come and see it? We could go over to Rum Point. Or out to the reef if you liked."

She had not been prepared for an invitation and it took her some time to answer. She should say no; she should claim, quite rightly, that she had to go to the supermarket. But now, in his presence, she found it impossible to do what she knew she should do.

"How long would it take?"

"As long or as short a time as you want. Fifteen minutes to get there. Ten minutes to get things going. Then forty minutes out and forty minutes in, depending on the wind and what the sea's doing."

She looked at her watch.

"What's everybody doing?" he asked. She realised that this was his way of asking where David was.

"I think that Clover's with James. Out on their bicycles, I think. Billy's at that dolphin place with Margaret. David's working."

"Does he ever take any time off?"

"Sundays, usually. Otherwise ... no, he's pretty busy." She looked at him. His eyes were registering pleasure at what she said.

"How about it?"

The sea was calm as they edged out into the sound. They had boarded the boat in the canal along which he moored it – a thin strip of water that provided access to four or five rather run-down houses. Dogs barked from the bank as the boat made its way towards the sea; a large Dobermann, ears clipped, kept pace with them, defending its territory with furious snarls.

She pointed to one of the houses. "Who lives in these places?" she asked.

"You can tell from the dogs," he said. "That Dobermann belongs to a man who owns two liquor stores, and a bar." He made a calming gesture towards the dog. "Dogs are aspirational here. Like boats."

She laughed. "That's his boat there?" She pointed to a gleaming white vessel. A towering superstructure was topped with a bristling forest of aerials and fishing rods.

"Must be."

Once in the sound he opened the throttle and the boat surged forward across the flat expanse of sea. The sky was high and empty of all but a few cumulus clouds on the horizon, off towards Cuba. The water was a light turquoise colour, the white sand showing a bare six feet below. Here and there, patches of undulating dark disclosed the presence of weed. In the distance, a line of white marked their destination, the reef that protected the sound from the open sea beyond. That was the point at which the seabed began to drop until, a few hundred yards further out, it reached the edge of the deep and fell away into hundreds of feet of darkness. The dive boats went there, dropping their divers down the side of a submarine cliff. It was dangerous: every so often divers went down and did not come up; nitrogen-drunk on beauty, they went too deep and forgot where they were.

It was hard to make oneself heard against the roar of the engine. He signalled to her where they were going, and she strained to make out the break in the reef that provided a passage out into the open sea. A small cluster of boats congregated not far away – the boats that took people out to see the school of giant stingrays that swam into the sound to be fed by the boatmen. The rays, accustomed to people, would glide obligingly round the legs of swimmers, taking fish from the hands of the guides. They had taken the children there on numerous occasions – it was one of the few outings the island afforded – and the memory reminded her that she was a mother. She looked away, and thought: *I should ask him to go back.* She wondered why she had said yes to this. It was … what was the right word for it? Folly. That was it. Folly.

He had slowed the boat to negotiate the difficult passage between the outcrops of coral that made up the reef. It was a clear enough route, and everybody who took a boat out there learned it soon and easily enough. One had to line up several points and keep a careful eye on which way the current was flowing. One had to read the sea, which provided all the necessary signs, particularly on a calm day like this.

"Are you all right with this?" she asked as he steered them towards the gap.

"Yes," he said. "I've done it a few times. You have to watch out, but it's simple enough."

"I won't distract you."

She looked over the side of the boat. The water was shallow enough to stand in, she thought. There was weed, lines of drifting black. A large shell, she thought – a conch, perhaps; a blur of white against the sand. There was a flash of colour as a school of bright blue fish darted past. There was the shadow of the boat on the seabed below.

"There." He had brought them through, and the reef and the breaking waves were suddenly behind them. He opened the throttle again to put water between them and the coral. The sea now was a different colour – a darker blue – and it was rougher too, with a swell bowling in towards them.

He throttled back, making the bow drop down. Then, glancing at a dial on the console, he switched the engine off entirely.

"We might as well conserve fuel. These big outboards are thirsty."

She leaned back against her seat and closed her eyes. She felt the sun on her face; the breeze too. There was silence.

"It's the peace, isn't it?" she muttered, to herself as much as to him. "It's the peacefulness."

She opened her eyes. He was struggling with the catch of a small cool-box that he had brought with them.

"Somebody gave me a bottle of champagne," he said. "A grateful patient."

The catch shifted and the champagne was revealed. Two glasses nestled against the ice, alongside the bottle. She wondered why he had packed two glasses. He had had the cool-box with him when he had met her at the tennis club, but he would not have known that she was there. So this could not have been planned for her. For his wife? For Alice?

The cork popped, shooting up into the air to fall into the sea beside them. She watched it floating away on a swell.

"I didn't mean that to happen," he said. "I disapprove of people who shake champagne and pop the corks. It's one of the biggest causes of eye injury there is." He grinned. "Not that I'm a spoil-sport."

He handed her a glass of champagne. "Here. For you."

She took the glass, which was cold to the touch. She raised it to her lips. It's too late, she thought. This is it.

He took a sip. "You don't mind, do you?" he asked.

"Mind what? Being here? Drinking champagne instead of being at the supermarket?"

He looked serious. "You don't mind that I asked you?"

She shrugged. "Why should I?"

He was studying her reaction. "Because I can't pretend that I didn't hope that I would find you at the tennis club."

For a while she said nothing. It thrilled her: she meant something to him. There was no dismay; just pleasure.

When she spoke the words, it seemed to her, came from somewhere else.

"I hadn't envisaged this happening. But it happens, doesn't it? It … well, it comes over one. I never thought it would. I never thought about it. It just happens."

He nodded. "I hadn't anticipated this either."

"So what do we do?"

The question hung in the air.

"Do?" he said. "I hadn't thought that far."

"Neither had I." She put down her glass. "Because we both have children to think about."

"Yes," he said. "And others."

"By that, you mean …"

She thought that he did not want her to see his wince, but she did. "Alice and David."

It was a mistake, she thought, to mention the names. They had not been present until then, but now they were. And there were only two glasses of champagne.

She drew in her breath. "I think maybe we shouldn't take this any further. I'm sorry."

His mouth opened slightly. She saw that he was gripping the glass tightly, as his knuckles were white. *I've said the wrong thing. It's entirely the wrong thing.*

"Is that what you feel?"

She nodded, and glanced at her watch. "I think it would have been nice. But it can't be. It just can't."

"If that's what you feel ..."

"It is. I'm really sorry, George. I wish that I were free to say yes. I wish that. But I'm not. And I don't think you're free either."

He looked down at the deck. "You're probably right." He drained his glass and put it back into the cool box. Then, picking up the bottle of champagne, he looked at it, held it up against the sun, and then poured it out over the side of the boat. She watched in astonishment, noticing the tiny bubbles, visible against the surface of the sea for a few instants before they disappeared.

"I'm so sorry," she said.

He replaced the bottle and took her glass from her.

"You don't have to say sorry," he said. "I'm the one who should apologise."

"No. You don't have to."

He reached for the ignition. "I suggest we write the whole thing off to experience. That's the civilised way of dealing with these things, I think."

It could have been said bitterly, but she did not detect any bitterness in his voice. He was a kind man, she thought. He was exactly what she thought, and hoped, he was.

9

When George turned the key in the ignition, the outboard engine spluttered into life briefly, but did not catch. He attempted to start it again. Sometimes it took a second try for the fuel to get through; a small blockage, a bubble of air could starve the injectors of fuel but these would right themselves. This time there was no response at all. He looked down at the safety-cord – this was a small key-like device that operated against a sprung switch and had to be in place for the engine to fire. It was correctly slotted in. He tried once more, and again there was no response.

She had not noticed the first failure, but now she did.

"Trouble?"

He raised an eyebrow. "I don't know. It won't start."

"Are we out of fuel?"

He pointed to the gauge. "We've got at least ten gallons. Maybe more."

"Perhaps you should try again."

He reached forward and turned the key. There was complete silence.

"I can check the batteries. A lead might have detached itself."

He opened a hatch, exposing two large twelve-volt batteries. All four leads were in position, and secure. He tried the key again, with the same result.

She glanced over her shoulder. After they had cleared the passage, they had gone half a mile or so out onto the open sea. Now, carried by the swell, they were little more than several hundred yards off the line of surf marking the location of the reef. In ten minutes or so, possibly less, they would have reached the point where the waves would carry them onto the reef itself.

"Have you got a radio?"

He shook his head. "I've got my phone. We're not too far out. We'll get reception."

She felt a surge of relief. "Then phone somebody."

"Who?"

She frowned. "The police. They'll know what to do."

He reached into his pocket to retrieve his phone. As he did so, he looked about, scanning the sea. On the other side of the reef, in the protected waters of the sound, he could see three or four boats still bobbing at anchor round the sting-ray feeding grounds. He could make out the heads of swimmers in the water.

"Could we attract their attention?" she asked.

"I'm not carrying any flares. If we had a flare they'd see it. But I haven't."

She stood up and looked over in the direction of the knot of boats. She had been frightened, but the human presence not too far away reassured her. If the worst came to the worst, they could abandon ship and swim back through the passage in the reef. They would be seen then, or they could even swim over to join the boats at anchor. It was not as if they were far out at sea; and the water, as usual, was invitingly warm.

She saw that George was looking anxiously at the reef, to which they were slowly being carried by the swell. She looked down: they were in about forty feet of water, she thought, but as they approached the reef that would diminish. Could they not anchor and then wait for help – boats regularly used the entrance to the sound and they would not have to wait too long.

"Your anchor," she suggested. "Couldn't we ..."

"Yes," he said. "I was thinking that."

He moved to the bow and opened a locker. Reaching in, he

lifted out a rather shabby-looking anchor to which a line of rusty chain was attached. He looked over the side of the boat.

"We'll have to get a bit closer to the reef," he said. "It's too deep here."

The swell seemed to pick up, and they found themselves being pressed closer and closer to the breaking waves and the jagged points of coral. When they were only a few boat's lengths from the first of the outcrops, George heaved the anchor over the side, paying out the chain and line.

She felt the boat shudder as the anchor line took the strain.

"She might drag a bit," he said. "We'll have to watch."

But it held, and the boat was soon pointed into the incoming swell, riding it confidently.

George sat down. He wiped his brow and smiled at her. "There we are. Emergency over."

She scanned the sea. "No sign of anything."

He seemed confident that help would not be long delayed. "Something will come by. A fishing boat. A yacht. Less than an hour, I'd say." He looked at her apologetically. "I'm sorry about all this. You went off to play tennis and ended up shipwrecked."

"Not quite."

"Near enough. And I rather wish I hadn't disposed of the rest of the champagne."

She made a sign to indicate she did not mind. "I'm fine."

He was about to say something, but did not. She was pleased that he did not, as she did not wish to discuss what had gone before. Some lovers, she thought; some affair.

She steered the conversation to neutral topics. They discussed the plan to extend the system of canals to sensitive mangrove swamps. They discussed the ambitions of the developers who were setting out to cover the island with concrete and pastel-coloured condos. He became animated on the subject of corruption. She listened, and found herself agreeing with everything he said. David was far less harsh in his judgement of developers; in fact, he spoke up in favour of them. That was the difference.

She looked at her watch. They had been anchored for forty-five minutes and there had been no sign of any boat. It was barely noon, and there were another six hours of daylight, but what if nobody came? Who would report them missing? David had no idea where she was and she did not want to ask George whether Alice knew that he was going out in the boat. If she did, then she would raise the alarm and they would send out a search party, but if she did not know, then it could be the next day before anybody came and found them. Did they have enough water, she wondered. And there was no food, although one could last for a long time without anything to eat.

"You aren't worried?" he asked.

"Not really." She hesitated. "No, maybe a bit."

"We'll be all right. In fact ..." He broke off, as he had seen something and was standing up, shading his eyes with his hand. "Yes. Help's on its way."

She stood up too, and he pointed out the direction in which she should look. He took her hand in his, to do so, which was not strictly necessary – he could have pointed. But she felt a stab of excitement at his touch.

There was a boat in the distance – a powerboat churning the sea behind it, heading their way.

She squeezed his hand in relief, and he returned the pressure. Then he leaned over and kissed her gently on the cheek.

"See," he said. "We're saved."

She felt herself blushing at the kiss, like an innocent schoolgirl. He should not have done it, she thought, because they had agreed, had they not, that they were not going to take this further. But she was glad that he had because the kiss had felt so wrong and so right at the same time.

As the boat approached, George began to move his arms from side to side in the maritime gesture of distress. Figures could now be made out on the deck of the other boat and there was a response. The boat slowed and changed course towards them.

"Thank God," said George.

"A relief," said Amanda.

"I'm going to have to get a new outboard after this," George said.

The other boat was a rather larger cruiser, set up for deep-sea fishing, although not sporting any rods. Gingerly it came alongside, taking care to leave sufficient distance so as not to be pushed by the swell on to the anchored boat.

"What's the trouble?" asked the man at the controls.

"Engine failure," shouted George. "We'll need a tow."

The man nodded. "We'll throw you a line. Ready?"

Amanda had been looking at the other skipper. Now she looked at the crew, of whom there were four. With a start she recognised John Galbraith, one of David's partners in the firm. He saw her at much the same time as she saw him, and he waved.

"Amanda!" he called out.

She acknowledged the call.

"I didn't expect to see you," he shouted out. "Are you all right?"

She cupped her hands and shouted a reply. "Fine. Absolutely fine."

John gave the thumbs-up sign and then busied himself fixing

the line to a cleat at the stern of the boat. Then the other end of the line was thrown across to George. It went into the sea the first time, but was retrieved and thrown again. This time it was caught and secured to the bow of the stricken vessel. The anchor was pulled up and the rescuing boat took the strain.

Progress under tow was slow, but once through the passage in the reef there was little to do but to sit back and wait. Amanda went to the stern and sat by herself, deep in thought. The implications of what had happened were slowly sinking in. The odds against being rescued by somebody she knew were not all that high. The island was small and people knew one another. If she had imagined that she could go anywhere – anywhere at all – and not be spotted, then she was mistaken. Yet it was particularly bad luck that it should be John, of all people. He and David saw one another every day, for most of the day; he would be bound to mention that he had rescued his colleague's wife.

She felt raw inside. Dread, she thought. That's what dread feels like. Rawness. Hollowness. She would have to speak to John. She would have to ask him not to say anything. And that meant that she would have to confess that her presence on George's boat was being kept secret from David. It was nothing short of an admission of adultery.

The rescuing boat took them all the way back to the canal. One of their crew jumped out onto the dock to pull them in, and they were soon safely attached. Amanda went ashore. The other boat was standing off and was about to leave to go back to its own berth at a marina some distance away.

John waved to her. "Happy ending," he called out. "But I'll have to claim salvage from David!"

She shook her head. "No," she called out. "Don't."

He laughed. "Only joking."

The other boat was beginning to pull away. She looked at John desperately. She was unable to shout out a request that he say nothing. She waved again, trying to make a cancelling gesture. He waved back, giving her a thumbs-up sign. Then they moved off, leaving behind them a wake that washed sedately at the edges of the canal. She heard the barking of the liquor store man's Dobermann, and laughter from the other boat.

George was at her side.

"You knew him?"

She nodded miserably. "David's partner."

He was silent for a while. Then: "Oh. Not good."

"No."

He looked at her expectantly. "What do you want me to do?"

"You? Nothing."

She thought of what she should do. She would go back to the tennis club, collect her car, and then drive straight to the Galbraith house and wait for John to come home. She would explain to him that she did not want him to mention to David that she had been out in George's boat. She would tell him the truth; she would explain that there was nothing between them but that she understood that it looked suspicious. She would appeal to him through truthfulness.

10

John Galbraith lived on his own in a house overlooking South Sound. The house was older than others around it, having been built when the land in that area was first cleared. It was modest in scale compared with more recent constructions, and less ostentatious. A recent storm had brought down several of his trees but the house itself was still largely obscured by vegetation when viewed from the road, and it was only once on the driveway that one could see the full charm of the Caribbean-style bungalow. A deep veranda ran the length of the front, giving an impression of cool and shade. The exterior was painted light blue and the woodwork white – a local combination that could still be seen on the few remaining old Cayman cottages. It was a perfect colour scheme for a landscape dominated by sea and sky.

John, who was in his early forties, had been in the Caymans for almost fifteen years, having arrived several years before David and Amanda. He was now the senior local partner in the accountancy firm in which David worked, and would become, so everybody said, an international partner before too long.

He was unmarried – a fact that led to the usual speculation, but none of it substantiated. There were rumours about his private life, of course, about boyfriends, but if these ever reached him, he showed only indifference to gossip, and cheerfully enjoyed the company of women, who found him sympathetic and a good listener.

Amanda encountered John socially at drinks and dinner parties. She and David had been to his house on several occasions, and had entertained him themselves. As a spare man who was good company at a dinner party, he was much in demand by hostesses seeking to balance a table. He could be counted on to talk to any woman he was seated next to without giving rise to any complications. He could be counted upon, too, never to mention business, which formed the core of many of the other men's conversation. People said there had been a tragedy in his life somewhere, but nobody had discovered what it was. There was one wild theory – risible, Amanda thought – that he had killed somebody in New Zealand, where he originally came from, and had come to the Caymans to escape prosecution.

He was not in when Amanda arrived. She had thought that she would probably arrive too early – it would have taken time for them to dock the other boat – but she wanted to be sure that she did not miss him. She had no idea what plans he might have, but she thought there was a danger that he had been invited to the Hills' – she knew he was friendly with them – and she would have to see him before that. At the Hills' it would be too late, as he might say something to David.

She parked her car on his driveway under the shade of a large Flamboyant tree and began her wait. The minutes dragged past; after half an hour, she got out of the car and stretched her legs; after an hour she began to wonder whether she should write him a note and slip it under his front door. It could be brief – a request that he say nothing about seeing her in the boat and offering to give him her reasons later on, when they could meet to discuss it.

She had a notebook with her in the glove compartment of the car, and she took this out and began to compose the note. She was writing this when she heard the car and, looking up, saw John's dark blue Mercedes coming up the drive. He slowed down as he drew level with her and peered into the car. Recognising her, he gave a wave and continued to the garage at the side of the house.

Amanda left her car and walked up the drive to meet him.

"Twice in one day," joked John. "Is everything all right?"

"I wanted to thank you," she said. "But you dashed off."

He smiled, and gestured to the front door. "Come in. I'll make some coffee, or something cooler?"

She followed him into the house.

"I must say," he began, "that I've often thought about what would happen if one lost power out there. I don't have a boat myself, but I'd always have an auxiliary engine if I did. Something to get one back through the reef."

She agreed. "It seems reasonable."

He led her into a sitting room at the front of the house. From the windows at the end of the room, there was a view of a short stretch of grass and then, framed by trees, the sea. On the walls there were paintings on Caribbean themes: a Jamaican street scene, a small island rising sharply out of the sea, a couple of colourful abstracts.

He invited her to sit down while he went to prepare coffee. "Where's David?" he asked. His tone was level. "Working, I suppose."

"Yes."

"Not my fault," he said. "I keep telling him to work less. He puts the rest of us to shame."

"Yes, I think so too. But ..."

He looked at her expectantly.

"This isn't easy for me," she said.

He stared at her, and then sat down. He would make the coffee later.

"It's about today? About that business out at the reef?"

She nodded. "I know what you're probably thinking."

He held her gaze. "I try to keep out of other people's private affairs," he said. "It crossed my mind that it was a bit ... how should I put it? Surprising that you were out there with ... what's that doctor's name again?"

"George Collins."

"Yes. George Collins." He paused. "I hardly know him. I've met him once or twice at the usual functions, but they seem to keep to themselves for the most part, don't they?"

"They do."

He sighed. "I didn't think it was any of my business what was happening on that boat."

"But there wasn't anything happening," she blurted out. "We just went out in the boat together."

He stared at her for a moment, as if he was deciding whether to say something. Then he shrugged. "Well, that's fine then. You've made the point that it was just a casual trip. I'll go and make coffee."

"No," she said. "That's not the point. The point is that David doesn't know that I went out. I didn't tell him."

He stared at her. "Oh."

"Yes. I didn't tell him. George bumped into me at the tennis club and asked me on the spur of the moment." That was not strictly true, she thought, but it would become too complicated if she had to explain further.

"He just suggested it? Like that?"

"Yes." She wondered if that sounded implausible.

He seemed to be weighing up the likelihood of her telling the truth. "So what you're saying is that this was an unplanned outing that you didn't tell David about. And now you think that David will be …"

"Will be suspicious."

He looked out of the window. "You must forgive me," he said. "As a bachelor, I'm not sure that I understand how these things work. Are you saying that a husband would automatically be suspicious if his wife went off on an outing with another man?"

She wanted to laugh. Was he that unaware of how the world worked? "Yes, that's exactly what I'm telling you. And he would be. As would a wife."

"Always?"

She thought about this. "Well, it depends on the circumstances. You couldn't go out for dinner with another man, for example, unless you discussed it with your husband first."

He asked about the position of an old friend of both husband and wife. Could he take the wife out for dinner if the husband was away?

"Of course. An old friend could do that, yes. As I said, it depends on the circumstances."

"Well, that seems reasonable enough. But …" He frowned. "But you're telling me that David would think that you and this doctor … George Collins were having an affair?"

She did not answer him immediately. It was possible that David would not form that impression, but there was a good chance he would. She explained her anxiety to John, who listened attentively. But halfway through her explanation, she faltered.

"I suppose I should tell you the truth."

She saw the effect that this had on him. He drew back slightly, as if offended.

"I would hope you'd tell me the truth," he said stiffly. "Who likes to be lied to?"

"I'm sorry. Of course you wouldn't want to be lied to. The problem is, you see, that I've felt attracted to George Collins. I like him. I'd go so far as to say that I'm interested in him, but I haven't been having an affair with him. We discussed it – yes, we did talk about it, but it hasn't gone anywhere."

He looked at her intently. "I'm sorry that you feel you can't trust me with the truth."

She was aghast. "But what I've just told you is absolutely true."

"Is it?"

She became animated. "Yes, it is. It is the truth."

He held her gaze. There was an odd expression on his face, she thought; it was as if he were just about to pull the rabbit out of the hat.

"Well," he said evenly. "If that were the case, then I must have imagined what I saw from our boat."

She looked puzzled.

"I saw," he continued, "the two people in that boat kissing. I'm sorry, but that's what I saw. I just happened to be looking through my binoculars at the time. We'd seen the signalling and I was interested to see what was going on. I looked through my binoculars."

She stared at him in silence. George had kissed her – that brief, entirely chaste kiss of relief. It was not even on the lips. A kiss on the cheek. And he had been seen.

"That's not what you think it was," she stuttered.

He spread his palms in a gesture of disengagement. "I saw what I saw. Forgive me for jumping to conclusions."

"He kissed me when he saw that you were coming to our rescue. It was the equivalent of ... of a hug. That's all. There was nothing more to it than that." She paused. "I promise you, John. I give you my word."

She could tell that he did not believe her. And had she been in his position, she would not have believed herself either.

"Well, I don't think it has anything to do with me," he said. "As I said, I like to avoid getting involved in other people's entanglements. I know that these things happen, by the way. I'm not standing here being disapproving."

"I feel so powerless. I can't make you believe …"

He interrupted her. "You don't have to make me believe anything, Amanda."

"I'm not cheating on David," she said, putting as much resolution into her voice as she could muster. "I want you to know that."

"Fine. So you've told me."

"But I need to know: will you tell David about what happened today?"

He rose to his feet. His tone now was distant. "I'm sorry, but I'm not going to lie. I know you may have little time for it, but I happen to hold a religious position on these things. I will not tell a lie." He looked at her. "Does that make me sound pompous? Okay, it does. But that's where I stand."

She struggled to control herself. Tears were not far off, she felt, but she did not want to break down. "You don't sound pompous, John. And I'd never ask you to lie. All I'd like to ask you is not to tell him about my being out there in the boat. That's not a lie. It's just …"

"Concealment?"

She tried to fight back. "We don't have a duty to tell everybody everything. That's not concealment, for heaven's sake."

He seemed to reflect on this. He walked to the window and looked out across the grass to the sea beyond. She thought: he's never been involved in the messiness that goes with relationships. He doesn't know. He's a monk, with a monk's understanding of life, which is not how life is for most of us.

"I'll not say anything," he said after a while. "I won't mention the incident to David, but, and I'm sorry to say you won't make me change my mind on this, if he were to ask me about it, then I would have to tell him the truth." He turned to face her. "And that truth would be the whole truth."

She knew what he meant by this. If he were asked, he would mention the kiss.

She nodded her acceptance. Then she said, "John, may I just say one thing more? I haven't lied to you today. I promise you that. I've got nothing to hide."

He raised an eyebrow. "Apart from what you're hiding from David."

She looked down at the floor. She would not lose her temper.

"You know something?" she said. "You think that you understand things. You don't, you know. You've kept yourself apart from the messy business of being an ordinary human being with ordinary human temptations and imperfections and … and conflicts. You're looking at the world through ice, though, John."

His look was impassive, but she could tell that she had wounded him. She had not meant to do that, and she immediately apologised. "I'm sorry. That came out more harshly than I intended. I'm very sorry."

He held up a hand. "But you're right," he said. "I have kept myself away from these things you mention. But have you any idea – any idea at all – of what that has cost me? You don't know, do you, about how I've come back here sometimes, at night, by myself, and cried my eyes out? Like a boy? You don't know that, do you?"

"I'm sorry, John ..."

He shook his head. "I didn't mean to burden you with that. It's nothing to do with you."

She got up and went towards him. She put an arm around his shoulder, to comfort him. He flinched at her touch.

"I understand," she whispered. "I understand."

"Do you? I don't think people do."

"They do. Some may not, but most do."

After that, they were, for a time, quite silent. She moved away from him and told him that she would not stay for coffee after all. He nodded, and accompanied her, unspeaking, to the door. The heat outside met her like a wall.

II

Teddy's father was arrested four days later. It was done with the maximum, and unnecessary, fuss, with two police cars, sirens wailing, arriving at the front of the house shortly after eight in the morning. Amanda was taking the dog for a walk round the block at the time, and saw what happened.

"They made a big thing of it," she said to David that evening. "There were six or seven of them – one or two senior officers, I think, and the rest constables. It was totally over the top."

He snorted. "Role playing."

"Anyway, they bundled Gerry Arthur out of the house, put him into one of the cars, and then drove off, sirens going full tilt."

"Ridiculous."

"Then one of the constables came out carrying a computer, put that into the other car, and off they went."

"A show – that's what it was."

She looked at her husband. He had a built-in antipathy to officials.

"What was it all about?" she asked. "Have you heard?"

"I met Jim Harris," he said. "He told me that Gerry Arthur is being charged with being party to some fraud or other. Something to do with the scuttling of a ship to get the insurance payment. Apparently that sort of thing happens. You sink your boat and claim the insurance."

"I'm surprised. They go to that Baptist church, don't they?"

David laughed. "Baptists are every bit as capable of sinking ships as anybody else, I suspect. But I wouldn't have thought that Gerry Arthur did that sort of thing anyway. He's one of our clients. We audit his books, and they're always scrupulously clean. This'll be a put-up thing."

She asked him to explain.

"You know what it's like here. You make a remark that offends somebody high up in the political food-chain. All of a sudden, it's discovered that there are problems with your work permit. Gerry has status, I think, which means they can't chuck him out, even if he's not an actual citizen. So the next best thing is to get him into trouble with the police."

She pointed out that it would be difficult to set up the sinking of a ship.

"No," he said. 'The ship would have sunk anyway. So all you have to do is to create some evidence of an instruction to the captain that points to the thing being deliberate. You've got your case. You leak something to the police and they're delighted to get the possibility of a high profile conviction. Off you go."

"What will happen?"

He was not sure. "I heard that they've let him out on bail. They might drop the charges if he agrees to go off to the British Virgin Islands or somewhere like that. It'll die down. It usually does."

"It's very unfair."

"Of course it is."

She looked at him. "To be accused of doing something you haven't done. That must be very hard."

He returned her gaze. "Yes. Certainly." Then he said, "To be accused of doing something you have done – that must be hard as well, don't you think?"

She caught her breath. "Yes, I suppose so."

He was still watching her, and it was at that moment that she became certain that he knew.

Clover said to Teddy: "Your dad was taken off to jail, Teddy. The police came. Is he still in jail?"

The boy bit his lip. "They brought him back. They made a mistake."

"Really? Why did they take him anyway? Was he spying?"

Teddy shook his head. "Don't be stupid."

"It's not stupid. We know there are spies here."

Teddy kicked at the ground in his frustration. "He hadn't done anything. They said he'd sunk one of his boats, but he didn't. You'd have to be stupid to sink one of your own boats."

She nodded. The world of adults was opaque and sometimes difficult to fathom; but the proposition that one would not normally sink one of one's own boats seemed reasonable enough. "I'm sorry for you, Teddy," she said. "It must be awful having your dad taken away by the police."

"Thank you. But he didn't do anything."

Later, she talked to James about it. He agreed with her that the sinking of the boat might just be a cover for the real charge of spying. Now that the police had become involved, though, he thought there was no need to continue with their observations. "It's in their hands now," he pronounced. "We can stop."

He had lost interest, she sensed, and so the notebook, and the photographs they had collected, were filed away in a cupboard in James's room. The photographs, of which there were about fifteen, had been printed on James's computer and labelled with the date, time and place when they had been taken. *At the tennis club, Saturday morning. Suspect 1 gets into the car with Suspect 2.* And *At the tennis club, Suspect 1 talks to Suspect 2. Details of conversation unknown.*

She sensed that he was more concerned with other things. She invited him to the tree-house, but he rarely came now, and when he did, he seemed detached, as if he wanted to be somewhere else. He never stayed long.

She made suggestions. "We could fix the tree-house; I could get some wood. We could take more things up there. If you wanted, I could make you a shelf of your own for your stuff."

He shrugged. "Maybe."

She persisted. "We could take the walkie-talkies up there. I could leave one there and you could take the other to your house. We could speak to each other."

He looked bored. "Out of range," he said. "You have to be able to see the other person, or they don't work. Those are useless walkie-talkies."

He looked at his watch. "I can't stay for long."

She said, "You're always saying that. You're always saying you have to go and do something else."

"I'm not."

"You are. You do it all the time."

He looked at his watch again.

"Well, it's true," he said. "I've got stuff to do."

She felt frustrated at not being able to pin him down. She wanted to have his full attention, but he seemed now to be reluctant to give her that. It was as if he were holding back; as if he were away somewhere, in a different place – a place that she could not get to, or understand. And yet he was not rude to her. He was kind, and, unlike other boys, behaved gently, without any of the pushing or shoving that boys seemed to use. That was part of his appeal – that, and the way he looked. She thought nobody could ever look more beautiful. She had, hidden away, a photograph that she had taken of him without his knowledge.

Amanda sensed her daughter's unhappiness.

"Something's wrong, darling. I can tell."

"Nothing."

"No, you can't just say nothing. If something's wrong, you should tell me about it."

"I told you: everything's fine."

Amanda put an arm about her. "James? Is that it? Has James been nasty to you?"

She shook her head. The denial was genuine. "He's never nasty. He's too nice for that."

"Doesn't want to play any more? Is that it?"

This was greeted with silence, which was an answer in itself. Amanda gave Clover a hug. "My darling, here's something that you're going to have to get used to. Boys are different – they have things that keep them busy and sometimes they don't seem interested in the things that girls want to do. Boys can ignore you when you really want them to take notice. That can be really hard. They break our hearts, you see. Do you know what I'm talking about? They make us girls feel sad because they don't want to be with us. There may be no special reason for that – they might just want to be by themselves. You're just beginning to see this now; when you're a teenager – a bit older, maybe – you're going to see it all much more clearly. And there's no easy answer, no magic wand. I can't make James want to spend time with you. I can't make him be your friend. I wish I could, but I can't."

She nestled into her mother. She just wanted to be James's friend. She just wanted to be with him. He had been happy with that before, but now no longer.

Amanda kissed Clover's forehead. So precious, she thought.

She tried to remember what it had been like at that age. The problem was that we so quickly forgot that even young children have intense feelings for others. Passionate adoration does not suddenly arrive, ready made, when one is fifteen or sixteen – the stage of the first fumbling romance. Falling head over heels for another can occur years earlier, and we would understand these things better if only we bothered to remember. That intensity of feeling for a friend was usually not expressed in any physical way, but it represented a yearning that was already knocking on the door.

12

Clover knew all along that there would come a day when she would have to go away to school. The Cayman Prep School took children up to thirteen before handing them over to the High School. Many children made the transition smoothly and completed their education in the senior division next door, but for a considerable proportion of expatriates the expense of sending children for their secondary education abroad was outweighed by the risks involved in staying. The island had a drug problem, as well as a problem of teenage pregnancy. Stories circulated of girls who had stayed being seen as an easy target by boys from West Bay. Sending children abroad might have its drawbacks, but at least the teenage years would be passed, for the most part, in the supervised conditions of a boarding school. There the day-to-day headaches of looking after adolescents were borne by people paid to bear them – and experienced in doing so.

Clover knew, and accepted that boarding school awaited her. She was ready to go; several girls who had been in the year above her at the Prep School were already there and seemed to enjoy it. They came back each school holidays and were full of stories of a world that seemed to her to be unimaginably exciting and exotic. There were stories of school dances and trips to London. There were accounts of clandestine assignations with boys – meetings that took place under the threat of dire punishment if discovered. It all sounded to her like a rather exciting prison camp in which girls and boys pitted their wits against the guards. But unlike a prison camp, you could have your own pictures on the wall, perfectly good food, and outings, admittedly restricted, to the cinema and shops.

Her parents talked to her about the choice of school. David wanted something in Scotland, and identified a school in Perthshire that seemed to offer everything they wanted. They showed her the pictures in the school brochure.

"You see how attractive it is," said David. "You'd be staying in one of those buildings over there. See? Those are the girls' dormitories."

She looked at the photograph. It was of an alien landscape, all hills and soft colours, but it was a world that she had been brought up to believe was where she belonged. The Caribbean, with its dark greens and light blues, was temporary; this was permanent.

"And that's the pipe band," said Amanda, pointing at one of the photographs. "You can learn the pipes if you like. Or the violin. Or any instrument, really. They have everything."

There were misgivings. "I won't know anybody. Nobody I know is going there."

"You'll make plenty of new friends. It's a very friendly place."

Silence.

"And if I'm sick?"

"Why should you be sick? Anyway, they'll have a sick room. There'll be a nurse. Really, darling, you'll be fine."

"I suppose so."

"What about James?" asked her mother. "He's going off to school too, isn't he?"

James had not told her very much. "I think he's going to a school in England. I don't know what it's called." She looked at her mother. "Couldn't you tell them about Strathearn? Couldn't you show them this?" She pointed to the brochure.

Amanda smiled. "It's nothing to do with us," she said. "They're not Scottish, like Daddy. James's father is English. He'll want James to go somewhere in England. It's only natural."

"But Scotland and England are close together, aren't they? Aren't they next door?"

"They are. But the schools are different, I think. They want him to go to an English school."

"They could change their minds if they saw this brochure."

Amanda looked at her daughter fondly. "You'll be able to see James in the holidays. He'll be here, and so will you. You'll still see him."

Clover became silent. She stared at the photographs of the school and imagined that it was her face in one of the pictures. And standing next to her was not that boy with ginger hair who was in the picture, but James. She wanted to share what lay ahead with him. She did not want to be with strangers.

Her mother touched her arm lightly. "You'll get over it," she whispered.

"Get over what?"

"You'll get over what you feel for James. I know right now he's a very special friend, but we meet other people, you know. There'll be plenty of boys at – different boys. You'll get to know them and they'll be your friends."

She stared at her mother. How could somebody as old as that understand what it was like? What did she know?

That night, lying in her bed, she closed her eyes and imagined, for the first time, that James was with her. It made her feel warm to think of his being at her side, under the covers, as if they were lost children. His feet felt cold as she moved her own feet against his. She held his hand and she listened to his breathing. She told him about her school and he told her about his. They were together and they would stay together until morning. Nobody could take him away from her; no school in England could keep him from her. They would stay together forever. From now on. Forever.

It was the day following the conversation about schools. Amanda and Clover went to the supermarket near the airport to stock up for the week. Outside in the car park, as they were unloading the trolley into the back of the car, a car drew up beside them. A woman got out. Amanda paid her no attention and was surprised when she suddenly realised that it was Alice Collins.

Amanda moved to the side of the car to greet her. "Sorry. I didn't recognise you behind those sunglasses."

Alice took off the sunglasses, folded them, and then placed them in her hip pocket. "Better?"

"Yes. I wasn't paying attention."

She saw that the other woman was not smiling. There was tension in her face.

"Is something wrong?"

Alice turned away; it was as if she had not heard the question. Then, without saying anything, she walked off. Amanda opened her mouth to say something, but Alice had walked round the side of another parked car and was lost to view. From within the car, she could hear Clover operating the electric window.

"What did Mrs Collins say?"

"She didn't say anything," said Amanda. "She's in a rush, I think."

She finished the unpacking of her trolley. She felt quite weak with the shock of the deliberate snub. It was the feeling one has after some driving error on one's part brings a snarl from another driver – a feeling of rawness, of surprise at the hostility of another.

Clover was listening to music, her ear buds in place. Amanda drove off, her heart still racing after the encounter with Alice. She must know; but how? Had John said something? She was not confident that he could be trusted; it was not that he would gossip – there was a far greater possibility that he would speak about what he had seen on principle. But if he spoke to anybody, would it not be to David, rather than to Alice? She considered the possibilities. One was that John was friendly with Alice and felt that he had a duty to warn her. Or he could have spoken to David, who had told Alice in order to get her to warn George off. That was feasible only if David would *want* to warn George off, which was far from clear. Another possibility was that George had decided to make a clean breast of things and had told Alice that he had almost embarked on an affair but had not done so. He might have done that had he thought that news would leak out somehow – probably through John – and that it would be better to raise the matter himself rather than to protest innocence once his wife became aware of it.

"Look out!"

Clover had spotted the car making the dangerous attempt at overtaking. Amanda pulled over sharply, and the two vehicles that had been heading straight for one another avoided collision by a matter of a few inches.

"Didn't you see him?"

Amanda looked in the mirror. The other car, now behind them, was being driven erratically – far too fast, and halfway into the other lane.

"That was his fault. He shouldn't have been overtaking there. The road's clearly marked."

"Maybe he's drunk."

"Could be."

They drove on in silence. As was always the case with such things, notions of what she should have done came after the event. She should have pursued Alice and asked her what was wrong. She should have said to her that whatever she had heard was not the real truth – the real truth was that there was nothing between her and George and there never had been; accepting the brush-off was tantamount to an admission of guilt.

Clover switched off her music. She looked at her mother.

"I hate this place," she said.

Amanda turned to look at her daughter. "What place?"

"Here. This. This whole place. Cayman."

"I thought you liked it."

Clover shook her head vigorously. "There's nothing to do. And I've got no friends."

Amanda's gaze returned to the road ahead. The plane from Cayman Brac, a small twelve-seater, was coming in to land; its shadow passed across the road and the mangrove swamp on the other side.

"You need to get away to school. That's soon enough." She paused. "And you have got friends. You've got Holly ..."

"She doesn't like me any more. She spends most of her time with that American girl."

"You've got James."

This was greeted with silence.

Amanda shot her a glance. "You still like James, don't you?"

Clover moved her head slightly.

Amanda spoke gently. "He's special to you, isn't he? It's good to have a special friend."

Suddenly Clover turned to her mother. "Do you think that

when we're both grown up ..."

"Yes? When you're both grown up?"

"That maybe James and I will get married? Do you think that might happen?"

Amanda suppressed a smile. "Possibly, but it's far too early to even think about that. You never know whom you're going to marry. But what you really want to do is to marry somebody who's kind. That's the most important thing, you know. They don't have to be good-looking or rich or anything like that – but they have to be kind."

"James is kind."

"Yes, I'm sure he is. But it's very early to talk about what may or may not happen. You're going to meet plenty of other boys, you know, and it's highly likely that some of them will be every bit as nice as James. You've got years and years to meet other people, and so you shouldn't make your mind up too early."

"But he's the one I want."

"But that could change. You might think very differently when you're ... say, twenty-five, twenty-six. You may have very different ideas."

"I won't."

"I think you'll find that you will."

"No."

The conversation ended there. They had reached the turn-off to their house and Clover would shortly have to get out to open the gate.

Over the next few weeks, James's visits, which had become less frequent anyway, stopped altogether. Clover waited several days before summoning up her courage to call him on his phone.

He sounded friendly enough when he answered, but when she asked if he would like to come round to listen to some music, he sounded wary.

"Maybe I'd better not," he said.

"Why not? Just for half an hour?"

"Because …"

"Because what?"

He did not reply immediately, but after a while he said, "Ted's coming round."

She waited for him to invite her too, but he did not.

"I could come too."

This was greeted with silence.

She tried again. "I could come, if you'd like."

She heard his breathing. "Actually, Clover, it was just me and Ted. We were going to do some things."

"What things?"

"Ted's got a metal detector."

She persisted. "Couldn't I …"

"No, Clover, sorry. Maybe some other time."

There was silence.

"Don't you like me any more?" It was a wild gamble. He could easily say no, he did not, and that would be the end of the friendship. But he did not. "Of course I like you, it's just that my mother says that you and I should … shouldn't spend so much time together."

She absorbed this.

"What's it got to do with her?"

He sounded surprised. "She says …"

"You don't have to do everything your mother tells you, James." And with that she hung up. She hoped that he would call her back, chastened, apologetic, but he did not. She sank her head in her hands. Why did she feel so empty, so unhappy? Why should a boy do this? She had never asked for this to happen; all she wanted was to be his friend, forever if possible, but at least for that day, for that moment. She wanted to see him again and listen to the way he laughed. She wanted him to look at her and smile. She wanted it to be the same as it always had been. Which is, of course, what we all want. We all want love, friendship, happiness to last forever, to be as it was before.

13

There was nothing in David's behaviour to indicate that he knew. She watched him closely over the days that followed the encounter with Alice in the car park. But there was nothing unusual in the way in which he spoke to her; nothing to suggest a change in the polite, but somewhat distant, relations between them. He was busy preparing for a business trip to New York that would take place two weeks later – a trip that he said would be awkward. There were Internal Revenue Service enquiries into the affairs of one of the firm's clients and he had been requested to attend a hearing. It was entirely voluntary – the Cayman Islands were outside the jurisdiction of the American tax authorities, but the client was asserting his innocence vigorously and had waived any privilege of confidentiality. David was sure that the client had nothing to hide, but he knew that he would be treated as a hostile witness, that he would be disbelieved.

She heard that John Galbraith would be going too. He disclosed this casually, but her heart thumped when she heard it.

"Why does he have to go? It's your client, isn't it?"

"I took him over from John," he replied. "He looked after him for part of the period they're interested in."

She searched around for something to say. "John would be good in court ..."

"It's not actual court proceedings. It's an enquiry."

"He'd be good at that."

He was looking at her. They were sitting in the kitchen; he had just returned from work – late – and was drinking a beer at the kitchen table. The air conditioner wheezed in the background. He said: "That damn air conditioner. Has the man been?"

"He came and looked. He did something to it. He was here for only fifteen minutes or so. He was singing some sort of hymn while he worked – I heard him."

"They've all got religion."

"Well, at least they believe in something. What do air conditioning men believe in ... in New York, for instance?"

He raised his bottle of beer to his lips. "The dollar. And at least that's real."

She turned up the gas under the pasta she was reheating for him. The smell of garlic was too strong for her, and she wrinkled her nose; but he liked to souse things in garlic; he always had.

"Is John travelling with you?" She tried to make the question sound casual.

"Yes. There, but he's coming back before me."

"And staying in the same hotel?"

He looked up sharply. "What is this?"

"Nothing. I was only asking ..."

He smiled. "What's it with John? Do you think we share a room?"

She brushed this aside. "Of course not."

"You think he's gay, don't you?"

She shrugged. "How can you tell? I know what people say, but how can they tell? He's never said anything, has he?"

"He doesn't have to."

She wanted to get off the subject, but he had more to say.

"He's discreet, of course. People like that often are. Conventional, high-achieving background – a very prominent New Zealand family. His father's a general, I think, or an admiral – something of the sort. He's used to not giving anything away."

She did not react.

"For instance," David continued, "if he knew something, he wouldn't speak about it."

"Oh yes?" Her voice was small, and she thought he might not have heard her. But he had.

"Yes."

She had her back to him, but she felt his eyes upon her.

She stirred the pasta. It was already cooked and it would spoil if she over-heated it. But it was hard for her to turn round. "That's good."

"You know what I think?"

She struggled to keep her voice even. "What?"

He finished his beer, tilting the bottle to get the last few drops. "I think he rather likes me."

She reached for the plate she had put on the side of the stove. "Likes you? Likes you as a friend? As a colleague?"

A mocking tone crept into his voice. "Come on, Amanda. Come on."

She dished out the pasta. The odour of garlic rose from the plate, drowning the tomatoes, the onion, the slices of Italian sausage. "You mean he likes you ... like that?"

He nodded. "Who knows? I've done nothing to encourage him in that view. And he knows that I'm not interested."

She put the plate in front of him at the table. She and Clover had eaten earlier, but she usually sat down and kept him company when he came in late like this. "He may not know. Or he might think that you ... well, that you liked men as well as liking women."

He began his meal, spearing pieces of pasta on his fork. "I doubt it. And anyway, frankly I wouldn't care to try ..."

"I'm glad to hear that."

"I'm going to have another beer."

She rose to her feet. "I'll get it."

It was while she was reaching into the fridge that he told her. "He came to see me the other day, you know. In the office. He stood in the doorway for a few seconds, as if he were hesitating. Then he came in. He said that he wanted to speak to me about something."

She was holding the bottle of cold beer. Her hand was wet. She did not turn round.

"Then he kind of clammed up. He shook his head and said it had been nothing. He said: some other time. Something like that."

She straightened up. "Your beer. Here it is."

He opened the bottle. "Poor John. It must have been something to do with his private life. I would have been perfectly happy to listen to him – he maybe doesn't have anybody else to speak to – living on his own, as he does."

She sat down.

"Mind you, it could have been something to do with the office. Jenny is being a real pain in the neck right now. She's taken it into her head that we need to change all our internal procedures. It's chronic." He went on to describe Jenny's plans and nothing more was said about John. After a few minutes, she made the excuse of going to check that the children had finished their homework. She left the kitchen and made her way along the corridor that separated the living quarters from the bedrooms. She stopped halfway, in front of a poster listing the islands of the Caribbean. She remembered how she had stood in front of it every day, with one of the children in her arms, and read out the list of names and pointed to the islands on the map. They had been taught to identify them all, from Cuba down to Grenada. Now she found herself staring at Tortola – a small circle of green in the blue of the sea. She thought, inconsequentially, of something a friend had said the other day – "Tortolans – they're the rudest people in the Caribbean, by a long chalk. They have a major attitude problem." But could one generalise like that? And people sometimes appeared rude for a reason; here and there, history had left a legacy of hatreds that could prove hard to bury.

If John had not told him already, then he would probably do so on the trip to New York. They would be together, at close quarters. He would say something when they had drunk a beer or two. But why?

The answer came to her almost immediately. Because John was jealous of her and would like to prise him away. Perhaps he thought they would separate, and then David might move in with him – temporarily, of course – but when you had to rely on scraps of comfort, then that would be consolation enough.

She lay awake that night, not getting to sleep until two in the morning. David slept well – he always had done – and did not wake up when she got out of bed to find a sleeping tablet in the bathroom. She did not like taking pills, but these ones worked, and were for emergencies.

The next morning she slept in, and by the time she woke up David had gone to work. The children were up, but Margaret had fed them and prepared them for school. They came into her bedroom to kiss her goodbye, while Margaret hovered at the door, saying that she would drive them, and then go to the supermarket to buy things they needed for the kitchen.

Amanda lay in bed in the quiet house, staring up at the

ceiling. If she had been uncertain what to do last night, now her mind was made up. She would speak to John and ask him, once again, to refrain from telling David. She would remind him that David had told her that he had clearly wanted to say something. She would shame him; she would accuse him of breaking his promise.

She dressed quickly. She knew that John was always one of the first to get into the office in the mornings; she would phone him there and arrange to meet him for coffee somewhere down near the harbour; there was a place that she knew they sometimes went to with clients.

She reached him; he sounded hesitant when he realised it was her. But he agreed to meet her for coffee an hour later.

"I can't be long," he said, as he sat down opposite her. "I have a meeting. There are some people coming in from Miami."

"I won't keep you."

He looked at her enquiringly.

"It's about the other day," she said. "When I came to see you …"

He cut her short. "We don't need to go over that ground again. I told you what my … my position was. It hasn't changed."

She raised an eyebrow. "Hasn't it?"

He frowned. "No, it hasn't. And David hasn't said anything. It's water under the bridge as far as I'm concerned."

"David said that the other day you wanted to say something to him and then changed your mind."

He seemed puzzled. "Me? I wanted to tell him something?"

She thought that his surprise was genuine. Now she was not so sure that she should have sought him out. "He told me you came into his office and said that there was something you wanted to say, and then you seemed to change your mind."

The waitress brought them coffee. He reached for his cup and half-raised it to his lips; then he put it down. "Oh yes. I remember that." He seemed relieved. "That had nothing to do with this, I assure you. Nothing at all."

She looked at him silently.

"It was an office thing," he volunteered. "Somebody had taken money from the petty cash. I had an idea who it was, but I wasn't sure. I wanted to sound David out, because this person works for him, but then I thought that it was wrong of me even to voice my suspicions. It could amount to casting an aspersion over an innocent person's character – if he was innocent, that is." He looked at her. "Which we all are, of course, until somebody unearths proof against us."

She realised that she had been holding her breath. Now she released it. "So."

"Yes, that's all there was to it."

"I'm sorry, I thought that you were going to tell him. I jumped to conclusions, I suppose."

He looked at her over the rim of his coffee cup. "So it would seem." He glanced at his watch. "I'd better dash."

She nodded. "May I say one thing – just one thing?"

"Of course."

"What I told you was absolutely true. I promise you that. I'm not having an affair with George Collins. I'm just not."

He sat quite still, looking at her. "You know something? I believe you. So even if he were to ask me, I wouldn't say anything." He paused. "Is that better?"

She reached out to take his hand, and held it briefly, squeezing it in a gesture of gratitude – and friendship. "Thank you, John."

He smiled at her, weakly. He was tired; at forty-three, he was tired. 'The problem with Cayman," he said, "is that it's too small. We all live on top of one another and spend far too much time worrying about what other people are thinking."

"You're right."

"I know I'm right. That's why I'm getting out five years from now. To the day. My forty-eighth birthday. I'll be in a position to stop work. I don't want to be an international partner. I don't want any of that. That's me off."

"Back to ..." She was not sure where he was from.

"Not back to anywhere. Somewhere new. I've been thinking of Portugal. I know people who have moved there. They bought a vineyard – which is as good a way of losing one's money as anything."

"I can see you being happy there."

He seemed to be weighing what she said.

"It's not that I see you as being unhappy here," she said hurriedly.

He smiled, and stood up. "But you know I am – you know I'm unhappy. So why say that I'm not? Is unhappiness something we're ashamed to admit to?"

She shook her head.

"To cheer me up?" he prompted.

She met his gaze. "Maybe. We don't want others to be unhappy, do we?"

He agreed. "Not really. But perhaps we should allow them their unhappiness, don't you think? Just allow it?"

"Of course." She let her gaze wander. It was bright outside, as it almost always was, with that intense Caribbean light that left no room for subtlety. It was a light that seemed to demand cheerfulness, that somehow went so well with a steel band. Just inside the door, the bored waitress answered her phone, starting an animated conversation that became louder and louder as the emotion behind it rose. *Why you think that? Why you do that?*

John caught Amanda's eye, and the glance they exchanged was eloquent. She looked away; she did not feel superior to that woman, which is what she felt the glance implied.

"She's the victim," she muttered. "She's his victim."

He shrugged. "Life," he said.

Something rose within her. "You're above all that?"

He studied her. She noticed the coldness that had appeared in his eyes. "You don't imagine that I have feelings like that?"

She back-tracked. "I'm sorry. I didn't say that. Or I didn't mean to." She hesitated. "It's just that you seem to be so detached. You seem to be so in control of yourself."

He looked at his watch. "I don't see what's wrong with self-control." He looked at her. "Do you have a problem with it?"

For a moment she wondered whether this amounted to a retraction of what he had said earlier, when he had assured her that he believed her. Was he now implying that it was a lack of self-control that had led to an involvement with George? Was that what he really believed?

She answered him quietly. "No, I don't. But there's a difference between self-control and repression, don't you think?"

Her words seemed to hit him physically, as words can do when they shock the person to whom they are addressed. It can be as if an invisible gust of wind, a wall of pressure, has had its impact. For a short while he did nothing, but then he looked at his watch, fiddling with the winder, as if to adjust it.

She immediately relented. "I shouldn't have said that."

He raised his eyes to hers. "But it may be true." He paused. "Repression may have something to do with a lack of confidence, don't you think? In fact, it probably does. But I've decided to live with it. You see, I can't find what I want to find and I know that I never will. It's different for you."

She reached out to him again. "John …"

"No, it's fine. I don't mind."

"I'm the unhappy one," she said. "It's me. Or it's both of us, maybe."

"You?"

She spoke without thinking about what she was saying. "I no longer love David."

The coldness had disappeared; the distance between them seemed to melt away. "I'm sorry to hear that."

She suddenly felt reckless. The initial unplanned admission seemed to lead quite naturally to what she went on to say. "I love somebody else. I didn't want to. Of course, falling in love with somebody is never a result of wanting to do it …"

"No, I suppose you're right."

"It just happens," she went on. "It's like finding that you have a cold. It's just there."

"You could say that." He was looking at her with interest. "Is it reciprocated?"

"What?"

"Your feelings for this other person … are they reciprocated?"

She hesitated. "I think so."

"So, do you mind my asking: who?" He immediately thought better of the question. "I'm sorry, I shouldn't ask. It's none of my business."

It did not occur to her to keep it from him now; it was too late to dissemble. "George." But then she went on. "But I'm not having an affair with him. I haven't been lying to you about that. He's … he's off-limits."

"Because he's married? That doesn't seem to stop people round here."

She smiled. "Maybe not. But we have children. Alice is in love with him and he's a good man. So put that all together and you have a fairly impossible picture."

He looked thoughtful. "I'm sorry about that."

"So whatever your situation is, John – I think I understand."

He looked at his watch again. "I really have to go. These people from Miami …"

He signalled to the waitress, who looked at him, vaguely irritated by the disturbance to her call. He stood up, which persuaded the waitress to act. He paid for them both.

"I don't think we need to have this conversation again," he said to Amanda as they went out into the light. "You needn't worry."

She felt that he was closing off two subjects: her and him.

14

The ceremony at the Prep School to mark the end of the school year took place while David was in New York. The leavers, now aged twelve or thirteen – thirteen in the case of Clover and James – were presented with a certificate bearing the school motto and a message from the Principal about embarking on the journey that was life. The Governor attended and the school band played a ragged version of "God Save the Queen"; the Governor, in a white tropical suit, stood stiffly to attention, and seemed to be interested in something that was happening on the ceiling; one or two of the younger children, fidgeting and giggling, attracted discouraging looks from the teachers. Then the choir trooped onto the stage and sang "Lord Dismiss Us, With Thy Blessing". Hymns had made little impression on Clover, but the words of this one were different, and touched her because she sensed that it was about them. "May thy children may thy children, Those whom we will see no more …" The children were sitting with their parents; Clover was with Amanda and Margaret, because David was away. Margaret knew the hymn, and reached for Clover's hand. "That's you, isn't it?" she said quietly. "Leaving your friends, saying goodbye."

Clover turned away, embarrassed; she did not want to be told how she felt. She looked around the hall, searching for James, and found him just a few rows away, seated between his parents. He was whispering something to his father, and George nodded, whispering something back. She watched them, willing him to turn his head slightly so that he would see her. I'm here, she thought. Here. I'm here.

At the end of the ceremony, the parents left, and the children returned to their classrooms. The leavers were each given a large bag in which to put the things they wanted to take away with them: the drawings, the exercise books, the pictures from the walls that the teacher said could be shared out amongst those who wanted them, as mementoes of the school.

James was in a different class, and once outside in the corridor, she lingered until she saw him emerge from his own classroom with a few other boys. They were talking about something under their breath; one gave a snigger; boys were always doing that, laughing at something crude, something physical.

She waited until the other boys were distracted before she approached him.

"Do you feel sad?" she asked.

He looked round. "Clover ..."

"I mean, do you feel sad about leaving everybody? All your friends?"

He shrugged. He was smiling at her; he seemed pleased to be talking to her, and this encouraged her. "I'm really sorry to be saying goodbye to everybody," she continued.

"We'll see them in the holidays. We're not going away forever."

"No, but ..."

She felt her heart beating loud within her. She could ask him; there was no reason why she could not ask him. They were meant to be friends, and you could ask a friend to your house if you wanted to.

It was as if somebody else's voice was speaking. "Do you want to come back to my place? We could have lunch there. Margaret's made one of her cakes."

He glanced at the other boys. "I don't know ..."

"Please."

He hesitated, and then replied, "Yes. All right."

She felt a rush of joy. He was going to be with her. The others – Ted, these boys she did not know very well – none of them would be there; it would just be her.

Her mother was out; she had said something about a lunch for the Humane Society after the event at the school; they were always raising money for the homeless dogs shelter. Billy was with Margaret, being spoiled.

"Those dogs are rich by now," she said, as they went into the kitchen. "They raise all that money for them – just a few mangy dogs."

"It gives them something to do," said James.

"The dogs?"

"No, the parents. The old people too. They raise money for the dogs because they haven't got anything else to do."

She frowned as she thought about this. Did adults play? Or did they just talk? "Have you ever thought what it'll be like when we're old? Twenty? Thirty?"

He sat down at the kitchen table, watching her as she took Margaret's cake tin out of the cupboard. "Do you mean, will we feel the same?"

She nodded. "Yes. Will we think the same things?"

"We'll feel the same inside, maybe, but we won't think about the same things. I think you feel tired when you're that age. You run out of breath."

"When you're twenty?"

"I think that's when it starts."

She cut two slices of the lemon cake that Margaret had baked the day before, and slid each onto a plate. He picked his slice up eagerly.

"Everything's going to start to get different," she said. "From today onwards."

"Because we're going to boarding school?"

She said that this is what started it. But there would be other things.

"Such as?"

She did not have an answer. "Just things."

"I don't care," he said.

"Neither do I." But it was bravado; she did. She had lain awake the night before and fretted over what it would be like to be with a group she had never met before, sharing a room with another girl, which would be a new and confusing experience.

"How do you decide when to turn the light out?" she asked.

"When?"

"At school – when you're sharing."

He was not sure, but he thought they probably told you. "There'll be a rule. There are lots of rules. You just have to follow them."

She watched him lick the crumbs off his fingers. "Are you nervous?"

He affected nonchalance. "About going off to school? No, of course not. What's there to be nervous of?"

Everything, she thought.

He finished the last of the crumbs. "I'd better go home."

She caught her breath. "Why?"

"I don't know. I suppose I just should."

She asked him whether he would stay – just for a short while. He looked at her, and smiled. He likes me, she thought; he likes me again because he wouldn't smile like that if he didn't.

"We could have a swim."

He looked through the open kitchen door; the pool was at the back of the house, on the edge of the patio, and the water reflected the glare of the sun back into the building.

"I haven't brought my swimming trunks."

"There are some in the pool house. We keep them for visitors. Come on."

He got up reluctantly, following her to the pool house under the large sea-grape tree that dominated that end of the garden. Inside, it was dark and cool. There was a bench used for changing and a shower. The shower could not be completely shut off, and dripped slowly against the tiles beneath. There was the smell of water.

She opened a cupboard. There was a jumble of flippers and snorkels, used for the sea; a rescue ring, half eaten away by something; a long-poled net for scooping leaves from the surface of the water. The net slipped and fell onto the floor.

"The pool-men bring their own stuff," she said. "They come to clean the pool every week. The man who supervises them is almost blind now. My mother says he'll fall into a pool one of these days."

"He should stop," said James. "You shouldn't do jobs like that when you're blind."

"No, you shouldn't."

She moved the flippers, looking behind them. "There were some trunks. We had some. Maybe the pool-men took them ..."

"It doesn't matter."

She looked away. "You mean you don't need them?"

He hesitated. "I didn't mean that. I meant that I don't have to swim."

She felt her breath come quickly. "Have you ever skinny dipped?"

He did not answer for a moment, and she repeated her question. "Never?"

He laughed nervously. "Of course I have. Once at Rum Point. Off my dad's boat too."

"I dare you," she said.

"You serious?"

She felt quite calm. "Why not?"

He looked about him. "Now?"

"Yes. There's nobody around."

"And you too?"

She nodded. "Of course. I don't mind." She added, "Turn round, though. Just to begin with."

He turned his back, and she slipped out of her clothes. The polished concrete floor was cool against the soles of her feet. She felt goose-bumps on her arms, although it could not be from cold. Is that because I'm afraid? she asked herself. This was the most daring thing she had ever done, by far; and the goose-bumps came from that, obviously.

He said, "And you have to turn round too."

"Okay."

She turned round, and faced the wall. But there was a mirror, for doing your hair after the shower; her mother used it; he had not seen it, or it had not occurred to him that she could see him in it. She saw it suddenly and found herself watching him. She could not help herself. She thought: he's perfect. And she felt a lightness in her stomach that made her want to sit down, it was so overwhelming, so unexpected.

Naked now, he turned round, and immediately he saw the

mirror. Their eyes met in the glass, and she saw him blush.

"You shouldn't cheat," he mumbled. "It's cheating to look in the mirror."

She made a joke of it. "I didn't mean to. I didn't put the mirror there."

He put his hands in front of himself, to cover his nakedness. But she saw his eyes move down her own body. She did not say anything; she wanted the moment to last, but was not sure why she should want this. There was a feeling within her that she had never before experienced. She recognised it as a longing, because it was like other longings, other experiences of wanting something so much that it hurt. This hurt, she thought; it hurt and puzzled her.

He said: "I'm going to get into the pool. Are you coming too?"

She followed him. She watched him. She wanted to touch him, but she thought: I should not be thinking this. I should not. And it frightened her that it should be so strong, this confusing, odd feeling, of wanting to touch a boy and put her hands in his hair and kiss him, which is what she had sometimes dreamed of doing, and she wondered what his lips would taste like.

He entered the water cleanly, and she followed. With the protection of the water, there was no embarrassment, and they laughed, not at anything in particular, but because they were aware that something had happened, a moment had passed. He splashed her, and she responded, the water hitting him in the face and making him splutter. He swam up to her and would have ducked her head under the water, but she dived below the surface and escaped him, although his hand moved across her shoulder. He dived too, but she kicked him away; she felt her foot against his stomach. She said, "Sorry, I didn't mean to hurt you," and he said, "You didn't."

He swept back his hair, in the way she liked him to do, and then he looked up at the sun and said, "I've got to go home now."

"Don't. I don't want you to go. Can't you stay?"

"No."

He swam back to the edge of the pool and he climbed out on the curved metal ladder, and she could not help but watch him and feel again that lurch in her stomach. He ran to the pool room; she saw the water dripping down from him, and she noticed something she had been told about but never seen, and thought: *it's because of me.* She stayed where she was, and was still there in the pool when he came out, clothed, and shouted to her that he would see her again, sometime, and thanks for the cake. She whispered goodbye and then, after he had gone, climbed up the steps and ran, as he had done, to the pool room although there was nobody to see her naked. She sat down on the bench where he must have sat, for there was a puddle of water on the floor below it, and she put her head into her hands and felt herself shivering.

15

Amanda usually went to the airport to meet David when he returned from one of his trips abroad. Going to the airport was something of a ritual in George Town – the outing to the small building that served as the island's terminal where, with Caribbean informality, disembarking passengers walked past palm trees and poinsettias and could be spotted and waved to from the terrace of the coffee bar. She took Billy, but left Clover with Margaret, who liked to take her with her to the ballroom dancing academy she frequented where, if one of the instructors was free, Clover was sometimes treated to a lesson.

On the way back to the house Billy dominated the conversation, asking his father about New York and telling him a long and complicated story about an iguana that, injured by dogs, had limped into the back yard of one of his friends from school. She slipped in a few questions, about her father, whom David had visited. Her father had been widowed a few years previously and had taken up with a woman they were not sure about.

"She drags him off to exhibitions all the time," he said. "He was about to go to one when I arrived to see him. She kept looking at her watch while I was talking to him; it made me like her less than ever."

Billy said: "This iguana, see, had a big cut on the side of his head. A dog had bitten him there, I think, and you'd think that he would have died, but he hadn't, you see."

"I think she must feel frustrated. He's obviously not making up his mind."

And Billy said: "There was another iguana – not the one that had been bitten by dogs but another one. Maybe it was his brother. He had these big spikes on his back and …"

"I wish he'd come down here to see us. She discourages him, I think."

"That happens. Perhaps you need to let go." And to Billy, he said: "How big was the iguana again?"

When they reached home, he took a shower and then swam in the pool. It was hot, and the doors of the house were kept closed to keep the cool air inside; in the background, the expensive air conditioners hummed. There was a cost here to everything, she had once remarked; even to the air you breathed.

She watched him through the glass of the kitchen door. It was like watching a stranger, she thought; she could be standing in a hotel watching one of the other guests, an unknown man, swimming in the pool. He was towelling himself dry now, and then he threw the towel down on the ground, and she thought: *I'll have to pick that up.*

She went outside, taking him the ice-cold bottle of beer that she knew he would want. He took it from her without saying anything.

"Thank you," she said quietly. It was what she said to Billy, to remind him of his manners. It was what every parent said, time after time, like a gramophone record with a fault in the grooves.

He looked at her sharply. "I said thanks."

She went over to examine a plant at the edge of the patio. He followed her, beer in hand; she was aware of him behind her, but did not say anything.

"Tell me," he said. "Tell me: did you have coffee with John the other day?"

She answered without thinking. "John Galbraith? No. Why would I have coffee with John?"

He took a swig of the beer. "That's what I'm asking."

"I told you: I didn't."

She had lied instinctively, self-protectively, as people will lie to get more time.

It was as if he had not heard her answer. "It seemed odd to me, you see," he continued. "Because you never mentioned it to me."

"I didn't mention it because it didn't happen."

He looked at her in disbelief. "But it did."

She sighed. "You're picking a fight."

"No, I'm not. I'm simply asking you something."

She struggled to remain calm. "I told you. I didn't have coffee with John. I don't know why you should think I did." She paused, thinking of how rumours circulated. It was a small place; inevitably somebody had seen her and had talked about it. Why should she be in the slightest bit surprised by that?

"Whoever told you must be mistaken," she said. "Maybe it was somebody who looked like me."

"Or looked like John?"

There was an innuendo in his comment that she ignored. "People think they've seen somebody and they haven't. It happens all the time."

"It was me," he said.

This stopped her mid-movement.

He was staring at her. She noticed that he was holding the bottle of beer tightly – so tightly that his knuckles were white with the effort. For a moment she imagined that he might use it as a weapon; instinctively she moved away.

"Yes," he said. "I saw you because I had called in somewhere earlier that morning and was coming back to the office. I walked past that coffee bar near the entrance to our building. I walked right past and saw you sitting there with him."

She said nothing. She averted her eyes.

"And then," he continued, "when I was in New York, I asked John directly. I said: what were you and Amanda talking about the other day?"

It felt to her as if there were a vice around her chest.

"And do you know what?" David went on. "He said: I don't know what you're talking about. That's what he actually said. He flatly denied it. I let the matter go."

She felt a rush of relief, of gratitude. John was covering for her. He was as good as his word. "Well, there you are," she said. "You must have imagined it. Or you saw two people who looked a bit like us. The eye plays tricks, you know."

He took a step forward, bringing himself almost to the point where he was touching her. Now he spoke carefully, each word separated from the word before with a pause. "I saw you. I did *not* make a mistake. I saw you."

"You *imagined* you saw me."

"I *saw* you. I *saw* you."

She fought back. "Even if you did, then so what? So what if I have coffee with one of your friends. I know him too, remember. And anyway, are you seriously suggesting that there's something between me and John, of all people?"

"It's not that," he said. "It's why you should lie to me – which you've done recently on more than one occasion."

She tried to be insouciant. "Oh, so many occasions then ..."

"The Grand Old House. You went there with somebody – I don't know who it was – but you didn't tell me. You gave an account of your evening that very specifically omitted to say anything about your being there. But you were, weren't you?"

She faltered. "The Grand Old House ..."

"I didn't see you myself, but one of the girls from the office said you were there. She told me. She said: I saw your wife. I saw her yesterday. I wanted to say 'hi' to her, but she was with a man I didn't know."

"Your spies are everywhere, I see."

"Don't make light of it," he hissed. "It was another lie. It can't have been John you were with. But John's involved in some way, though I don't know how."

She felt a growing sense of desperation at being accused of doing something of which she was innocent. And yet she could assert that innocence only by confessing to something else – something that would implicate George, who was also every bit as innocent as she was. But then she thought: am I completely innocent? I entertained the possibility of an affair; I sought out George's company; I went some way down the road before I turned back.

When she spoke now, there was irritation in her voice. "I am not seeing John. If you can't understand that, then you can't understand anything."

He appeared to think for a while before responding to this. "I don't understand why you should tell me lies unless you have something to hide. And if I conclude it's an affair, then, forgive me, but what else am I expected to think?"

"But you yourself think he's gay."

He became animated. "Yes, I did think that. Not any more. I don't think he is. I asked him, you see."

She was incredulous. "And he discussed it with you?"

"John is impotent. That's the issue with him."

She was at a loss for anything to say.

David watched her. "Yes. That's quite the disclosure, isn't it?"

"Yes, I suppose it is."

"He gets fed up with people thinking that he's gay. He says that it's nothing to do with being anti-gay – which he isn't – it's to do with people making an assumption. He says that he understands how gay people might resent others treating them differently. Patronising them, maybe; pitying them. They put up with a lot."

"So he opened up to you about this to stop you reaching the wrong conclusion."

"So it would seem."

Of course it added up; it might explain the sense of disappointment that she felt somehow hung about him. But was that its effect? Did men in that position mourn for something, in the same way that a childless woman might mourn for the child she never had? Was it that important – that simple, biological matter: could it really count for so much?

David continued. "He told me when we were in New York. He became very upset when he talked about it. He said that it's been with him all his life, and it has spoiled everything – his confidence in particular. He's never had a girlfriend – never."

She had not expected that, but it made sense of the conversation she had had with him. He had said something about confidence; she tried to remember what it was, but could not.

She considered telling him the real truth now. She could do that, of course, but the problem was that the truth would sound implausible and he would be unlikely to believe it. And why should he believe her anyway, in the light of her lies? So she said, instead: "Don't you think I'm entitled to a private life?"

The question surprised him. "You mean ..." He struggled to

find the words. "Are you talking about an open marriage?"

The term sounded strangely old-fashioned. She had not meant that, but now she grasped at the idea. "Yes."

He shook his head in disbelief. "Are you serious?"

"Never more." She was not; she had not thought about it until a few seconds ago.

He put down the half-empty bottle of beer. "Listen," he said. "We've fallen out of love. We both know that, don't we?"

She met his gaze now. Anger and resentment had turned to acceptance; to a form of sorrow that she was sure they now both felt.

She fought back tears. She had not cried yet for her failing marriage, and now the realisation came that she would have to do this sooner or later. "I'm so sorry, David. I didn't think this would happen, but it has."

He spoke calmly. "I'm sorry too. I don't want this to be messy."

"Of course not. Think of the children."

He picked up the bottle of beer and took a sip. "I've thought about them all the time. I'm sure you have too."

"So what shall we do?" She marvelled at the speed with which everything had been acknowledged.

They were standing outside on the patio. He looked up. Evening had descended swiftly, as it does at that latitude; an erratic flight of fruit bats dipped and swooped across the sky. "Can we stay together for the children's sake?" he asked. "Or at least keep some semblance of being together?"

"Of course. They're the main consideration." She was thinking quickly. Now that they had started to discuss their situation, the whole thing was falling into place with extraordinary rapidity. And the suggestion that came next, newly minted though it was, bore the hallmarks of something that had been worked out well in advance. "If they're going to school in Scotland, I could live there. I'll live in Edinburgh. Then we could all come out here to see you in their school holidays."

He weighed this. He had thought that she might mention the possibility of returning to the United States, which is what he did not want; he would lose the children then; lose them into the embrace of a vast country he did not understand. "I'd stay in the house here?"

"Why not? It's yours, after all."

He seemed reassured. "I'd still meet all expenses."

That was one thing he had never cavilled at; he had been financially generous to her – very financially generous – and she thanked him for it. "You've been so good about money."

He laughed. "It's what I do, after all."

"But you could have been grudging, or tight. You weren't – ever."

He said nothing about the compliment, but he reached out to touch her gently. "Friends?"

She took his hand. "Yes." She paused. "About John …"

"You don't have to."

"John saw me, seeing George. I was worried that he would misinterpret what was going on. And he did."

He caught his breath. "George Collins?"

"Yes. It didn't mean anything – or maybe it did. But we were never lovers. I enjoyed his company and … Why can't a married person have friends? Why not?"

"Don't tell me," he said quietly. "I don't want to know."

"It's not what you think." But then she said, "I feel something for George. I just do. I can't help it."

"What everyone says."

She felt that she did not have to explain. He was the cold one; he was the one who had chilled their marriage. "You're to blame too," she said. "You lost interest in me. All you ever thought about was your work, and that's still the case, I think."

"I don't think that's fair. Don't try to transfer blame. The fact remains – we're out of love."

"Which is exactly the position of an awful lot of married couples. They just exist together. Just exist." She looked at him. "Is that really what you want, David?"

He turned away. "No," he said. "And now that we've made a plan, let's not unstitch it."

"You don't plan your life just like that, without thinking a bit more about it."

"Don't you? Some people do. They make decisions on the spur of the moment. Big decisions."

There was one outstanding matter, she thought, and now she raised it. "And we each have our freedom?"

"In that sense?"

"Yes. We can fall in love with somebody else, if we want to."

He shrugged. "That's generally what happens, isn't it? People fall in love again."

It sounded so simple. But what was the point of being in love with somebody who was not free to be in love with you?

He said, "I must go and get changed."

She nodded absent-mindedly. Marriage involved little statements like that – I'm doing this; I'm doing that – little explanations to one's spouse, a running commentary on the mundane details of a life. She was free of that now; she would no longer have to explain. But still she said, "I'm going inside," and went in. She stood quite motionless in the kitchen, like somebody in a state of shock, which in a way she was. She crossed the room to the telephone. She knew George's number without looking it up, as she had made an attempt to remember it and it had lodged there, along with birthdays and key dates. The mnemonic of childhood returned: *In fourteen hundred and ninety-two, Columbus sailed the ocean blue.* Those were the last four digits of his number: 1492. It would be so easy to dial them.

16

"All right. I've told you all about me. Now it's your turn. Tell me all about yourself. Everything. I want to hear everything. Don't leave anything out."

There were just the two girls in the room, which was a small study, plainly furnished with two desks above each of which a bookcase had been attached to the wall. These bookcases had been filled with textbooks – an introduction to mathematics, physics, a French grammar – and a few personal items – a framed photograph of a dog, a lustrous conch shell; mementoes of home.

It was Katie who spoke, and she waited now for Clover's answer.

"It'd be boring to tell you everything."

'No,' said Katie. "It wouldn't. I want to know. Everything. If we're sharing, I have to know. I just have to."

"I come from the Cayman Islands. Well, that's where my parents went to work and I have lived there all my life. It's home, although my mother's moving to Edinburgh now and my father is going to stay out there – for his job.

"I have one brother, Billy. He's all right, I suppose. You said you have a younger brother, so you know what I mean. He's going to school in Edinburgh and will be living with my mum. That's why she's moved, you see – to be there for Billy while he's at school.

"There was somebody back in Cayman who helped look after us. She's called Margaret. She's a brilliant cook, but she's got this husband who's really thin – you should see him – you wouldn't think he was married to somebody who was such a great cook. She's from Jamaica. Those people put a lot of hot spices in their cookery and they have this pepper that they call Scotch Bonnet. You can't actually eat it or it would burn your mouth off. You put it in a stew and then you take it out – it leaves some of the hotness behind it."

She made a gesture of completeness. "That's all."

"Come on!"

"There really isn't much more."

"What about friends? Who are your friends?"

She told her about friends at school.

"And any boys?"

She did not answer at first, and Katie had to prompt her. "I told you about Andy. You have to tell me."

"There's a boy called James."

"I love that name." Katie rolled her eyes in mock bliss. "I wish I knew somebody called James. Is he nice?"

Clover nodded. "He's the nicest boy I've ever met. You know how boys are – how they always show off? He's not like that. He's the opposite."

"He's kind?"

"Yes. He listens to you. He's easy to speak to."

"I love him already," said Katie. "Have you been out with him?"

"We went to a movie once – with some other people."

"That doesn't count. Not if there were other people. That's not a proper date."

"You didn't go out with Andy."

"I never said I did. I said I *wanted* to, but he never asked me."

"Well, James asked me to go to that movie. And he's been to my house loads of times."

Katie took time to ponder this. "He must like you."

She hesitated, and Katie seized on the hesitation. "He doesn't? That's really bad luck, Clovie. Really bad luck."

'I didn't say he didn't like me. He's just not ready. Boys are a couple of years behind us. You know that."

The conversation switched to mothers. "Mine won't leave me alone," said Katie. "She wants to interfere with everything I do – everything."

"Maybe she's unhappy," said Clover.

It had never occurred to Katie that her mother, a socialite, could be anything but in the mood for a party. "She's never unhappy," she said. "But that doesn't stop her trying to ruin *my* happiness."

"Poor you," said Clover.

She thought of Amanda in her flat in Edinburgh, which seemed so diminished after the house in the Caymans. The whole world here seemed diminished, in fact; the horizons closer, the sky lower, the narrow streets affording so little elbow room; the sea, which they could just make out in the distance from the windows of the flat, was so unlike the Caribbean that it could be a different thing altogether. Instead of being a brilliant blue, as the sea should be, it was a steely grey, cold and uninviting.

The move made it seem to Clover that their whole world had been suddenly and inexplicably turned upside down. The decision had been presented to her as a slight change of plan – "just for the time being" – but she knew that it was more than that. No modern child can be unaware of divorce or of the fact that parents suddenly may decide to live apart; Clover knew this happened because there were friends at school for whom it had been the pattern of life: adults moved in with one another, moved out again, and took up with somebody else. It was what adults did. But this was something that happened to other people – like being struck by lightning or being eaten by a shark – it never happened to oneself.

The move may have been precipitate, but the truth was revealed slowly. "Daddy and I are happier, you know, if we're doing separate things. You'll understand that because you know how friends often want to do something different from what you yourself want to do. It's just the way it is."

"Yes, I suppose so."

"And if you're living with somebody you can sometimes want to have a bit more time to yourself. You must feel that sometimes – when Billy's being a nuisance. It doesn't mean that you don't like the other person any more – it's just that you feel a bit happier if you have more time to yourself."

"Maybe. But if you love the other person, won't you miss him?"

That had been more difficult for Amanda to answer. "Love changes, darling. At the beginning it's like a rocket or one of those big fireworks – you know the sort – that sends all sorts of stars shooting up all over the place, and then it dies down a bit. That happens with love. You don't necessarily stop loving somebody, but you might just decide to live in separate places so that you can have that time to yourself. That's the way it works."

She thought about this. Lying in bed on that first night in Edinburgh, a few days before she was due to be taken up to Strathearn to begin her first term at boarding school, she thought about what her mother had said about love. *It dies down.* That was what she had said: *it dies down.* Love was very important; it was something that people talked about a lot. They also sang about it – just about every song she heard was about being in love. And some of these songs, she had noticed, were unhappy.

People sang because they were in love with somebody who did not notice them nor love them back. This saddened them, and they sang songs to express the sadness.

She lay in her bed looking up at the darkened ceiling. *Am I in love?* It was a question she had never thought she would ask herself because love, she had felt, belonged to some unspecified future part of her life; it was not a question to be asked, or answered, at this stage, when she was just embarking on life.

But there was only one person she really wanted to see. It was such an unusual, unsettling feeling that she wished that she could talk to somebody about it. She was close to her mother, and they had had that earlier conversation about James, but she now felt that she could not say anything more because her mother would discourage her. There was something awkward in her parents' relations with James's mother and father – something that she could not quite put her finger on. They did not like one another, she felt, but she was not sure why this should be so.

On the day before she left for Strathearn, she sent an e-mail to Ted and asked him to pass on a message to James. She had an address for Ted, but not for James, to whom she had not had a chance to say a proper goodbye. "Please pass on this message to James – I think you have his address. Tell him to send me his e-mail address so that I can write to him. I know he's going to be starting school in England soon, but he must have an address. So please ask him to send it to me, just so that we can chat."

Ted wrote back almost immediately. "I asked James and he said that he doesn't like getting lots of e-mails as he doesn't have the time to answer them all. He says sorry, and he hopes you don't mind. He says that he'll see you in the school holidays in Cayman. Maybe."

She re-read this message several times. It occurred to her that Ted might not have spoken to James at all – Ted was quite capable of telling lies, as everybody seemed to be. He had never wanted to share James as a friend, and this was his way of thwarting her. On the other hand, he might be telling the truth. It might be that James did not like dealing with e-mail – some boys were like that – and the important thing then was that he had said that he would see her in the school holidays. That meant that he wanted to see her, and that gave her comfort.

But when the much anticipated school holidays came round for the first time, the Christmas holiday, her mother told her that they would not be returning to Cayman but would spend the time in Edinburgh. "Daddy will come. He has to be in London for a meeting, and so you'll see him here. We'll all be together as a family."

She could not hide her disappointment. "But it's so nice in Cayman at Christmas. It's the nicest time of the year."

"I know, darling. I know the weather's gorgeous …"

"Which it isn't here – not at Christmas. It'll be cold."

"Of course it'll be cold. It might even snow. Imagine that – a Christmas with snow lying about. Imagine how you'll like that."

There was no persuading her mother, who eventually revealed that the decision had been taken by David. "Your father wanted it this way. I suggested that it would be good for us all to get a bit of sun, but he wouldn't shift. I'm sorry, darling, but that's the way it's going to have to be."

For the first few days, having her father in the house seemed to her to be almost like having a guest, an ill-at-ease stranger. He spent more time with Billy than with her, taking him out on expeditions that ended with the boy being spoiled with the purchase of yet another expensive present.

"He likes Billy more than he likes me," she said to her mother.

"That isn't true. You mustn't think that, darling. Daddy likes you both exactly the same. And the same goes for me. You're both the most precious things we have in this world."

"Really?"

"Yes, of course."

"Then why don't we go back to the way it was before? Why don't we go home?"

"To Cayman?"

"Yes, that's home, isn't it? That's where we grew up."

Amanda tried to explain. "But remember that you're not Caymanian. You're half Scottish and half American. That makes you different from real Caymanians. They don't have somewhere else to go back to."

"They aren't any different from me. Just because their parents …"

"That's exactly what makes the difference, darling. Parents. You get to be something because your parents are something. That's the way the world works."

"So I have to live somewhere I don't want to be just because you come from somewhere else?"

This was answered with a nod: the injustices of the world – the rules and red tape – could be difficult to explain to a child.

"And James?" she asked.

Her mother made a gesture of acceptance. "It's different for him, I think. His father has Caymanian status and I believe that James has that too. It's because his father is a doctor. You know all about that, don't you? The right to stay there? He can live there for the rest of his life if he wants."

"That's unfair."

"Yes, it is. You're right – it's very unfair." Amanda paused. "Have you heard from him? I wonder how he's getting on at his new school."

"I haven't heard."

"You could write to him. Send him an e-mail."

She looked away. "I tried to. I sent my address to Ted and asked him to pass it on to James. But then Ted said that James didn't want to write to me."

Amanda glanced at her daughter; the pain of love at that age was so intense – one might easily forget just how bad it could be. It would be transient, of course, but children did not know that; what they felt, she had heard, they thought they would feel forever. "Darling, that can happen. People can make new friends. They don't mean to upset us when they do that – it's just the way that things work out."

"I'd never say I wouldn't write to a friend," said Clover.

"I'm sure you wouldn't."

"I hate him."

That meant, Amanda knew, that she loved him. She had hated somebody once because she loved him; she remembered. Yet there would have to be a parental reproach. "No, you don't hate him. You mustn't hate somebody else because they drift away from you. That's very unkind."

Clover went to her room. She lay down on the bed and stared out of the window at the December sky. It was getting dark already, and it was only three in the afternoon. Everything had changed. She had been happy at home with the light and the sun, and now suddenly she had been taken to a world of muted shades and misty light and silences. She thought of James. If only she could see him, then all this would be bearable; he would be like the sun, his presence dispelling the cold, the damp air, the pervading grey.

She took a piece of paper and wrote on it. *I love James. I love James. I said that I hated him, but that's not true. I said I hated him because I love him so much. I love him and have always loved him. Always.* The writing of these words gave her a curious feeling of relief. It was as if she had made a confession to herself – admitting something that she had been afraid to admit but that, now acknowledged, was made much easier to bear, as a secret when shared with another is deprived of its power to trouble or to shame.

17

A pattern became established. Although there was talk of their making trips to Cayman, a reason was always found as to why it would not work. David would be away on business, or there were workmen renovating the house, or there had been an invitation to spend a few weeks in France and they could not turn this down without giving offence.

"We're never going to go back, are we?" Clover said to her mother. "And you don't want to, do you?"

"I'd love to, darling. And we will – some day. It's just that there's so much going on here, and Daddy is in the UK so often that it makes more sense for us all to be together in Scotland, or even in France. It really does."

"I want to go back to George Town. It's not the same here or in France. I want to see our house again. I want to swim at Smith's Cove. I want to do the things we used to do."

"All in good time. We'll go some day."

"Billy's even forgetting what it was like. He thinks he's Scottish now."

"Well he is, in a way. As are you. Half of you."

But in the year she turned sixteen, they went to Cayman for a month, a week being added to the three-week break the school allowed over Christmas. Amanda told Clover of the trip at the beginning of October, and the intervening months were spent in a state of eager anticipation. Three years had elapsed since they had left George Town, during which time she had settled into and accepted her new existence. There was no shortage of new friends – Strathearn was a friendly school and strong bonds were formed with her new classmates. There were boys she liked, one in particular – a studious boy from Glasgow whose passion was ornithology. He painted birds and had a collection of feathers and bird eggs. He seemed a lonely boy, and they slipped into a comfortable friendship that was, from her point of view, a long way off romance. He sent her a Valentine card one year, slipped unseen into her French dictionary, and although it was anonymous she could tell it was from him because it had a picture of a bird perching on a red heart, and he was the only boy in the school who would have chosen a card like that. She was flattered, but these cards were not something to become excited about. There was only one Valentine card that she really wanted to receive and of course it never came.

David sent her a message. "I can't wait to have you all back home," he wrote. "You and Billy and Mummy; we'll have a great time together. And you'll be able to catch up with all your old friends, which I expect you're really looking forward to. Counting the days now!"

She wrote back to him: "I know that it's soon now because the dreams I'm having are all back in Cayman – it's as if I was already there. I think this is a sign, don't you?"

He replied: "Of course it is."

The days before they left passed slowly. She made a list of things she would need to take – swimming costume, sunblock, clothes for parties. They were going to what had remained a family home in spite of her parents' separation, but she knew that everything that she had left there would be the possessions of childhood and nothing would fit her any more.

"Your room's still here," her father had written. "And it's exactly the same as it always was."

Yes, she thought; but I'm not the same. And that led her to

wonder whether James would have changed. She had looked at his Facebook page, cautiously, as if trespassing, but he did not seem to bother very much with it and there were only a few out-of-date photographs. She wondered what he would look like now; it was only three years and people did not change all that much in three years; or did they? He had still been a boy when she had seen him last, and now, at sixteen, he could look quite different. Boys changed; they became thicker and coarser. The fact that they had to shave changed everything about their faces, it seemed to her; or so it seemed with the boys at school. Some of them did not use electric razors and came to class in the morning with cuts on their chin or on their neck; she shivered at that; she hated to think of how people dragged razors across their skin that could so easily slip and slice into it and … It did not bear thinking about.

She could not imagine James doing that. His skin was smooth, and like the colour of light honey, as he tanned so easily; that was how she remembered him, anyway. She was careful about the sun because with her colouring her skin could turn red and itch. She closed her eyes. In a day or two she would be seeing him, talking to him, and everything would go back to the way it was when it had just been the two of them; before Ted started to get him involved in things that excluded her; before something happened between her mother and his and he started talking about seeing her less. They would go back to that time. That would happen; she was sure of it.

They caught a plane from Edinburgh to London, and then boarded the flight to Grand Cayman via Nassau. On the ground in the Bahamas, when all the Cayman passengers had to stay on board, she looked out of the window into the Caribbean glare, watching a man driving a small airport truck, a shepherd of great jets, fussing about on some errand opaque to others. The cleaners came on in a bustle of energy, removing the detritus left by the passengers who had disembarked in Nassau; she heard the patois of their conversation and found that she understood; she had not heard it for a long time, but she understood it, and realised that this was the language of home. She wanted to join in, but did not, as the cleaners looked straight through the passengers, who were simply not there for them; they were too rich, too alien. She wanted to say something that would tell them that this did not apply to her; that she was Caymanian and she knew what it was like. But she did not.

She turned to her mother in the seat beside her.

"Are you looking forward to getting there?"

Amanda smiled. "Of course."

"To seeing Daddy?"

"What?"

"Looking forward to seeing Daddy?"

"Of course I am."

She was silent. "Can't you get together again?"

Amanda reached out and took her hand. "Sometimes these things happen. People find it easier to live apart."

"Because they don't like each other any more?"

Amanda hesitated. "Sometimes it's like that. But that's not really what it's like between Daddy and me. Not really."

Clover took her hand away. "I wish you would. I just wish you would."

Amanda's gaze moved to the window. A young man was driving away a refuelling truck, describing an arc across the shimmering concrete; another, wearing earmuffs against the whine of the engines, was signalling to their pilot, looking up at the cockpit as he did so. The cleaners had vanished as quickly as they came, dragging behind them the bags of litter like sacks of loot.

"Would you like me to try?"

Amanda was not sure why she said this; it had not occurred to her that the subject would come up, and she had not intended to raise it, but now she had asked her daughter whether she would like her to mend her relationship with David and Clover was going to say yes.

"Please try."

"I will." Again the words had come out without being planned, like an off-hand agreement to do something minor. But this was not minor.

"Good."

Beside Clover, Billy struggled with sleep; he had stayed awake the entire previous night – out of excitement – and now it was catching up with him. Clover tucked him up in his airline blanket; the plane's ventilation system breathed cool air upon her; she felt a welling of joy: they were going home; her mother and father would be together again, which is what she had always wanted; things lost were to be returned to her, made safe, secured.

Amanda could tell that David was nervous. He had a way of speaking when he was unsure of himself – a clipped, guarded form of speech that she had noticed before and that she had put down to the tightening of muscles that went with insecurity. It was the vocal equivalent, she thought, of sweaty palms or a thumping heart.

They had seen him on the observation terrace – standing slightly apart from a family group of Jamaicans excited at an imminent reunion. The Jamaicans waved madly, flourishing tiny Jamaican national flags, the children issuing whoops of delight; David stood stiffly, but waved enthusiastically to the children when he saw them.

"There he is!" shouted Billy. "See him, Ma? See him?"

She raised her eyes against the glare. It was early evening and the light was gentler, but it was so much brighter than in Scotland. She had forgotten just how strong it could be, this Caribbean light; how it could penetrate. Scotland, with its attenuated light, soft at the edges, allowed one to hide; to conceal, if one wanted to do so; to live in ambiguity.

She felt the warm air on her skin, and shivered. The touch of the air was what had struck her most forcibly all those years ago when she had first come here. She used to go out at night, out from the air-conditioned cocoon of their bedroom, and stand in the darkness with the night air about her like a mantle. The air clothed you here. It was like swimming. It was like that.

They moved through immigration quickly. In the baggage hall, the luggage carousel seemed tiny – a toy so small that it could have been operated by clockwork. It was silent when they went through, but about ten minutes later burst into life and started to bring suitcases. Theirs were out early, and placed on a cart that Billy had retrieved. She led them through the customs area and into the hall where David, having come down from the observation deck, was now standing. Billy ran forward and embraced his father, who lifted him up briefly before turning to Clover and kissing her on both cheeks. Then he turned to his wife.

The nervous voice: "You made it."

She nodded. "Yes. Here we are."

He took a hesitant step towards her. "Thanks. Thank you so much."

She was not sure what she had expected, but somehow she had not imagined that he would thank her.

"Margaret wanted to come," he continued. "But she couldn't."

"Something on at the church?"

He laughed, but his voice still sounded strained. "How did you guess?"

"Things don't change," she said. And she thought: but they do.

In the car he seemed to relax. Billy, delighted to discover that he recognised everything, revelled in pointing out landmarks. 'There's that tower – that radio thing. See, I remember. And there's that place that sells fishing stuff. Remember that? Remember, we went there once?"

David said, "Of course I remember." Then he added, "You're talking like a Scotsman, Billy."

"I'm not. I talk the same as everybody else."

"And everybody else around you is Scottish these days."

"Maybe."

And from Clover: "He talks too much, don't you, Billy?"

They swerved to avoid a car that had failed to signal.

"Home," Amanda muttered.

Clover would have stayed up, but she too was tired and was in bed by half past eight. Billy had managed a swim before he had fallen asleep at the table, and was helped to bed by his father. David had been tactful and had asked Margaret to prepare a separate room for Amanda at the back of the house. "You'll be all right there?" he had asked. "Margaret went out of her way to make things comfortable."

In the Caribbean winter, air conditioning was unnecessary, but Margaret had left it on at high pitch, making the room feel like a walk-in fridge. David had gestured to the thermostat and rolled his eyes. She said: "Yes. Down. If you've lived without it for years …"

"In Scotland? I suppose so."

She shook her head. "No, that's not what I meant. I meant Margaret. In Jamaica they wouldn't have had it – not at home. It would have been an impossible luxury – something dreamed of."

"And then you get it …"

"And you think you've arrived in heaven."

He smiled at her. "It's the same with food. I was reading somewhere or other …"

"*The Economist.*"

He laughed. "I do read other things. Occasionally."

She bit her tongue. She did not want to start off on the wrong foot. "Of course. Sorry. I didn't mean it like that."

He had not taken offence. "It probably was in *The Economist.* Anyway, it was about average weight in Germany. It goes up and down, apparently – just like everywhere else. But what they were saying was that in the post-war years, once their economic miracle got going, they became heavier and heavier, because they remembered when they did not have enough to eat and made up for it."

"Pigging out. Insecurity does that."

"Yes." He paused. "I've prepared something for dinner, if you've got an appetite … They keep feeding you on planes. I suppose it keeps you busy and stops people asking for things all the time."

She was hungry; she had not eaten much on the plane.

"I'm quite the cook these days," he said. "Not that I'm boasting. It's just that necessity is the mother of invention."

"I'm sorry."

He smiled. "Oh, I don't say that out of self-pity. I actually rather like it. If you look in the kitchen you'll see all my books. Delia. Jamie. All those people."

"I'm impressed."

He moved towards the door. "Come through when you've unpacked. I only have to heat it up."

Standing in the doorway, for a moment it seemed that he was going to say something else, but he did not. She looked at him expectantly, and it seemed to her that in their exchange of glances, at one time both uncertain and regretful, was the whole history of what had happened between them.

She unpacked, throwing her clothes into a drawer that she now remembered clearing, years earlier, for visitors; little thinking then that she would be a visitor in her own house. That was the most painful thing about separation, she felt: the ending of the very small things, the ordinary sharing, the unspoken reliance; removing one's toothbrush from the bathroom was as big a step, in a way, as making an appointment with the divorce lawyer.

She went into the bathroom that led off the bedroom. There was a slight smell of mustiness about it – inevitable in that climate, when towels became fusty within hours of going on the rail. But he had put a small bag of lavender on a dish, and she picked this up and smelled it, holding the muslin to her cheek. He had remembered that she loved lavender, and the thought that he had done this, had bothered himself, touched her.

She had thought about it before, of course; had entertained the possibility that she could fall in love with him again – as suddenly, perhaps, as she had fallen out of love with him. People did that, sometimes going to the extent of remarrying the person whom they had already divorced. She had met a couple like that – an elderly couple from Savanna who spent several months of each year in Cayman; he had divorced her in order to go off with a younger woman. The younger woman had treated him badly, leaving him for a youthful band instructor. He had waited a few months and then gone round to see her to propose marriage again, and she had said yes; an example of forgiveness, she had decided, when it would have been so much easier to crow, to enjoy the *Schadenfreude* that such a situation could provoke.

She looked in the bathroom mirror. What exactly was one entitled to expect from life? Romance that could last a lifetime, or, at best, the comfort of friendship with a chosen person? Had she been naïve, she wondered, to imagine that she should have remained in love with David rather than just to have lived with him in reasonable comity? Husbands and wives did not stare fondly into one another's eyes; that required mystery and a sense of wonderment at the other, which surely could not last very long. And she knew – as everybody did – that you had to accept that marriage could not be a fairy story, that you could not go through life feeling as if you have just had a glass of champagne, that all you could hope for was a sort of unchallenging companionship – an understanding not to judge each other too harshly.

Yet even that required a form of belief in the other, and that could be so quickly ruined by the wrong words, by an expressed doubt, an act of disloyalty, that would weaken the pact that you both wanted to exist. It was rather like saying that you do not believe in God; God can be a fine pretence, can give all the comfort that you need, until you doubt his presence; and with that you find that he is indeed not there.

She turned away from the mirror. She would try.

She started to leave the room, but stopped. She closed her eyes. Standing below the air conditioning vent, the cool air blew directly on her skin. And she thought: insecurity. He had brought it up when they had been talking about over-eating but now she was going over it in her mind and realising that if she went back to David it might just be because she felt at some subconscious level that this was where her best chance of security lay. She needed him because he had the money and paid for everything.

She opened her eyes again and started to make her way to the kitchen, where she heard the sounds of his preparing whatever it was he was heating up for her.

"Bouillabaisse," he announced. "Made with red snapper."

"And …"

"And conch."

She raised a hand to her lips in a gesture of gastronomic anticipation. She did not carry it through, as she felt the tears well in her eyes. How stupid of me to cry, she thought; how stupid.

"Onions," she stuttered.

But he knew that it was not the onions that she could see he had been cutting that were making her cry, but memories. He put an arm around her; and this was the first proper touch of him for years.

"Start again?"

She was unprepared for this. The move, she had thought, would come from her, not from him, and now she felt gratitude, sheer gratitude, that he had chosen to make it so easy for her. She moved against him, into his embrace. Three years, she thought, of pointless misunderstanding and separation are coming to an end in a simple touch. There had been no elaborate discussion, no rehearsal of pros and cons, and she felt that she was falling into this decision without thinking things through. But she had had enough; she had had enough of loneliness; as he had, too, she imagined.

He kissed her, and she wondered whether she really still liked it. She remembered what a friend had said to her at high school, all those years ago: *if you wouldn't use a boy's toothbrush – and you wouldn't, would you? – then why kiss him?* The things people say can ruin the things we would otherwise like to do, and kissing – or the prospect of kissing – had never seemed the same to her after that. She had forgotten what it was like to be this close to him; it was familiar and yet unfamiliar; she had become used to his separateness and had not given thought to the physical. *Perhaps I have shrivelled within me. Perhaps I can't.* "Tonight?" he said. "Or you can wait if you like. You mustn't feel under pressure."

She said that this was not the way she felt. "I feel so silly crying like this. This was not the way it was meant to be."

"But it is," he said.

His embrace turned into a playful hug, and then they broke apart, each as surprised as the other by what had happened. "Are they both asleep?" he asked, nodding in the direction of the bedrooms along the corridor.

She said she thought they were.

"Clover's very excited," he said.

She nodded. "There's a reason for that."

He looked at her enquiringly.

"She wants to see that boy," she said. She looked at him hesitantly. "James. He's the reason."

"Ah."

"Yes. I fear she's in for a disappointment. These teenage romances ... Particularly one-sided ones."

"Poor girl."

"We want to protect them, don't we? We want to protect them from the pain that we know is coming their way, but what can one do?"

He shrugged. "We can warn them. We can tell them the truth."

"That won't work," she said. "You think you know what the truth is at sixteen. All other versions of it are wrong."

"Just like us?"

"Yes. Just like we did at that age."

He sighed. "My little girl ... thinking about other men."

She laughed, and she realised that this was the first time she had laughed in his company for more than three years. He seemed to sense this too, and he grinned at her. She thought: he's changed, and of course I can fall in love with him again, or at least fall in friendship, if there is such a thing.

18

Clover saw Ted before she saw James. She had gone with her mother to the supermarket – an everyday trip but one that, after three years' interruption, was like performing once more an important ritual of childhood. It was exactly the same as she remembered it – the car park with its hotly contested shady spots; the line of shopping carts along the front of the building; the cool exhaled breath of the air conditioning as the automatic doors parted to admit you. The smell was familiar too: the ripe, sweet smell of the fruit at the entrance, and then the piquant notes from the trays of ready-made dishes. The man at the fish counter was the same man whom she had last seen standing there three years ago; his white straw hat at the same angle and the apron with his embroidered name and the printed picture of a jumping marlin. The same tired woman was spraying water over the salad vegetables and she glanced at Clover and then looked at her again before deciding that she recognised her, and nodded.

Ted was standing at the section where magazines were displayed. He was reading something about cars and he looked up and smiled broadly at Clover.

"Clove," he said. "It's you, isn't it?"

"Yes, me."

He put the magazine down. "It's great to see you."

"And you."

"I mean it," he said.

"I know you do."

They looked at one another awkwardly before she broke the ice. "I'm here with my mother. Shop, shop, shop."

"Me too."

She looked over her shoulder. "We could go and have a coffee round the corner. They're going to take ages."

"Yes, they always do."

In the coffee bar, the awkwardness that Ted had shown seemed to melt away. He told her about the school he was at – an international school in Wales – and asked her about Strathearn.

"You haven't changed," he said.

"Nor you." That was not true, she thought, but she said it nonetheless. Ted had changed; his face was thinner, she thought, and that slightly puppyish look he had at twelve was no longer there.

"But I hope I have," he said.

"Then you have."

Their order of coffee arrived.

"What are you going to do?" he asked.

"Now?"

"No. While you're here. For the next two weeks."

'Three." She paused. He was watching her. "Nothing much. Chill, I suppose."

"There's going to be a party."

She caught her breath, but tried not to look interested. "It's that time of year."

"James is having one."

He was watching for her reaction, and she could not help herself blushing. He'll be able to tell, she thought.

"Yes?"

"Yes, the day after tomorrow." Ted paused. "Would you like to come?"

She shrugged. "I don't know. He hasn't invited me."

"Oh, that doesn't matter. Nobody's being invited as such. All his friends can come."

"I'll have to think."

Ted sipped at his coffee. "I hate this stuff," he said. "I've never liked coffee. I only drink it because everybody else does."

She stared at him. "You don't have to be the same as everybody else."

He wiped cappuccino foam from his lips. "I know."

"Just be yourself. It's easier."

"Yeah, sure. Is that what you do?"

She did not answer.

"You like him, don't you?"

She affected ignorance. "Who?"

"James."

"He's all right."

Ted smiled. "No, it's more than that. You really like him, don't you?"

She turned the questioning back to him. "Well, what about you? You like him, too. You really like him."

He stiffened. "He's a friend. I like my friends."

"But some more than others."

"Sure. Who doesn't?"

He was watching her warily. She had strayed into something she had not expected, and her instinct was to move away. "I might come to the party," she said. "Will you tell him?"

"What?"

"That I'm coming."

He shrugged. "It'll be fine. I don't need to tell him … but I will, if you like." He paused, as if weighing up whether to continue. "By the way, you know how people can't stand other people?"

She said nothing. Was he going to say that James could not stand her?

"Your mother," he went on. "Your mother and James's mother. Don't go there."

She looked at him wide-eyed. "What do you mean?"

He seemed to be enjoying himself now. "You remember years ago? You remember how when we were kids we played at being detectives, or whatever. We took photographs at the tennis club."

"Sort of," she said. "It wasn't my idea – it was James's. He liked to do that sort of thing."

"Maybe, but he took them of your mother talking to his dad. And he made some sort of note about their meeting one another. Kids' stuff."

She remained silent.

"James's mother found them – the photographs. She thought that it showed that your mother and James's father were … you know … seeing one another."

She felt a sudden coldness within her. "Oh."

"James told me," Ted continued. "He said that his folks had a major row. Big time."

She could only think to say that it was not true.

"I know," said Ted. "Adults get it seriously wrong sometimes. But the point is that she hates your mother."

Clover struggled to control herself. "I don't care." She did.

"I don't think she hates you, though," said Ted. "What your mother does has nothing to do with you."

"She didn't do anything."

"I'm not saying she did. All I'm saying is that if she did something, then it wouldn't be your fault. You see the difference?"

She nodded. She felt miserable.

"James doesn't hold it against you," Ted went on. "He's cool with what happened. I suppose he's more embarrassed than anything." He paused. "He likes you, you know."

She struggled to control herself. She wanted to ask him what James had said; she wanted to hear the exact words. But she did not want Ted to know how desperately she wanted this knowledge.

"I'm not saying that he's *keen* on you," Ted said. "Not in *that* way."

She bit her lip. She tried to laugh. "I didn't think you meant that."

"He's got a girlfriend, you see."

Now she lost the battle to remain aloof, and Ted noticed. "I can tell you're upset," he said. "Sorry about that. It must be tough if you're really keen on somebody ... and they don't notice you."

She tried to look scornful. "I'm not *really keen* on anybody. I don't care."

He looked unbelieving. "Don't you? You don't have to pretend with me, Clove. Remember, we've known one another since we were six, or whatever."

She looked at her watch. "I have to go." But then she added, "Who is she anyway – this girlfriend?" She stumbled on the word *girlfriend*, and had to repeat it. Ted noticed; she could tell by the way he looked away in embarrassment.

"She's called Laura," he said. He turned back to face her. "I can't stand her myself. He's only known her since the summer."

"You don't like her?"

"Of course not ..." He checked himself, but she wondered why he had said *of course*.

"Why not? Why don't you like her, Ted?"

He shrugged. "You can't like everybody. You like some people, and you don't like others. It's a matter of ..."

"Chemistry?"

"Yeah, sure. Chemistry comes into it." He played with the handle of his coffee cup. "Chemistry's important, but there are other things. The things people say, for instance. Their attitude. She's keen on him – you can tell."

She tried to keep her voice level. "How?"

"She's all over him – know what I mean? She looks at him in a really intense way. Like this." He glared at Clover. "See? What do you call that?"

"I don't know."

"It's *the* look. That's what they call it. *The* look. You can always tell."

There was a straw to be clutched at. She heard her friend at school: *if you're keen on a boy, never show it – it's the quickest way of scaring them.* "That sort of look can put people off. Maybe he doesn't like it. She could be much keener on him than he is on her."

Ted was doubtful. "I think he likes her – at least that's the impression I got when he spoke to me. And when I've seen them together." He seemed to consider something. "But then you know how kind he is – he's always kind to people, isn't he?"

Yes, it was why she liked him; or one of the reasons for the way she felt: his kindness.

"So maybe he's just being kind to her?" But then Ted seemed to reject his own suggestion. "No, I don't think so. I think she's managed to get him to like her. And then there's the way she is. She's really hot. You can tell. I think he likes all that."

She stared at him. She hated hearing that, and something

made her feel that Ted did not like it either, although he was the one who said it.

"Why's she here?" she asked. People came and went in Cayman; perhaps she would not last.

"Her folks. Her dad has a job here. He's with one of the American banks, but they're Canadians themselves. She's at school in Vancouver. They have different holidays from British schools, but the summer holidays are more or less the same."

She listened to this carefully, trying to envisage Laura. "Are you sure? How do you know she's his actual girlfriend?"

"Because he told me."

"He said he was seeing her?"

Ted smirked. "More than that. He said ..."

She cut him short by standing up. "I have to get back."

"Me too. But what about the party? You can come with me if you like."

She almost said that she had no interest in going to the party – that she didn't care about James. But those were not the words that came. Instead, she nodded, and said: "All right."

They walked back to the supermarket, to meet their mothers. She separated from him at the entrance, saying goodbye without letting him see how upset she was. She felt that he probably knew, anyway, but somehow she wanted to salvage her dignity by not revealing the despair that now engulfed her like a sea-fog, as cold, as dispiriting. He could not have a girlfriend because he belonged to her. She should be his girlfriend, not some girl from Vancouver who had only just met him.

When Amanda saw her, she could tell that something was amiss. "Is it Ted?" she asked. "Did Ted do something to upset you?"

She shook her head. "He didn't."

"You look as if you're about to cry."

She turned away. "I'm not. Don't be ridiculous."

"And you should stop being so moody."

She said nothing. Her mother could not possibly understand. She was an ice maiden when it came to these things; she had no idea, none at all, about how it felt when the only boy you could ever love was seeing some Canadian girl and telling Ted about it. They were standing at the supermarket check-out now, and the woman behind the till was looking expectantly at her mother, waiting for her to unload the cart. The woman had a dull, passive look to her, and behind her, ready to pack the purchases, stood a boy with a scowl. Clover looked through the plate-glass window behind them, out into the supermarket car park; a large white vehicle, a luxury SUV, was pulling up at the kerb. She watched as a young couple got out, and said something to one another, laughed briefly, and then went back to looking bored. That's the trouble, she thought: everybody here is bored. She did not want that. She wanted something different, and that, she knew, was James. I want him more than anything I've ever wanted. I want to be with him. I want to feel him beside me. I want to be far away from everybody else, just with him. I want him to whisper to me and kiss me and tell me all his secrets and that he thinks of me all the time. That's what I want, and that's what's going to happen – it really is. It will happen if I want it hard enough.

19

"There," said Billy, pointing to a spot where the land jutted out into the sea. "That's the place. You can put everything down there and then we can swim."

Amanda had suggested a picnic, and they had agreed – Billy more enthusiastically than his sister. She had said initially that she wanted to stay at home, having things to do. Amanda had said, "To mope?"

"No. Things to do."

"Then do them after our picnic – there'll be plenty of time."

It was a place they had often visited – a place where the mangrove met a cluster of sea-grape trees and where there was enough sand to make for a small swimming beach. The beach gave way to rock formations on either side through which the sea was making slow ingress, wearing away at the basalt to produce strange indentations and incipient caves. When an onshore wind whipped up waves, the movement of the sea, though dissipated here by the protective ring of reef a mile or so further out, was sufficient to produce the occasional plume of spray from a blowhole, shooting up like a displaced ornamental fountain. As a young girl, Clover had been fascinated by this, and had been prepared to sit for hours on end, under Margaret's watching eye, waiting for the sudden eruption of white.

"Don't dive," warned Amanda, as Billy rushed to the edge of the water. "Remember what happened to that boy …"

Billy stopped in his tracks. "Timmy …"

"Yes, Timmy. He was lucky not to have been much more badly hurt."

Billy stared at the water. "He was knocked out, wasn't he?"

"Concussed – not quite knocked out. But it could have been much worse."

Clover joined in: "You shouldn't dive into water if you don't know exactly how deep it is."

"Your sister's right," said Amanda. "Listen to her."

"He never does," said Clover.

While the boy waded into the water, Clover and her mother unpacked the bag of picnic provisions they had brought with them. There was a flask of iced juice, and Amanda poured some for her daughter. Clover took it, drained the glass, and then lay back on the picnic rug and looked up at the sky.

"Happy to be here?" asked Amanda.

"Yes."

Amanda lay back too. "I love looking at this sky. You can't lie back in Scotland and stare at the sky."

"It would rain on you."

"Yes."

Flat out on the sand, Amanda turned her head to look at her daughter. She was an attractive girl – still obviously a teenager, but getting to the point where the adult butterfly finally emerged, where all vestiges of the vulnerability and softness of the child gave way to the grown young woman. "Happy?" she asked.

"I've already told you. Yes."

Amanda persisted. "Not just to be here, but happy in … in general. With life?"

"Yes. Of course."

"I wanted to talk to you."

Clover was still staring at the sky. "Well, we're talking, aren't we?"

"About me and Daddy."

This was greeted with silence. Above them, a high-flying jet curved a line of white across the sky.

"You see," said Amanda, "I have some rather good news for you. Or I think you'll find it good news."

There was little reaction.

"You're listening to me, I hope. You aren't going to sleep, are you?"

This brought a muttered response. "No, I'm not."

"Daddy and I are going to live together again. We've talked it through. We're getting on better and we ... well, both of us have been lonely. You understand that, don't you?"

She saw her daughter stiffen. She continued to lie still, but the effect had been immediate.

"Yes, I understand. I'm a bit surprised, though."

"It's a surprise for me, too. So I'll go back to Scotland, but only to close up the flat. Then I'll come back home. Billy will go back to the Prep." She was aware of the fact that she said *home*. There had been a change, as slow, in human terms, as the erosive action of the sea on the rock: home was no longer New York, or America; it had become this place in the middle of nowhere, under a familiar, but still alien flag.

"So everything will go back to how it used to be." She paused, and reached to the flask to pour more juice. "I hope you're pleased."

Clover had raised herself onto an elbow and was looking at her mother. She was smiling. "I'm really pleased, Mum. I'm really pleased."

"Good. Then give me a kiss."

Clover leaned forward and kissed her mother on the cheek. She wanted to cry, and the tears now came, sobs, almost painful in their intensity.

"Darling, you mustn't cry …"

She struggled with the words. "It's because … because I'm so pleased."

"I'm glad."

Clover wiped at her eyes. "And Billy? Does he know?"

"I'll tell him later – after his swim. Both of us – we can both tell him. Not that he'll pay much attention."

Clover shook her head in disagreement. "He misses Dad. Surely you've noticed that."

It was a reproach, and Amanda tried to explain herself. "Yes, you're right. I suppose I was just thinking how boys don't feel so intensely about these things."

This caught Clover's attention. "They don't?"

"Well, it's a bit of a generalisation, of course, but these generalisations are often true. Or at least, I think they are. Boys – men too – are more interested in the outside world than the inside world."

"The inside world?"

"How we feel. Of course there are plenty of men who feel these things, but generally speaking they're too busy *doing* things to ask themselves how they feel about them. That's why it sometimes seems to us that they don't care about people's emotions."

"Because they're selfish?"

"Not selfish – it's more a question of indifference."

"What exactly is indifference?"

Amanda glanced across the beach to where Billy was examining something washed up by the waves – a cuttlefish, she thought. "Indifference is not worrying about others. And that may be because you don't know what they're thinking, or because you know and don't care."

"Indifference," muttered Clover, as if savouring the new word, like a new taste, experienced for the first time.

Amanda glanced at her. We let our children grow up under our noses without talking to them about these things; now she was. "Which is one of the worst things you can experience."

Clover frowned. "Why?"

"Because when we want somebody to notice us and they don't, there's a particular sort of pain involved." She paused. Billy had picked up something else – an abandoned sandal – and was waving his discovery at them. "Put it down, Billy."

"He picks everything up," said Clover. "The other day I saw him pick up a handkerchief somebody had dropped. Think of the germs."

"We need a certain number of germs – just to keep our immune systems in trim."

Clover was not convinced. "Yuck." She was looking up at the sky again; but it was indifference that was on her mind. "You were saying ..."

Amanda hesitated. She knew what her daughter was going through, and this discussion of indifference went to the heart of it. "We all want to be loved, you know. We want that rather badly."

Clover said nothing.

"And so," Amanda continued, "that's why indifference can be so painful. We may decide that we want to be loved by a particular person – and we can't really control who that will be – and if they don't love us, if they take no notice of us, we hurt. It's the way we're made, I suppose. It just is."

Clover propped herself up on an arm and stared at her mother. "Why are you saying all this?"

Amanda took a deep breath. "I'm saying it, darling, because I think that's what you may be feeling. I think you're very keen on a boy whom you haven't seen for the last three years and who is probably rather different from when you saw him last."

"He isn't," muttered Clover.

"Have you seen him? You haven't, have you?"

"I saw Ted. He told me."

Amanda smiled. "Maybe. Maybe. But the point is that you don't really know whether you're going to be able to resume the friendship you had. And you don't really know how James feels, do you?" She reached out and took Clover's hand. She felt the sand upon it; the fine white grains that would cling to your skin, like face-powder, long after you had left the beach. "I think you may be in love with an idea of a boy, rather than with an actual boy."

She did not take her hand away, allowing it to remain in her mother's clasp. "I don't think I am."

"But you don't know yet whether James sees you in the same way that you see him. That's the problem. And it might not be a good idea to allow yourself to love somebody you don't see very much and who may not feel the way you feel. It's just likely to make you miserable, I'd have thought."

Amanda pressed Clover's hand. She had never spoken to her with this degree of intimacy, and it felt to her as if she had been admitted to a whole new dimension of her daughter's life. It was like coming across one's child in some private moment and seeing the child, perhaps for the first time, as a person who was quite distinct from you, with a moral life of his or her own. Perhaps that was a transition that every parent experienced as a son or daughter moved from being an extension of the parent to having a life led separately from the parent, with its own tides of feeling, its own plans.

"Darling," she said, "there's an expression that people bandy about: love hurts. It sounds like one of those things that people say without thinking because they've read about it somewhere, or heard it in a song. But those things are often true, even if they sound corny and over-used. Love really does hurt. It hurts when you realise how much you love somebody. It hurts whether or not that person loves you back and everything goes well, or whether they don't and they ignore you or treat you badly. It just hurts, because that's the way love works. Does any of this make any sense to you?"

There was a murmur – nothing more.

"So as you go through life, you work out a way of dealing with it – just as you work out a way of dealing with the other things that happen to you. You could deny your feelings and try never to fall in love – lots of people do that – but that's no way to live. So you work out how to control the impact of love. You learn to protect yourself from being too badly bruised by it. You let yourself go, but always remembering that you have to keep part of you from being … well, I suppose, from being too badly hurt – from being drowned."

Clover looked away. "I like James. That's all."

"That's all?"

"Yes."

Amanda looked at her watch. "We need to begin our picnic. Perhaps you could go and fetch your brother from the water."

"He'll come if you shout *food*," said Clover. "Like a dog." She paused. "Do you think boys are a bit like dogs?"

Amanda laughed. "In some respects," she said.

20

They welcomed Amanda at the tennis club as if her absence had been three months rather than three years. Although there was a floating population of expatriates – those who came for a few years before going on somewhere else, or returning to the place they had come from – there were others who stayed for years, for the greater part of a lifetime in some cases. These people might spend much of their time elsewhere but seemed drawn back to the sheltering skirts of the place that having asked so little from them in terms of tax, then made no demands of them other than that they pay their bills and refrain from challenging corrupt politicians or well-connected developers. If they had the bad taste to be rich, then they might at least have the good taste to keep a low profile politically, and certainly not give others their advice.

With money, there came an ability to escape the normal constraints of geography. Most people did not have much choice about where they lived, and they stayed there year upon year. By contrast, the wealthy could move about as they wished, following the tides of whim and fashion. But too much absence could be a bad thing: being *off island* meant that you were away, but would probably return when you had had enough of the grind of existence in London or New York or wherever it was that you had gone to.

So the secretary of the tennis club merely added Amanda's name to the club competition ladder and sent her the bill for a renewed membership even without asking her whether she still wanted to play tennis.

"I heard you were back," she said when Amanda first visited the club. "I took the liberty of adding you to the doubles ladder:

we needed another woman for the mixed doubles and I thought of you."

Amanda had not objected. "My tennis is rusty," she said. "I joined a club in Edinburgh but you know how it is in Scotland. They have all-weather courts but that doesn't really help all that much if there's wind."

"You can book the pro."

"I will."

Clover went with her mother for her first lesson, and watched as Amanda returned serve after serve and responded to shouted instructions.

"He shouldn't shout at you like that," she muttered at the end of the lesson. "You're paying him, aren't you?"

"That's the whole point, darling. This island is full of people ..." – she almost said rich people, but stopped herself – "who pay others to shout at them. Personal trainers, and so on. There are hundreds of them."

Clover did not come to watch the second lesson, which took place the next afternoon, in that crucial hour before evening fell when the temperature was right for activities that involved exertion. The coach was impressed with the progress they had made and shouted less; her backhand, he said, was improving and would obviously get stronger with practice. At the end of the lesson, she made arrangements for the next session and then went into the club house for a shower. She did not intend to stay, as David would be back for dinner in an hour or so and she had nothing prepared, but she stopped by the noticeboard to look at the latest postings. The ladder was there – she saw her name in the mixed doubles section – and there was a poster advertising an exhibition match between the top-ranked player in Florida and a finalist from the Australian Open. It was to be on Boxing Day and there would be a dinner afterwards in aid of club funds. There was an appeal for a lost racquet – "of purely sentimental value" – removed accidentally, of course, from a car. No questions would be asked if the racquet were to be returned.

There was a voice behind her – so close that it startled her.

"See – there *is* a crime wave, whatever the Commissioner of Police may say."

She turned round to see George Collins. He was dressed for work, in a smart white shirt with buttoned-down collar and a red tie with a worked-in motif – a rod of Asclepius, the snake twirled round the physician's staff. In the confusion of the moment, her eye was drawn to the tie; he noticed, and smiled.

"People sometimes misunderstand this," he said. "One of my patients even asked if I was a snake-handler. I think she was disappointed when I explained that it all just had to do with an old Greek god."

She looked up at him, and she felt a sudden emptiness in her stomach. She had imagined that she would meet him on this trip; the island was too small for people to avoid one another. That could be done, of course, at the cost of some effort; two warring *grandes dames* who had left Palm Beach precisely to avoid contact with each other and had, by coincidence, both chosen Grand Cayman as their refuge, had been obliged to work out an unspoken rota that allowed them to frequent the same parties, but at different times; one came early and left early; the other arrived once the coast was clear.

She had thought it would be at a party, when she would have time to prepare herself. She had rehearsed in her mind how she would behave; how she would appear unfazed by the meeting;

how she would indicate by a casual, friendly demeanour that she bore no resentment or disappointment; that whatever had happened was a long time ago – three years was sufficient for people to get over most things, she felt, except, perhaps, sexual involvement: that was more difficult – the memory of intimacy was always there in the background, no matter how casually treated; the other had been admitted to the personal realm as others, acquaintances, friends, colleagues, had not.

But none of the scripts she had prepared came to her in this setting, before the tennis club noticeboard, where the opening remark had been about crime and a missing tennis racquet.

Banality came to her rescue. "Sometimes I wish somebody would steal my racquet," she said. "My game might improve with a new one."

He laughed. "I saw that you were having a lesson. I'm beyond all professional help, I'm afraid."

He looked at her, as if expecting her to comment on his tennis – she had never seen him play – but she said nothing. He waited, before continuing: "I thought you were never going to return."

She looked askance. "Why shouldn't I?"

"I just made the assumption."

"Well, you were wrong. Here I am."

He nodded. "You have the kids with you – so I assume it won't be for long."

She confirmed it would be for the duration of the school holidays and then she would return to Scotland, but only for a short while. "I'm coming back more permanently. Billy's going back to the Prep."

She saw that he seemed pleased to hear this news, and she became guarded. "I don't think that we should …"

He interrupted her. "Should what? Talk to one another?"

"I didn't say that. But I don't think it would be wise, after what happened, for us to be seen together too often."

Again he queried her. "What counts as too often in this place? Once a month? Once a year?"

She spelled it out. "Too often means ever. I suppose I'd say that we shouldn't really see one another at all."

He raised his voice in protest, causing her to glance anxiously down the veranda; they were still by themselves. There was a note of frustration in his voice now. "I don't see what harm there is in two friends occasionally seeing one another."

"George," she said, "there's such a thing as disingenuousness. We can't pretend that we didn't, well, fall for one another."

He looked away, as if it was painful to be reminded.

"We can't pretend," she went on, "that people don't know that our marriages suffered as a result: you know what this place is like for gossip. We happen to live in a village of married couples. There are the keepers, with all their money, and the kept – and I'm one of the kept – and there are lots of us; it's just the way it is."

He interrupted her. "I've never heard it described that way …"

She ignored the interruption. "My marriage more or less came to an end and now I'm rekindling it. I don't want to go through a separation again – or, worse still, a divorce."

"Don't sell yourself short. You've got a mind. You're not one of these women with nothing in their heads but thoughts of their next cocktail party or shopping trip to Miami. You're not that at all."

"Maybe not, but the reality of the situation is that I have no career. David and I can get on. We have children, and one of them is still quite young."

He looked at her with a mixture of disappointment and pity. "So you've made your bed and you're going to lie in it."

"You could put it that way. I'm being realistic."

He stared at her mutely.

"I'm sorry," she said. "I was very anxious about meeting you again. And now I've upset you."

He looked away. "You're right, though. We can't, can we?"

"Not really."

"It would have been ..."

"It would have been good for both of us, yes, but I don't think we can."

He took a step away, and lowered his voice. "Let me tell you something," he said. "For the last three years, there has not been a day – not a single day – in which I haven't thought about you. Not necessarily for long periods, but even just for a few seconds – a fleeting thought, you'd call it – in which you have been there, in my mind, and I have let you in, so to speak."

She wanted to say: *me too, me too.* But she remained silent. *Do not tell your love.*

"Sometimes," he went on, "when I've been driving to work in the car, doing something as mundane as that, I've thought of you and I've whispered your name, or called it out, even, as if in agony. Why should I do this? Why should you have got under my skin to such an extent that I behave in a way that my psychiatric colleagues would find interesting? In fact – and this may amuse you – I mentioned this – disguising details, of course – to a psychiatrist friend and he said to me, 'Oh, that's not all that unusual; that's how agony is released, by shouting out the name of the person or the thing that haunts the mind.' And he said, too, that it was a way in which we tempt Fate to bring down upon us the thing that we dread could happen – the disclosure of our secret. Shout it out and control it that way. That's how he explained it.

"But I didn't really care about the explanation; what moved me was the fact that I had found something that I didn't think could exist. And that thing – the thing that I found – was very simple. Most people know all about it and have never really doubted it because their lives have been such as to give them a glimpse of this thing that they were not sure about, which is love, of course: the sheer fact of feeling love for another, of finding the one person – the only person, it seems – who makes the world make sense. It's like discovering the map that you've been looking for all your life and have never been able to find – the map that makes sense of the journey."

"George ..."

"No, I don't expect you to love me back, because that doesn't always happen, does it? So I accept that this is the way it is to be."

"Can't we just somehow get over this? I wanted ..."

He brushed this aside; it seemed that he was determined to finish what he wanted to say. "I shall continue to do what I'm doing, which is to be a doctor sorting out people's minor medical problems most of the time and every so often, I suppose, being able to do something more important for them. And I shall do this in a place that I don't really like – a place that I think has a tainted notion at its heart – that money should be able to be stashed away without doing anything for the people who actually do the work to produce it. I'm stuck with all that because even in places like this there are poor people and people who are treated badly and who need help with their varicose veins and digestive problems and their conjunctivitis and, yes, their deaths. And I'll do that because I'm the one who happens to be around to do it. I'm not being Albert Schweitzer or anything like that, I'm just doing a job that I happen to do. And I won't mind too much that I can't talk to anybody about this – other than you – because I can't find the words with which to open up to them. So, fine, I give you your freedom from this thing that happened to us and I promise you I'll respect what you have to do, which is what you've told me."

He stopped, and she reached out to him instinctively. "George …"

She withdrew her hand. A man and two women had appeared at the end of the veranda and had tossed their racquets down on a table. One of the women had looked in their direction and had seen her reach out to George. She was sure of that.

21

Ted had said to Clover: "Listen, if you feel awkward about going to the party, then why not come with me? Why not?"

He did not wait for her to reply. "We could walk," he said. "It's not far. I'll swing by and collect you."

She was at pains to say that she felt no awkwardness, although she was not sure that he believed her. Ted had a way of looking at you when you spoke as if he were weighing up the truthfulness or otherwise of what you said; Ted could tell. "I don't mind," she said, looking away to avoid his scrutiny. "It's just that I'm not sure that I want to go."

"But everybody …"

She chided him gently. "You don't have to do something just because everybody else is doing it."

He grinned at her. "You do, actually."

"I don't know what you mean."

He had written an essay on conformity, and he told her about it. "I got an A for it, as it happens."

"Clever you."

"Well, I got quite a lot of it from the web, although I put it in my own words. There's this fantastic site about personal psychology – it's called something like *The Authentic You*. It says that at some stages in your life you really want to conform – you really don't want to stand out. And you know when that is?"

She shrugged.

"Now. Right now. The stage we're at. Where we are."

"That is – if we're at the same stage."

He looked at her blankly. "We're both sixteen."

She pointed out, half-playfully, that boys and girls developed at different rates. "Sorry about that, Ted, but we're more mature."

"That's what you think."

"No, it's what psychologists think."

He was not convinced. "You wish."

"It's true."

He returned to the subject of the party. "Please come. James will be pleased."

She looked away. "You said something about a Canadian girl."

"Laura."

She had remembered the name, but had not wanted to utter it. "Her. You said that she and James are seeing one another."

"Yes, they are. But you know something?"

Her heart gave a leap; perhaps he had heard that it was over. "What?"

"I don't think it's going to last."

She asked him why he should think this, and he replied that he thought that James was bored. "He may like her, but ..."

"But what?"

"She looks at him all the time, you see. I think I told you. Imagine what it must be like to have somebody looking at you all the time. Just think of it."

Her voice was even. "He probably feels ... probably feels guilty, or something. You shouldn't look at people."

"Not at all."

She hesitated. "Well, maybe a bit. Now and then."

He thought that everybody looked at people. "You can't go around looking away all the time. How can you?"

"You have to be careful not to become obsessed."

He was staring at her. "Yes," he said, thoughtfully. "You have to." And then he continued, "Please say you'll come with me.

You can't have anything better to do round here. Come on."

"If you really want me to."

"I do, Clove. I do."

She wanted to go, of course, and did not want to go. She thought of her mother's advice – if it really had been advice, and if it had actually been given: it was not pressed upon her, as advice usually is – rather it was trailed before her, hinted at. You could make yourself unhappy so easily by wanting something that you might never get; that unhappiness could be avoided by the simple expedient of thinking of something – or somebody – else. Of course that was right. She had seen it a hundred times in the magazines that she and her friends read at school: the problem pages spelled it out with wearying familiarity: don't allow a boy to ruin your life; don't waste your time; move on. They were right, of course – she knew that – but it was easier said than done. She should ignore James's party, but Ted wanted her to go with him and she could at least oblige him. Ted liked James; he was perhaps a little bit infatuated by him; could boys be infatuated with other boys, and not be gay? She had talked about that with a friend at school who told her that her brother constantly talked about another boy. "He drives me mad," she said. "He thinks this boy is just great. The great Anthony: Anthony the Great. He tells me everything *Ant* says. It's all the usual stuff, but he still tells me. I think he wants to *be* him. That's what it is, I think. He wants to *be* him. Go and be *Ant*, I said to him, and he just stared at me. "

Their conversation had come back to her later. It was not so much the question of how boys felt about each other that interested her – she thought that for the most part boys were indifferent to other boys; they liked to impress each other, but there was not much more to it than that. What fired her imagination was the thought that people might want to be somebody else. Was that what happened when you fell for somebody? Did you really want to be him, or did you want to be yourself *beside* him? She tried to imagine what it would be like to be James. She closed her eyes and then opened them as if she were inside James, looking out at the world with his eyes. It did not work.

No, she yearned for something quite different from what she imagined James wanted. She wanted to be with him; she wanted to listen to him because everything he said was somehow … What was it? Was it anything different from what Ted or any other boy said? Yes, it was. It was different, but she could not decide why this should be so. James was funny. James looked at you in a particular way when he spoke and that made the words seem different. James was beautiful. James made everything seem special, as if the sheer fact of his presence cast a light upon what was around him that was simply not there in his absence. Margaret used to say that about Jesus. She said: *The Lord makes everything shine, you know. He makes it so different that you scratch your head and ask: is this the same place? Is this Jamaica? Is this Cayman? Or is it the Lord's special place?* Margaret had religion, and people who had religion said things like that; sang them too. But leaving Jesus and the Lord to one side, she wondered how one person, a boy, could do this? How could one person transform the world about him?

She had not allowed herself to use the word – at least about herself and James. But now she did. Now she thought she was approaching the heart of what was happening; she had fallen in love with him. This was the mysterious thing that people talked about so much, that was in almost every line of every song, written into the digital code of every mp3. Love. This is what it was. It was like a wave. It was like being covered by a great wave coming in off the open ocean; a wave that rolled you over and over, making you tumble helplessly in its force, rendering you unable to do anything about it because it was so strong. That was what it was like, and it was happening to her. She could admit that now. She loved James.

And what can you do if you are in love? What are you *meant* to do? Do you throw yourself at the person you love? Do you tell him how you feel and place yourself at his mercy? Or do you wait until the moment comes when what you are experiencing within yourself is somehow reciprocated and the feelings of two people coincide? The problem with that was that if she did nothing, James would be lost to her, and then somebody else – some girl from Vancouver – would step in and take him away. Lure him away with sex. Give him what every boy wanted and thought about all the time, if you could believe what you read about that.

Ted had hinted – in a smutty, childish way – that this is what had already happened. She could not bear to think about that. How dare she even *touch* him: slut. Even if they only kissed, that was too much. Her lips all over him, parted like the lips of a … mollusc. Mollusc. Her saliva in a little trail on his chin. Her teeth. Her disgusting, greedy lips. Her busy hands. Now she felt a new emotion: hatred. She hated that Canadian girl. She wished that she would die. No, she did not; you could not think that. She was a girl, just like she was. She had parents who probably loved her and would be upset if she were dead. You could not think that. Or just a little bit dead – dead for a short time – and then discovered still to be alive. No. Injured somehow. Run over, perhaps; not too badly, but enough to put her legs in plaster. No, that was cruel; you should not think cruel things about real people, and I will not. I will not. Sent away then. Sent back to Vancouver for doing something illegal in Cayman. Marched out of the country and being seen at the airport handcuffed to a fat Caymanian policewoman who ate too much unhealthy food and who wanted to get home to eat more fried conch and rum cake. Parents crying and waving goodbye; their only daughter disgraced on the front page of every newspaper; *We had no idea she was such a slut,* they said to the press. The Cayman Airways plane with its piratical, one-legged turtle painted on it waiting for her; people staring out of the windows and pointing at her. *Goodbye. Goodbye.* The sound of the plane's engine and its blast blowing leaves and sand back across the runway like one of those high winds. Back to a school in Vancouver – a girls' school – where there would be no boys to ogle or seduce. A school run by nuns, perhaps – if there were any of those left; they had them in Quebec still and they would come and scold you in French. A school where the dormitories were actually small cells with barred windows out of which, if you stood on a chair and peered, you might just see boys in the distance, all of them unaware of you; far away, out of reach.

She stopped herself. It was not in her nature to be unkind; in fact, she was naturally quite the opposite. *I am an ordinary girl, with ordinary feelings; that's all.* She would not think such thoughts; she would make a real effort to like Laura, to see her better points ... her hair, for instance. She stopped herself again.

In a moment of honesty, she said to Ted as they walked together up the short tarmac drive of the Collins house: "I feel nervous,

Ted. Sorry, but I do."

Ted turned to look at her. He smiled. "Of course you do, Clove. We feel nervous about people we like a lot. We feel worried in case they won't like us as much as we like them." He paused. "I feel nervous too."

It occurred to her that it was not just for her sake that he had suggested she accompany him to the party. "Because …" she began.

He hesitated. "Same as you," he muttered.

She reached out to him, but said nothing.

"I spoke to somebody once. He said I'd grow out of it. That's what he actually said."

"Maybe you will."

He laughed. "Nobody says that any more. But at least with James I know it's no use. I can be his friend – that's all."

She felt a rush of sympathy for the boy beside her. "Isn't that enough?"

"It'll have to be." He paused. "But don't think I'm unhappy – or all that unhappy. I'm not."

"Good."

"So let's go in."

James answered the door. She looked up and saw him; then she glanced at Ted. He was smiling, as was James.

"Clove?"

"Yes."

"Ages …" He stepped forward, grinning, and put his arms about her. "Ages and ages."

She felt his cheek against hers. "It's been …"

"Ages," he said. "Ted told me he had been in touch with you. Sorry, I haven't myself. I've …"

His explanation died away, and she helped him. "It doesn't matter."

"Cool. You must give me your e-mail."

He held her away from him, looking at her. She felt his eyes upon her, and she blushed.

James turned to Ted. "She's just as pretty as she always was, isn't she, Ted?"

Ted nodded. "More, even."

James gestured towards the inside of the house. "My folks are out until midnight. We've got the house till then."

"Great," said Ted. "Who's coming?"

James shrugged. "Everyone," he said. "You'll know everybody, or just about everybody." He smiled. "About twelve people max."

They heard voices from further inside the house, which, like many houses of its vintage on the island, was a rambling warren of cool interiors. "That's them," James continued. "In the kitchen."

Twelve, thought Clover, and winced inwardly. At a large party she could have avoided Laura if she chose to; with twelve it would be impossible. She glanced at Ted, who understood. "Laura?" he said. "Is Laura here?"

James shook his head. "They've gone to Florida for Christmas. Clearwater, I think."

For Clover, it was a release from dread. "I wanted to meet her," she blurted out, and immediately regretted it; he might ask how she knew; he might ask what Laura was to her.

But he did not. He smiled at her. "You'll like her. I think she wanted to meet you too." He paused. "She heard we were old friends."

"Oh."

"Yes. Next time, maybe."

They moved through the house, to join the other guests in the kitchen. There was music playing, and a couple of girls were emptying packets of snacks into bowls. There was a large container of popcorn and a bowl of what looked like fruit punch. One of the boys, whom she recognised as having been in the year above her at the Prep School, smiled at her as he poured a bottle of vodka into the punch. He poured her a glass, which she took gingerly. She did not like alcohol and would make one drink suffice for the evening.

They drifted out onto the patio, lit by a line of white lights strung along the eaves of the house. There was a pool, as there was with most of the houses in the area, shabbier than their own and with a water slide that leaned drunkenly to one side. "If you swim," said James, "don't get on that. Nobody's used it for five years."

She sat with Ted and James by the side of the pool, their feet resting on the first step below the water. For a brief moment she felt James's right foot touch her own, and remain there briefly until he moved it away. She glanced at him, and he returned her glance in a way that she thought was encouraging. She wondered whether she should move her foot back, but did not.

"I can't tell you how good it is to see you," he said. "And you, too, Ted. The three of us again."

"Like old times," said Ted.

"Yeah, like old times."

There was a burst of laughter from somewhere behind them; the party was getting going, but James seemed content to be talking just to them. He asked Clover about Strathearn and whether she liked it and whether there was anybody there he would know. Then Ted volunteered some information about the boarding school he was at. "It calls itself progressive," he said. "But none of us knows what progressive is meant to mean. Nor do the teachers. Nor do people's parents. Nobody knows."

"But it sounds good," said James.

Ted laughed. "Yes, it always sounds good to be progressive. *I believe in progress.* Great, so you believe in progress. Who doesn't?"

James looked thoughtful. "Some people," he said. "Some people want things to go backwards – to go back to what they used to be."

She asked why.

"Because they're conservative," suggested Ted. "Because they hate other people."

James looked sideways at him. "Not all ..."

"Yes," said Ted. "All."

"I don't think conservatives hate people," said James. "They're just ..."

"Uncool?" said Clover.

James shook his head. "Not necessarily. In fact, it's quite cool to be conservative these days. Ride a bike and so on, but be conservative."

"I'm not interested in politics," said Ted. "It bores me. Yabber yabber yabber. Build a road. Don't build a road. Build an airport. More taxes, no less taxes. Yabber yabber."

James looked at him indulgently. "So what gets you, Ted?"

There was a moment in which it seemed to Clover that Ted was wrestling with a question he found awkward. Then he said, "The same as you, James. The same things as you."

The answer came quickly. "I don't know what I'm interested in. You tell me."

"Things," said Ted lamely.

James teased him. "Come on!"

"Okay, sex."

She drew in her breath. Ted had looked away after he had said this, but James had looked briefly in her direction. He was embarrassed – she could tell that, and she decided to defuse the tension that had suddenly risen.

"What all boys think about all the time," she said lightly. "Or so we're told. Actually, I don't think they do."

"How do you know what boys think about?" challenged Ted.

"Boys tell me." It was untrue, and she could see that neither Ted nor James believed her.

Ted scoffed at this. "No boy is going to tell you what's in his head. He couldn't!"

"Maybe not," said James. "But the same applies to girls. Girls don't tell us what they're thinking. We have to try to work it out."

"Clothes," muttered Ted.

She rounded on him. "What did you say? Clothes? Is that what you think?"

Ted looked to James for support, but James put up a hand. "No. Don't go there."

"We do not think of clothes all the time," said Clover sharply.

"Some of the time then," said Ted.

They smiled at that, and were silent for a moment as the topic expired. Clover shivered. She wanted Ted to go away now, to leave her with James, but he showed no sign of moving. James looked over his shoulder towards the others, who were now standing around a pool table at the edge of the patio. Somebody had turned up the music, but nobody seemed to be paying much attention to it. "I have to go and talk to them," he said. "I haven't spoken to them very much."

He rose, leaving her sitting at the edge of the pool with Ted. He reached out and put a hand on her shoulder as he stood up. "I love your shoulders," he said.

She looked up at him in surprise. "What?"

"Just your shoulders," he said quickly. "They're so convenient for leaning on." Then he added, "Sis."

He turned to Ted. "And you, bro."

"Lean on me any time," said Ted.

James shook his head. "No thanks. I can stand now."

After he had gone, the two of them sat in silence. Ted moved forward and dipped his hand into the pool. His fingers made shadows in the water.

"Still like him?" he asked.

She nodded. "Yes."

"He called you sis," said Ted. "Nice."

"Do you think so?"

"It means that he sees you as a sister."

"And you as a brother."

Ted shrugged. "Okay with me." He hesitated. "But not with you?"

She stared up at the sky beyond the fronds of the palm trees that ringed the Collins's garden. "I suppose I'll have to settle for that. I can, I think. Maybe."

"Why does he get under our skin?" asked Ted. "What's it about him? What is it?"

She mentioned the first thing that came into her mind. "He's kind."

Ted looked doubtful. "Is that all?"

"That and other things."

Ted dipped his hand back into the water. "You won't tell anybody, will you?"

"Tell them what?"

"About me."

"About what you told me?"

He nodded.

"Of course not. Being friends is about keeping the secrets you've shared."

"Thanks. And I won't tell anybody about you. You and him, that is."

She thought there was nothing to tell, other than that she loved James and in return he regarded her as a sister.

Then Ted said, "You okay, my sister?" He had launched into a Caymanian accent – it was redolent of their shared childhood; the accent of the Caymanian children, the ones from West Bay, from the wrong side of the tracks, with whom they had played sporting fixtures at school, across such wide divides of wealth; of the Jamaican pool-man who scooped the leaves out of the water and cut the grass. It was comforting.

He touched her lightly on the arm. His hand was wet from the swimming pool. She liked him. She had always taken Ted for granted; she had never really seen him, in the way in which we see people we value.

She nodded. "Sort of, my brother."

He became serious. "Don't give up," he whispered. "Just don't."

Part Two

22

For the next two years, she did not see him, not by design, but because they were never on the island at the same time. James had slightly different school holidays, and often filled these with projects that took him elsewhere. There was a cricket tour of Australia, and a working trip to Malawi, where his school was renovating an orphanage. She heard about these things from Ted, whom she did see, and who sent her regular messages. She tried not to appear too interested – but in secret she was like an addict deprived, poring over each scrap of news Ted gave her about James as if it were a sacred text, an utterance to be dwelt upon, weighed for meaning.

"He doesn't do e-mails," Ted assured her. "It's nothing personal."

She was not convinced; Ted was trying to comfort her. "But you hear from him. He must e-mail you."

Ted explained that he heard the news indirectly, from other friends. "It's true, Clove. I swear. There are some people who just don't e-mail. It seems odd, but they don't."

"How can they? Everything's done by e-mail now. How can they do anything if they don't use it?"

He shrugged. "They use it a little. Now and then."

She shook her head. "They can't. They have to."

He did not want her in his life; that was clear to her. He was not hostile; he had been friendly, even encouraging, at that party, but it seemed to her that she was just part of his background – nothing more than that. Sensing this, she decided to fall in love with somebody else – she willed that to happen – but it did not. Unconscious, irresistible comparisons with James meant that other boys were found wanting. Nobody was as good-looking;

nobody made her laugh in quite the same way; nobody listened, as James did, was as sympathetic. In short, James had changed the world for her, had set a bar that others simply could not surmount.

Her education taught her self-awareness. Strathearn was a school that encouraged intellectual seriousness – it was what the parents who sent their children there paid for – and there was an English teacher, Miss Hardy, who opened eyes. Clover's reading was guided by her and she expanded the horizons of everybody in that particular class. Clover thought a great deal – about people and their emotions, about how things were in the world. By the time she was due to leave school at eighteen, she had as mature an understanding of the world as many in their mid-twenties – perhaps even more mature.

"University is not a finishing school," said Miss Hardy. "It is not a place to mark time for three or four years until you find yourself a job."

The conversation arose in Miss Hardy's study. Clover had called to say goodbye, and to thank the teacher. The following day, Commemoration Day, would be her last day at the school.

Miss Hardy closed the book that had been open on her desk before her. Clover squinted to read the title upside down: *Edward Thomas: A Life in Poetry*. She remembered that he was an enthusiasm of the teacher, and they had spent the best part of an hour talking about one of his poems about a train stopping at a station in the country, and steam escaping, and birds singing. She had wanted to cry, and almost did, because she knew the poet would be killed in the trenches of France.

"Edward Thomas," said Miss Hardy.

"I remember. That poem about the train."

Miss Hardy touched the cover of the book almost reverentially. "If you forget everything else I ever taught you, I suspect you'll remember that poem."

She assured her that she would not forget. "No, you're wrong. I'll remember a lot."

"You're kind … But, back to the topic of university. It's your one chance, you know. Or for most people it's their one chance."

"Of what?"

"Of opening the mind."

"Yes."

"Education – *educere*, the Latin for *to lead out*. How many times has somebody explained that to you while you've been here?"

"One hundred."

"Well, there you are. So choose carefully. And don't throw it away."

"Yes."

Miss Hardy looked at her thoughtfully. "Your family lives overseas, don't they?"

"In the Cayman Islands. My father's an accountant." Clover's tone became apologetic. "He works there."

The teacher smiled. "You don't have to explain. You don't have to justify it. At any rate, not to me."

She felt she had to; people had their views on the Cayman Islands.

"I didn't raise it for that reason," said Miss Hardy. "I mention it because I suppose it affects your choices. You're probably in a position to do what you want to do. Your choice need not be too vocational."

"What you mean is that I can do something indulgent if I

want to. Shouldn't you say what you mean? Haven't you tried to teach us that?"

It was not impertinence, although it may have sounded like it. This sort of bantering exchange was allowed – even encouraged – with the students about to leave; the school believed in independence of thought and in the ability to hold one's corner in debate. "Don't be too ready to read things into what people say. But, broadly speaking, yes. You can study something that isn't necessarily going to lead to something else. You'll have plenty of opportunity to do that later."

"Whereas most people can't?"

"No, they can't. A lot of people have debt to consider. They can't afford to study expensive subjects that don't lead to a paying career."

She looked down at the floor. "Should I feel guilty? Should I feel bad about it?"

"No. Not at all."

"Why?"

"Because sometimes in this life we're given things that we don't deserve – that we haven't done anything to merit, so to speak. We don't have to give those up if they come our way. And remember this: plenty of people are better off than you. Inequality is written into the way the world works, no matter how hard we try to correct it." Miss Hardy paused. "You may be fortunate in one respect and less fortunate in another. Nobody's guaranteed happiness across the board. Fate has her own ideas of equality."

"Nemesis? Isn't she the person you told us about?"

"Yes, Nemesis. She stalks us, we're told. If we get above ourselves, she may take action to cut us down to size."

"I'll be careful."

The teacher affected mock seriousness. "So you should be. But I suspect that you'll do nothing much to risk corrective action by Nemesis or any of the other gods and goddesses."

She laughed. "They were so nasty, weren't they – the Greek gods?"

"Horrible. Full of mean tricks and petty jealousies. Worse than the girls in the third form, although not by much."

"And punishing people too. Making them bear all sorts of things … Sisyphus."

Miss Hardy was pleased that she had remembered. In class they had read Camus's essay *The Myth of Sisyphus*. "Yes, Sisyphus – condemned to push a rock up a hill eternally. They certainly knew how to impose burdens." She paused, but only briefly. "Of course, we're quite good at imposing burdens on ourselves – without any assistance from Parnassus."

"I suppose we are," said Clover. "Unreturned love, for instance. That's a burden, isn't it?"

Miss Hardy looked at her with interest. She had not been able to make this girl out – not entirely. Other seventeen- or eighteen-year-olds were transparent – at least to those who spent their lives teaching them. Clover was more complex; there was something there that she could not quite put her finger on; some sorrow, perhaps, that was more specific, more focused than typical teenage angst. Now she had revealed it as clearly as if she had spelled it out in capital letters.

She would be gentle. She wanted to say: *don't worry.* Unrequited love was painful to begin with, but the passage of time dulled the pain – it always did. "The Greek legends have a fair dose of that."

Clover's voice was even. "Unrequited love?"

"Yes. Greek mythology may be full of instances of the revenge and pettiness we were talking about, but it also involved profound insights into the human condition – of which unrequited love is just one feature. Echo and Narcissus – remember?"

"Vaguely. She fell in love with him and he …"

"He was too preoccupied with himself to return her love. He gazed at his reflection constantly and eventually wasted away. As did she. All that was left of him was a flower by the water's edge, and of her a sound. That was it."

Clover was silent for a while. In their art class they had looked at a Pre-Raphaelite picture of Echo and Narcissus, with Echo watching Narcissus crouching by his pool, gazing at his reflection. It was a perfect depiction of what it was to be cut out of somebody's life.

Miss Hardy was smiling. "Would you mind if I said something critical of your generation?"

"Why should we mind criticism? We criticise people who are older than us. All the time …" She grinned.

"Oh, we know that," said Miss Hardy. "Any teacher who isn't aware of what is said about us must have her ears closed."

Clover waited.

"This is nothing personal," said Miss Hardy. "I'm not talking about the boys in this school."

"Of course not."

"It's a difficult thing to explain, but there are those who say that young men these days have been encouraged into narcissism. They've been presented with images of themselves that are essentially narcissistic. All those brooding pictures of members of boy bands sucking in their cheeks to make themselves look more intense. What's the message there? Be cool. Don't express your feelings. Gaze at yourself and your image … The problem is that this doesn't leave them much time – or emotional energy – for other people."

"Maybe …"

"Of course I overstate it a bit, but then you have to overstate some things if you're to see them in the first place. But there's a rather odd consequence to all this, I think."

"Which is?"

"It can leave the girls out of it. You end up with a lot of self-obsessed young men, all trying to fulfil the cultural expectation of the detached, moody young hero, and lo and behold, these young men don't have much time for the girls."

"But they do!"

Miss Hardy conceded. "For some things, yes. Disengaged sex, maybe. But not for others." She hesitated before continuing. "I think that's probably enough of that. You can make too much of a theory."

"It's an interesting one."

"You think so?"

"Yes, I do."

The teacher considered this. Then she said, "I suppose we can speak pretty frankly. You're about to leave this place, to go out into the world, and I don't have to treat you as a child any more. May I ask you one further thing?"

She waited for Clover to nod before she continued. "I get the strong impression that you've already been in love with somebody and that it hasn't worked out. I don't want to pry, and you don't have to speak about it if you don't want to."

Clover looked past Miss Hardy, out through the window behind the teacher's desk. The hills – gentle in that part of Perthshire – rose off towards the north; an attenuated blue now in the warmth of summer. She felt, more sharply now, the pang of regret that had first touched her a few weeks ago when she realised that she was shortly to leave a place where she had been happy. "I don't mind speaking about it. It's all right now."

"You're getting over it?"

"Yes, I think so. I'm forgetting him. That's what you have to do, isn't it?"

Miss Hardy sighed. "That's the conventional wisdom. And I suppose there's some truth in the conventional wisdom – there usually is. But it's not always entirely true. I'm not sure that you should forget entirely, because what you're forgetting may be something really rather important to you. Something precious."

It occurred to Clover that the teacher was talking about herself. "You didn't get married, did you?"

"I did."

"But your name ... Miss ..."

The teacher shook her head. "Don't go by names. I was married for three years. Just for three years – my fault as much as his, but I didn't want it to end. When it came apart, I went back to my own name. I'd been Miss Hardy, and I went back to that. My *nom de guerre*, so to speak – not that the classroom is a battleground."

"I'm sorry."

"Divorce happens. I hope it doesn't happen to you, but it happens."

"You said that we shouldn't forget."

"No, I didn't say that. I think that we need to forget a certain amount – just to be able to keep going – but we shouldn't forget everything. I suppose it's a question of forgetting to the extent that you don't think about it too much. But keep some of the memory, because it's part of what … of what you've had."

Clover's gaze returned from the window. "But if you keep thinking about …"

Miss Hardy interrupted her. "You don't have to keep thinking about him. You change the way you think about him – that way he won't dominate your life. What do they call it now? Moving on. I've always thought that a resounding cliché, but I suppose it has its uses, like any resounding cliché. Move on."

"I have. Or at least I think I have."

Miss Hardy looked relieved. "It's not easy to forget something, is it? But let's talk about university now. Where are you going?"

"Edinburgh. History of Art."

"Good. Where I was." She paused, and then added, with contrived wistfulness, "That's where I met him."

They both smiled.

23

"Colours," she said to a friend, much later. "That's how I remember the stages of my life – by the colours."

She had to explain. "I began in the Cayman Islands. The colours there were Caribbean – very intense."

"Blue?"

"Yes, of course. That was the sea. Blue or turquoise, depending on the depth. Deep sea was deep blue, like that intense blue ink. You don't find it elsewhere, I think. Or if you do, I've never seen it. But it wasn't just that blue. There was another blue that people liked – a much lighter shade that they used to paint houses. That and pink. They loved pink too. They were pastel shades, I suppose."

"I can see them. Houses with blue window-frames and doors."

"Exactly. Those were the colours I grew up with. And then suddenly I was in Scotland and ..."

"The colours were very different."

"Yes. Everything was gentler. There were no bright colours – just those soft greens and purples and, yes, white. There are lots of whites in Scotland. White in the sky and in the rain. Sometimes even the water seems white, you know. You look at a loch and the surface of the water seems white. White or silver, like a mirror."

"And grey."

"Yes, there is plenty of grey in Scotland. The buildings are made of grey stone – granite and so on – and they're grey. Hard and grey, though some of them are made of a different sort of stone. It's the colour of honey, actually; sometimes even almost red."

Honey-coloured … She looked up at the building that was to be her home during the university terms. The stone used for the four-floored tenement building was of just that stone. It was far softer than granite and had weathered here and there, softened at the edges, where the action of rain and wind had made its impression. The flat was on the top floor, tucked under the slate roof, reached by a shared stone stairway with a curving, ornate ironwork banister. The overall impression was one of nineteenth-century confidence and solidity. Stone was the right medium for that; stone was the expression of the values that lay behind these buildings; solid; designed to last for hundreds of years; crafted so as to allow the living out of whole lives within thick walls.

The flat belonged to a friend from school, Ella, who was starting at Edinburgh at the same time as Clover was. Or rather, it belonged to Ella's parents, who had bought it a few years earlier for their son, who had studied engineering at Edinburgh. The son had graduated and left for a job in Bristol, but the flat had been kept on for his sister. Ella had offered Clover a room, and had then let another by placing an advertisement in the student paper.

"I have no idea what she's like," she said to Clover. "I tactfully asked for a photograph, but she ignored my request."

"Why would one want a flatmate's photograph?" asked Clover.

Ella had looked embarrassed. "You never know."

"You mean that you want to make sure that you're not taking on a serial killer?"

Ella nodded. "Something like that. Don't you think that you can tell what somebody's like from their photograph?"

Clover was not sure. "Maybe. Maybe not. Some people look unpleasant but aren't really – not when you meet them."

"It depends on what you mean by unpleasant. I think I'd pay attention to what her hair looked like. And her make-up."

"Really?"

"If she was caked in make-up – you know, bags of mascara, and so on, then you'd think: this one's not going to be easy to live with."

"Why would you think that?"

Ella hesitated. "She'd hog the bathroom. We wouldn't get near a mirror."

They had laughed. And when Karen, the other flatmate, arrived – after Clover had moved into her room – they had been relieved to see that she was, outwardly at least, quite normal.

"You didn't send a photograph," said Ella. "But I assume it's you."

Karen looked blank. "Photograph?"

"I suggested that you should send a photograph – when you got in touch first. Remember?"

"No. I don't. I can give you one now, if you like."

"No, now we can see you. We don't need a photograph."

Karen later said to Clover: "Why did she want a photograph? Did you send her one before you got the room?"

"I didn't need to. We've known one another for ages. I was at school with her, you see."

"But why did she want one of me?"

"To check up."

"Why? What can you tell from a photograph?"

"Lots of things – or that's what Ella thinks."

The photograph was forgotten about; they liked Karen, who came from Glasgow and brought an entirely different perspective with her. "Glasgow," said Ella, "could be on the moon, you know.

It's that different."

Karen had the room at the front – a room that looked out onto the street four floors below – while Ella and Clover each had a room overlooking the drying green behind the building. This was effectively a great courtyard serving the line of buildings on every side and divided, like a medieval field, into small sections, each allocated to a different flat. In places the boundaries between these postage stamps of garden were marked with low fences, barely knee-height; elsewhere the owners had long since abandoned any attempt to distinguish their property from that of their neighbours and grass – and weeds – ran riot across human divisions. Cats, too, observed their territorial arrangements across the face of the map of human ownership, moving around any contested space on top of such stone walls as could be found, or surveying the green from windowsills or doorways.

It was Clover's first room. She did not count her room at home – mothers or younger brothers can enter your room at home with impunity – nor did she count the single room that she had eventually been given at school; that had been meant to be private, but never really was. Now she had somewhere that was at her complete disposal. She was paying rent for this and it was hers.

She stood in front of her window and looked down onto the green below. A woman in blue slacks, presumably one of the neighbours, was tending a small bed of discouraged-looking flowers; a pigeon, alighted on a branch of the single tree in the corner, was puffing up its breast in a display of bravado; the sky, a patch of blue above the surrounding rooftops, was enjoying one of its rare cloud-free moments. Greys. Greens. Light, almost whitened blue.

She thought about her mother. She would take a photograph and send it to her; she had asked for that. She looked at her watch; her mother would be up by now and might be having her morning swim in the pool. Or she might already have started a game of tennis at the club. She would not change places with her. Cayman, for all its colours, was boring, she thought. Money, money, money. Tennis. Parties. Gossip. And after that there was nothing, but the same all over again.

She smiled to herself, savouring the sheer joy of freedom. For the first time in her life – the very first – there was nobody to tell her what to do. If she wished, she could stay in this room all day. She could lie on her bed and page through magazines. She could drink as many cups of coffee as she liked. The course was due to start the following day with both morning and afternoon being given over to orientation. It was an odd word to use, she thought, and she imagined for a moment a group of confused and uncertain students standing in a room and being gently turned by assistants so that they faced north or south or whatever direction the authorities thought best. She smiled again.

Then lectures were to start the day after that, after everybody had recovered from the orientation party that she had already seen advertised. *Half-price drinks*, announced a poster, and underneath, somebody, presumably with experience of student parties, had written *Full-price hangover*.

She had already investigated the departmental offices in a restored Georgian house on one side of a square of such houses and had found out where the first lecture would be held. That first lecture would be at ten, she had been told, and since a large crowd was expected she should get there early.

"Some people sit on the steps," said one of the secretaries disapprovingly. "We don't encourage it, but if there are no seats, then there really is no alternative."

She went to the orientation party, which was solely for those enrolled on the art history course – almost three hundred and twenty students. The secretary who had advised her about sitting on the steps was there, standing at the entrance, at the same time giving the impression of being both disapproving and hesitant, as if undecided as to whether to join the party. "There are far too many people for this room," she said to Clover as she arrived. "I tell them every year to get a bigger room, but they ignore me. They just ignore me."

Clover, feeling that she was being drawn into some internal issue, some obscure matter of the workplace, was uncertain as to what to say. "They shouldn't," she said at last.

"Well, it's nice to hear that you think that," said the secretary. "Because others don't."

Clover looked around the crowded room.

The secretary noticed her wandering gaze. "And that's another thing," she said, taking a sip of her drink. "I tell them every year that they should recruit a few more young men. Look at all these girls." She sighed. "We used to have some very nice young men. But these days …"

Clover looked. There were a few boys, but those who were there were heavily outnumbered by young women.

"A group of women is always different," said the secretary. She glanced at Clover, appraising her reaction. "The atmosphere is more difficult. I don't think that women have as much fun as men, do you?"

"Oh, I don't know," said Clover.

"Well, I do," said the secretary. "Look at them." She gestured towards the group of students.

Clover's eye was caught by a group of three young women standing near a window. She was sure that she recognised one of them, but was not sure why she did. She stared harder. The ears were right. She always used to wear one of those odd hair-bands that showed the ears rather too prominently. She had some sort of patterned hair-band on now, although it was hard to make out exactly what it was. And the brow, too. That was unusually high, as it had been all those years ago.

It was somebody from Cayman, she thought; there was no doubt about it. She had met her. And then, as she detached herself from the disgruntled secretary and began to make her way across the room, the girl in the hair-band unexpectedly turned round and looked straight at her, as if suddenly warned of her presence.

They had not seen each other for some years. For a brief period, now suddenly remembered, she and Judy had been in the same class at the Prep; there had been a running argument over something – Clover tried to remember it – and sides had been taken, with each of them in a different faction. The *casus belli* was soon forgotten and they had briefly shared the same friend; then she had gone – somewhere, as people did when you were a child – although she had returned to the island with her parents some years later and they had acknowledged each other distantly, and somewhat warily.

Judy's face broke into a broad smile of recognition. "I thought it was you," she said as she came up to Clover. "You know something? I haven't met a single person – not one – I know since I came to Edinburgh, and now you ... Would you believe it?"

Clover shrugged. "Big world," she said. "Not small, as some people keep saying."

"Well, big and small," said Judy. "Here I am. Here you are. Small, maybe."

Clover noticed the bracelet – a thin band of tiny diamonds. Who would wear something like that to a student party?

"A present from my dad," said Judy. "My eighteenth birthday, last year. He said I should wear it."

Clover showed her embarrassment. "Why not? I like it." She glanced at Judy's clothes. They were expensive; expensive jeans could be frayed and distressed as much as you liked, but they remained costly-looking.

"So you're on the course too?"

Clover nodded absently. She wanted to know what had happened to Judy in the intervening years. "Where have you been?" she asked. "I mean, where have you been the last five years?"

"My dad moved to Singapore," Judy said. "He got remarried – remember my mum died?"

Clover nodded. It was coming back to her now; it had been an overdose, people said, and her mother had found it awkward explaining what that was. *Too many pills, probably by mistake. People get confused, you see.* What do you think, Clover asked herself at the time, if your mother takes too many pills – by mistake? How do you actually feel about that? She could not imagine it; she could not see her mother doing that; she counted things out; she never made a mistake. Other mothers took too many pills, not hers.

"So my dad married this Chinese lady – well, actually she's Singaporean. We moved to Singapore because her family had a company and my dad went and worked for them. They're quite important, actually – my Singaporean relatives."

"You went to school there?"

Judy shook her head. "No. I came to the UK. Boarding school. It wasn't too bad, I suppose."

"I went too."

Judy raised the glass she was holding. "Yeah, well, we're survivors, aren't we?" She paused. "I've got a flat in Singapore. I lived there for five months before I came here. I'll go back to it in the university vacations. Come and visit me."

"Your own place?"

"I told you – my stepmother's family is rich. Sorry, I'm not boasting – just explaining. There's a difference."

"Of course. I didn't think you were boasting."

Judy cast an eye back to where she had been standing earlier on. "That girl … The one in red. Dreary! Seriously dreary! She went on about that museum in St Petersburg – the whatever it's called …"

"The Hermitage."

"Yes, that place; she says that her aunt knows the head conservator there and they've offered her an internship for a month next year. She went on and on about it. I told her that Russia was a ghastly place and that I wouldn't ever spend a month there if I could avoid it. She became very defensive."

"Oh well …"

"But the boy she's talking to – see him? He's called Graham and he's seriously cute. I don't think he's gay either. You can tell, you know. They start talking about the High Renaissance or Michelangelo and you say to yourself *Here we go!* But he hasn't mentioned Michelangelo once – not once! That's almost like declaring yourself a rugby player round here."

Clover laughed.

"Did I say something amusing?" asked Judy disingenuously. "I should hate to miss my own jokes."

"Michelangelo ..." began Clover.

"Oh not you too!"

"No, I was going to ask why Michelangelo was ..."

"The litmus? Search me. It may be something to do with his statue of David. Who knows? But that guy, Graham, is seriously interesting." She paused. "And you know who else?"

"Who else what?"

"Who else is in Edinburgh. Not that I've seen him, but I gather he's here. He's doing economics or something like that." And then she added casually, without knowledge of the effect of what she said, "His dad was that doctor."

Clover caught her breath. "You mean Dr Collins?"

"Yes. He was my mother's doctor. She liked him a lot."

Clover battled to keep her voice even. "James?"

"Yes. That's him. I didn't know him very well – did you?"

"I did. Quite well. I'm a bit out of touch now."

Judy took another sip of her drink. "He was gorgeous, if I remember correctly. Or he looked as if he would be gorgeous ... with time." She smiled. "I heard he was here because that other guy who was in our class – the one who went to Houston – he's kept in touch in an odd sort of way. We never see one another and I never really liked him very much, but he still sends me e-mails sometimes and tells me that so-and-so has done whatever. Some people like that sort of thing – gossip, I suppose. There's no real point to it, but they don't seem to get it. He told me that James was coming to university in Edinburgh. That's how I know."

Clover was silent. She had been trying not to think of him, and had succeeded – at least to some extent. But every day, almost without exception, some thought would come to her unbidden; his name, or the memory of him, like a tinge of pain from tissue that has not altogether recovered from a wound – and perhaps never would.

When she spoke, her voice was level. "I didn't know that."

"Well, you do now. If I see him, I'll tell him you're here. We could all meet up – like a bunch of stranded expatriates – and talk about old times. Or maybe we won't. I can't stand that sort of thing. You know how it is? Remember how we ... that sort of garbage."

Clover nodded absently. She suddenly wanted to leave the party. She had come hoping to meet her future classmates – to make friends – but now she just felt empty. She did not want to talk to anybody; she wanted to get away, to go somewhere where she could just sit and think of James. It was precisely what she had been trying to avoid – she had sat and thought enough about him in the past – and now she was starting afresh. But tonight was different; this was a shock, and she could allow herself to think through the implications of what she had just been told. James was in Edinburgh. *In Edinburgh*. And he was at the same university as she was. That meant that he was one of – how many was it? – twenty-five thousand students, maybe a few more. Edinburgh was not a large city – not as cities went – and you were bound to bump into somebody else sooner or later. There would be parties – university life was full of parties – and that meant that they could find themselves in the same room together. She would see him.

The thought both appalled and excited her. It appalled

her because she had stopped thinking about him; it was over – whatever it was. No, it was love, she told herself. You can't dodge love by calling it *whatever it was*; it was love, and you might as well admit it. Use the word, Miss Hardy had said to them in English class; use the short, accurate, expressive word – not the circumlocution. And a boy at the back had muttered, "Circumlocution isn't a short, accurate expressive word." They had all laughed – Miss Hardy included.

"*Touché*," the teacher had said. "And here's another suggestion: if you can't find an English word, use a French one."

She extricated herself from the party as discreetly as she could. Just outside the doorway, though, she met one of the lecturers, a thin, rather worried-looking man. He had interviewed her the day before in his role as her director of studies, and now he frowned as he greeted her.

"Clover – it is Clover isn't it? You're not leaving, are you?"

"Well, I was ..."

"The Professor was going to make a speech – just going to say a few words of welcome. Can't you stay for that?"

She looked down at the floor. "I'm sorry, I just don't feel in the mood for a party. It's nothing to do with the Professor."

He looked at her with concern. "Are you sure you're all right? It can be a bit of a strain, the start of a new academic year; and this is your first year, which is always more stressful."

She looked up at him. "Thanks. I'll be all right."

But she felt the tears welling in her eyes and after a moment or two she could not disguise them.

His concern grew. "But you're crying ..."

She wiped at her cheeks. "I'm sorry. I'm all right. It's just that ..." Her voice tailed off. What could she say? *I'm in love with somebody who doesn't love me. I thought I'd got over him, but I haven't, I haven't at all ...*

He was looking at her expectantly. "Something's obviously wrong. It's not my job to pry, but I don't like to see you leaving in this state. I really don't."

She reassured him that she would get home safely and that she had just been a bit upset about a personal matter; she would feel much better in a few minutes. Really. Honestly. He did not have to worry.

She went outside into the street and began the fifteen-minute walk back to her flat. Yellow sodium street-lights glowed against the sky; a bus moved by with a shudder, one of the passengers looking out and briefly making eye contact with her as she walked past. She thought: *this is the last news I wanted to hear,* and for a moment she felt an irrational anger towards Judy for being the messenger who conveyed it. But after a brief struggle that stopped, and she felt calmer. I shall put him out of my mind, she said to herself. He is nothing to me any more; just a boy I once knew and to whom I can be indifferent when I see him again. I shall not be unkind; I shall not cut him nor ignore him; I shall simply be indifferent. Like this. She closed her eyes, expecting to see nothing, which is what she imagined a state of indifference should produce on the inner eye. But it did not. She saw James, and he was smiling at her.

24

It was easier the next morning. The anguish she had felt the previous night – and it had been anguish – a feeling of sheer sorrow, of loss – had dissipated itself in sleep; now she was back in the ordinary world in which she had breakfast to make and there were lectures to go to. The Edinburgh morning, which could be cold and windswept, was anything but – a brilliant display of the sunshine that could accompany an Indian summer. From her window the rooftops on the other side of the drying green were touched with gold, the rounded chimney pots like a row of amphoras against the sky. She found it hard to believe that she had gone to bed in such a state of misery; it was almost laughable, in fact, that a childish crush on a boy could make you feel as if there was nothing to live for; ridiculous thought. She was beginning a new life in one of the most romantic cities in the world. She had everything – everything – to live for; she had no reason to feel bad about anything.

Over the weeks that followed, she busied herself with her course and with the social activities that accompanied the start of the new semester. There were societies to join, and these involved new people and the almost immediate friendships that at eighteen – or on the cusp of nineteen – are so easily made. Karen and Ella both had a circle of friends already – people they had known for some years – and these friends welcomed Clover too. But she sensed the importance of having a life independent of her flatmates, and they understood that too. "I don't want to live in your pocket," said Ella, adding, "but of course that doesn't mean that you can't live in mine, if that's what you want."

But she did not. She made friends with several people studying her subject – Padraig, a young man from Dublin whose interest was in the Post-Impressionists and who had come to university slightly later than most of their classmates. He had worked in a bank in Ireland but had hated it, he said, because art was what he really wanted to do. He intended to write about it, he said, and he gave her criticisms that he had written of various art exhibitions. These he sent off to the *Irish Times* and other newspapers, although they had never been published. "You carry on," he said. "You send them your stuff and then eventually they publish something. Their regular art critic gets sick – or is arrested – and then they think, *There's this guy who's been sending us this stuff – let's ask him.* That's the way it works."

"Really? Is that the way it works?"

He shook his head ruefully. "No. But it gives me something to do."

In the second week, she went to a film at the Filmhouse, the arts cinema, with Padraig. He had invited her because he had a spare ticket and he thought she might like the film. "Iranian," he said. "They make pretty impressive films."

"I've not seen any."

"Nor me. But they do."

"About?"

He paused. "Oh, about the clash between modernity and the old ways. That's a good theme for an Iranian film. There are lots of clashes between …"

"Modernity and the old ways?"

"Exactly." He paused. "You go anywhere there and you see it. "

"You sure?"

He grinned. "I have no idea."

"You could be talking nonsense, you know."

"Of course it's nonsense. Life is nonsense, don't you think? How much of it actually makes sense? It's just us filling time because we know that we're tiny specks in a great broth of galaxies and black holes and gas clouds. We're nothing, and so we try to make structures and meaning for ourselves, but it's all nonsense underneath."

She thought that a bleak view, and said as much. "But some things aren't nonsense at all. Some things are deadly serious. Pain. Hunger. Human suffering. These things actually hurt people and only ..." She struggled to find the right way of saying it. "They only seem meaningless to people who aren't actually suffering them."

At the end of the film he turned to her and said, "You were right."

They were leaving the Filmhouse, but she felt she was still in Tehran, in the cramped house with the young woman arguing with her indoctrinated brother.

"I was right about what?"

"About suffering. About how simple human concerns mean a lot. How they mean everything, really."

She thanked him. "I'd forgotten our discussion. But thank you anyway."

"Like loneliness."

They were out on the street now. He had suggested they go to a bar – and there were plenty about – but she was tired.

"I have to get up early tomorrow." Then she asked, "Loneliness?"

"Yes. Being ... I don't know – separate from people and being unable to do anything about it. It's a form of suffering, isn't it?"

"Yes, it is." She smiled at him. "You're lonely, Padraig?"

He looked embarrassed. "I'm so cheesy. I say cheesy things. It's just that ..." He looked up at the night sky. "I like you. That's what I was trying to say."

"Good. That's nice to know."

"Can't we go for a drink?"

"I told you: I'm tired. Do you mind?"

He shook his head. "Of course not. I'm not much good at these things."

She said nothing.

"At dates," he said.

It had not occurred to her that they were on a date, and she was about to say, "But an Iranian film is not a date ..." but stopped herself. He now turned to her and said, "Maybe I shouldn't have asked you."

She told him not to be silly. "I'm glad you asked me. But ..."

He winced. "But ..."

"But, well, there's somebody else."

It took him a few moments to digest the information. "I thought so. I didn't imagine that somebody like you ... I mean, somebody who looked like you would be ... Not that I judge by looks, of course. I may study aesthetics, but philosophy and well, the way your hair looks and your ..."

She laughed. "Padraig ..."

"And you're three years younger than I am."

"So?"

"That counts. You're not going to be interested in somebody who's twenty-two."

"Don't be ridiculous."

"But you told me yourself. You've just explained. I'm Irish – I can take these things. We can take anything. Come to Dublin and speak to people and they'll say to you: *we can take these things ...*"

She took his hand. "Don't be silly."

They were standing at the pedestrian crossing opposite the Usher Hall. They had not crossed, although the light had changed several times in their favour. He said, "We can't stand here. There's a bar over there – look – the Shakespeare."

She did not resist.

"So tell me about him," he said as he brought the drinks to their table.

She had ordered a cider, and the glass was cold to the touch as she moved a finger down its side, tracing a pattern in the condensation. "He doesn't really exist," she said. "Or at least, I don't exist for him."

Padraig shook his head in puzzlement. "I'm not sure if I understand. You're not actually seeing him?"

"No. I never see him."

He frowned. "But you have actually *met* him? We're not talking about some film actor here, are we? You don't harbour a secret passion for ..." He named an actor. She would never fancy *him*, she said.

"Good," he said. "I can't understand why anybody would."

"Money, glamour, looks ..."

"Small things. Irrelevant." His eyes lit when he smiled; she noticed it. "So, you do know him, but you don't see him? I get it. He's in Africa or South America perhaps, doing something really important – selfless, too – and you promised him that even if it takes ten years you'll wait for him and ..."

"No."

She took a sip of her drink. She regretted telling him now, and she wanted to talk about something different. "I don't know if we should talk about it."

"I didn't exactly raise the subject." He looked at her over his glass. "I think that you probably need to talk about this."

She hesitated before replying. He was right, she thought.

"It's going to sound corny to you because ... well, because men don't think like this, I know, but I do. It's just the way I think – the way I am."

"Of course. We're all different."

"I've known this guy forever. Since we were kids. He was my best friend, I suppose, or that's the way I thought of him. Then I realised – a bit later – that he meant more to me than that. I wanted him to know that but I couldn't tell him, could I? I left it."

He interrupted. "But you should tell people." He shrugged. "Otherwise they don't know. How can they?"

"Yes, maybe. But I didn't, and all the time I thought of him. And so the years went by and nothing happened. That's all there is to it, I suppose."

He stared at her in silence. "You still love him?"

She avoided his gaze. "I suppose I do."

The admission – to Padraig – made her feel light-headed, and what was more, seemed to carry with it an unexpected sexual charge. In the past, on the few occasions when she had talked to anybody about her feelings for James, it had been to a girl friend or to Ted, and that was different. Now, talking to Padraig, she felt in a curious way that James himself was there – that she was talking to him about her feelings for him.

But then it occurred to her: the sexual charge had nothing to do with James, or talking about James; it had to do with Padraig.

He probed further. "And is he seeing somebody else?"

"I don't know. I never see him. I told myself I shouldn't, and

I haven't. I haven't spoken to him for … for months. A year maybe."

"He probably is. People don't stay by themselves unless there's a reason."

She felt a stab of pain. But she knew that what he said was true – and applied to her, too. James was the reason why she was alone.

He lowered his voice. "I think it's sad … I mean it's sad in the sense of being bad luck for you."

She nodded. "Yes, you're right."

"You need to forget him, I think."

"I know. But it's not easy."

He smiled at her. "Can't I help you? I'm not him, I know, but if you got to know somebody else, then that might help you to forget this other person … what's his name?"

"James."

"James. Predictable."

"Are you laughing at me?"

"I'm not. I'm being unkind, and I'm sorry. I'm called Padraig myself, for heaven's sake – how predictable is that, if you're Irish, which I happen to be? There's nothing wrong with being called James. But let's not mention his name." He made a slicing motion. "James is now an un-person. It's official. James has been *abolished.*"

He made her laugh. She liked that, and they had another drink. He said, "Feeling better?"

She felt the effect of the alcohol. The cider had not been very strong, but it had been strong enough. "Yes, much better."

He reached for and pressed her hand. "Me too."

She let her hand linger in his; returned the pressure.

That was the beginning of something that lasted for four years, throughout their university years in Edinburgh, until they both graduated. It was a friendship and a romance, but the emphasis was on the former rather than the latter. Each provided for the other what the other needed: Padraig was looking for something, for the perfect love, the head-over-heels affair that would bring him his life partner, but he knew that this would not be Clover. She had already found, she felt, exactly what she was looking for, and it was not Padraig – but it seemed that it was forever closed to her. Both settled for something less than they thought they might find; neither wished to hurt the other, and neither did. Clover, though, began to lead a secret life – out of desperation, out of disappointment, as most secret lives are led.

25

It was not until she had been with Padraig for a month or so that Clover first saw James. The beginning of the affair with Padraig had distracted her, and the upset that the news of James's presence in Edinburgh had brought to her had largely abated. She had decided that she could live with the knowledge that he was in Edinburgh and had persuaded herself that it did not matter to her. Padraig had suggested that James be abolished; very well, he was. And it surprised her to find out that the act of consigning him to oblivion in this way seemed to help. She thought of him, but only occasionally, and without the desperate tug, the almost physical sensation of pain, that such thoughts had previously triggered. I cannot have James, she thought. He is not for me. It was a form of self-hypnosis – a mantra of the sort that smokers used to abandon cigarettes or alcoholics their alcohol: *I do not need these things. I do not need these things.*

But if weaning from a dependence succeeds, it often does so intermittently, and there will be periods of back-sliding, of weakness, when the temptation to do the thing that you know you should not do is just too strong. For Clover that came shortly before her first sighting of James – a sighting that was not accidental in any way but was engineered by her in just such a moment of weakness.

It happened one afternoon. She had just attended a tutorial and was making her way out into George Square when she passed a university noticeboard. For some reason she stopped and looked at the notices pinned on that particular board. They had nothing to do with her course but she read the largest of them and saw that it was a schedule of classes in economics, which was the subject that she had been told James was studying.

The notice set out the names of those students in various tutorial groups and their time of meeting. Now she knew what she was doing, as her eye ran down the list. *James Collins.* She stopped at the words – words that were invested with such potent effect, as the name of someone we love always is. She thought, inconsequentially, absurdly: *the person who typed them can't have known what sort of person he was.* There were five other names in the groups. Olivia somebody; Jenny somebody; Mark, Mustafa, Terry. They would know, of course; these were his *companions.* She looked at Olivia's name and tried to picture her. She might even sit next to him, and if she did then she would be bound to want him – of course she would.

She turned away. These were ridiculous, stupid thoughts. They were unhealthy. This way lay obsession.

She turned back to look at the notice again. It gave the name of the building and the room number. It gave the time of the tutorial. She looked at her watch. James's tutorial would have started ten minutes ago, and it would be taking place not more than a few hundred yards from where she was standing. She went to the doorway and looked out. There was the other building. Third floor – the notice had said it would be on the third floor. She looked at the windows along the third floor façade. Behind one of those, Olivia, Jenny, Mark, Mustafa, Terry and James would be discussing whatever it was they discussed in economics tutorials. Prices, perhaps. Markets. Commodities. Rational economic behaviour – an expression she had seen in a newspaper article. Rational economic behaviour was behaving sensibly in response to economic incentives or disincentives. Irrational economic behaviour, presumably, was doing the opposite. *I, for instance, am now behaving irrationally …*

Why? Because a rational person does not stand and stare at a window because she thinks a boy she cannot get out of her mind is sitting with others behind that window. There was nothing rational in that.

She lowered her gaze from the third floor to the ground floor. She imagined that there was more than one door into the building and more than one door out of it. The front door, though, seemed to be the main entrance and exit, as she noticed, even as she was staring at it, students walking in and out. So when you went to your economics tutorial on the third floor that must be where you went in and an hour, or maybe slightly less, later where you came out. She looked at her watch again. Forty-five minutes from then he would walk out of that door. Forty-five minutes from then she could happen to be passing – the building was on the way to the main university library and everybody walked that way. She could be walking past just as James was coming out of the building and she would say …

"James! What are you …"

And, when it happened, as she managed to ensure it did, just over fifty minutes later, he said: "I don't believe it! I heard you were here and I was going to …"

Then why had he not? She put the question out of her mind. "Me too."

His smile was unforced. Even if he had not been in touch, the chance encounter clearly pleased him.

He had come out of the building with a girl and she was now standing next to him, smiling at Clover.

"This is Olivia," said James.

She looked at the other girl. She was a recognisable type; one of those well-groomed, expensively educated girls who chose to go to university in Edinburgh because it was a good place to find a husband. It was a crude generalisation, and one that Clover would have previously mocked, but once she had arrived there she had realised that, like so many stereotypes, it was simply true.

Olivia glanced from Clover to James.

"An old friend," he said. "We were at school together in Cayman back in the day."

Olivia smiled at her, and then glanced at her watch. "I have to meet Sue. I promised."

James nodded. "See you later."

"Yes."

Clover wondered what later meant. Later that day? Tomorrow?

"Eight-ish," said Olivia.

James nodded absent-mindedly. He was still looking at Clover; he was still smiling.

"We could get a coffee," he said. "It would be nice to catch up."

She felt her heart hammering within her. "Yes, of course. Why not?"

"There's a place at the top of Middle Meadow Walk. You know it?"

She did, and they walked there together, slowly.

"I don't even need to ask you what you're doing," he said. "Let me guess. History of Art?"

"How did you know?"

"Ted told me, actually," he said. "But it suits you. I always thought you'd do something like that."

"Well, maybe that's what people do. The things they're interested in."

"Most of the time," he said. "But not always. There was somebody in my year at school who's just started medicine and has realised it's a terrible mistake. He's squeamish. He threw up in the anatomy lecture theatre."

"I couldn't do it," said Clover. "I don't like the sight of blood."

"Blood doesn't worry me," said James. "It's spit that I can't stand. Mucus. That sort of thing."

"Well, you're not studying medicine. There's no mucus in economics."

"No," he said, and laughed. "Just sweat."

"And tears."

"Something missing there. Blood, I thought."

She glanced at him discreetly as he spoke. He had not changed; some softness had gone, perhaps, but that was what you would expect. He had been a beautiful boy, she thought, and now he was a beautiful man.

They sat down for coffee. Somewhere in the distance a bell chimed. He looked at her over the table.

"I'm glad that we bumped into one another," he said.

"So am I." She took a sip of her coffee. It was too hot, and she could feel it burn her lips. She wiped it away.

"Olivia," she said.

"What about her?"

"She doing economics with you?"

He nodded. "She's doing other subjects too. She wants to get a degree in economics and French."

The next question was blurted out unplanned. "Are you seeing her?"

He toyed with his coffee cup. "Yes, I am." He looked up. "And you? Are you seeing anyone?"

Her voice sounded hollow. "Yes. There's somebody on my course. He's Irish."

He looked away. "So. Good. I wouldn't like to think that you were seeing just anybody ..."

Her surprise at his remark made her laugh. "Why?"

He reacted as if her question were an odd one. "Because ... because we've known one another forever, more or less. Because you're a sort of sister to me, I suppose."

It cost her an effort not to wince. He had meant it well, but it was not what she wanted to hear.

"You don't have to worry about me," she said.

"Good," he said. "Well, what about ... what about everything?"

"Where do we start? Do you hear from Ted?"

"All the time," he said. "He sends me e-mails about all sorts of stuff. Music. Movies. The works. Ted has views on a lot of things."

"He always did."

They talked for fifteen minutes before he said that he had to get back to his flat.

"I'll phone you," he said. "If you give me your mobile number."

She gave him the number. She watched him write it down on a scrap of paper; she watched his hands. They were brown because of the sun that had been on them and that now was so weak, so distant, so unconvincing. It was strange seeing him here in Scotland, detached from the setting in which they had both grown up. She feared for him, somehow; she feared that something would happen to him in this cold, northern country; that the light that was within him, that was nurtured by the Caribbean, would somehow weaken, would flicker and be extinguished in Scotland.

She watched as he tucked the piece of paper with her number on it into his pocket. You lost pieces of paper like that. He would lose that, she was sure of it, and she would not hear from him. And she wanted, more than anything else, to feel that she was somehow part of his life – not of his past, but of the life he was leading now. But it was far more than that: she wanted to be able to see him, to be in his presence. It was a patently dangerous desire and she knew she had been foolish in courting it again, to allow it oxygen when she was only too aware that all that it would do would be to bring her unhappiness. It was what people did, though, she admitted to herself; they knew that something was wrong for them, and yet they did it. Women fell for the wrong men, time after time, and men did the same thing in falling for the wrong women. We repeated mistakes, and that was why our mistakes were often so recognisable to us – why we were able to admit to them, just as we self-deprecatingly admitted to weaknesses – an inability to resist chocolate, a streak of laziness, human failings like that; our mistakes were familiar because we made them again and again.

She waited for him to call her. She said nothing about it to Padraig, because she had not mentioned to him that she had met James. It was surprisingly easy to keep a secret – one just said nothing, which was hardly difficult – although he noticed that she was anxious not to leave her phone behind when he came to collect her to take her to a concert. "Why take it?" he said. "You have to switch it off during the performance."

She said nothing, and then he asked her whether she was expecting a call. She shook her head.

"Then why take it?"

"Habit," she said.

She did not like to lie, but she could not bear the thought that James might call and the phone would ring unanswered. But he did not, neither that evening, nor the next. She tried to remember his exact words. He said he would phone, but did he say when? She could not remember. And was it significant, she wondered, that he had asked for her number and not volunteered his? People did that, of course; and they did it not because they did not want you to phone them, but because they intended to be the ones to call.

After a week he called. It was in the early evening and she was alone in the flat. She thought it would be Padraig, who had taken to phoning her at that time, and almost said *Hello, Padraig*, but stopped herself in time.

James hesitated at the other end of the line. "Clover?"

"Yes. James?"

He laughed. "Oh, sorry: I wasn't expecting to get you."

She wondered whether it was a joke. "Well, it is my phone."

"Yes, of course. It's just that I've dialled the wrong number. I wrote down somebody else's number and I think I had yours on a piece of paper too. I've mixed the two up. I thought ..." He uttered a stage groan. "This is getting complicated, isn't it?"

She struggled to sound unconcerned. "A bit."

"I thought I was phoning somebody else, you see, but I was dialling your number. A silly mistake."

"I see."

"Not that it isn't nice to speak to you. How are things?"

They spoke for a few minutes. She hoped that he was going to suggest a meeting, but he did not. Eventually he said that he would have to go as he had to make the call he had intended to make in the first place. He did not give the name of the person he was calling, and she did not ask. It could be anyone, of course; she understood that; it could be somebody from his course, or a male friend – he played squash, she remembered, and he might just be phoning to arrange a game. Or it could be that girl she had seen, or any one of the other girls who would be flocking round him.

She sat down. She threw the phone onto her bed. It rolled off and landed on the floor, on the threadbare rug by her bedside, the rug she had bought, third-hand, for her room in the boarding house at Strathearn, loved in spite of its coffee stains, its bare patches, its tendency to crumple. She lowered her head into her hands. She would be seeing Padraig later. He had asked her to go with him to the pub. He would be witty – as he always was – he would make her laugh. He would whisper to her; he would share everything; he would invite her to be his co-conspirator in the word games he played with the world. He was honest and good – and she was keeping secrets from him. She should tell him that she could not love him entirely, that there would always be part of her that would be with James; she should say that that was the way it was no matter how hard she tried to make it otherwise. She should tell him the truth and then ask him to understand, to help her to get over this, as he had already tried, although in a jocular way, to help her to do. But she knew that she would not say any of this, because the whole point of the feeling that she had for James was that others, for all their sound advice, would be unable to understand how she felt.

And of course she should have said something to James. She could have let him know how she felt for him – there were ways of doing that short of the sort of declaration that could spoil everything; because that is what would happen, she knew it; James liked her, but he was not in love with her. James did not think about her as she thought about him; his day did not start, nor end, with thoughts of her. Kind and considerate though he was, he phoned her only by mistake. *I am the sort of girl who gets called only by mistake* ... It was the sort of thing that Padraig would say, with his occasional flashes of Oscar Wilde wit, that came from being Irish and from having a father who was a director at the Abbey Theatre. Or it could equally well have been that woman her mother sometimes quoted, the one from New York who made witty remarks.

She wondered where James would be. In his flat presumably, unless he had already gone out with ... her, whoever she was. She tried to envisage him in the shared flat which would be a mess, like all those flats that boys lived in; dirty socks all over the place and unwashed plates festering in the kitchen sink, and a smell. She could see it, but there were details missing because she had no idea where it was. Flats on the south side of the town looked different from flats on the north side. You could always tell. She thought James might live in the New Town, in one of those Georgian streets, with the Firth of Forth visible through the window and the coast of Fife beyond it. He would be sharing with boys called Henry and Charlie and names like that, and they would spend half their time in the pub and going to parties. And they would be surrounded at weekends by girls like Olivia, who would laugh at their jokes and cook for them on the dirty cooker and then do the week's washing-up without complaint. She tried to picture the place again, and failed. She should find out. There would be no harm in finding out where it was; there was no harm in just looking.

26

She sent an e-mail to Ted. "I saw James the other day. You're still in touch with him, aren't you? Have you got his address (not e-mail – I have that – but his snail-mail address)? I don't seem to have it. We're going to meet up some time soon."

She read and re-read the message. Was it a lie? No. She had seen James – that was quite true – and it was also the case that she did not have his address – she did not have to say that he had not given it to her. They were going to meet, too, as James had taken her number and you did not take a number unless you intended to do something about it. So there was no deception in this message, even if she had not disclosed why she wanted to know the address. But there was nothing to be ashamed of in that respect, she told herself. It was quite understandable, she thought, to want to know where your friends lived. That was normal curiosity. It was. *It was.*

Ted was usually good about answering his e-mails, but on this occasion it was three days before he responded. The delay made her wonder whether he somehow knew that she wanted to … to what? To *spy* on James. But it was not spying. All she wanted was to be able to imagine the place where he lived, and that was definitely not spying. Wasn't there a song about that; somewhere in one of the old musicals that her father liked? About being on the street where a lover lives?

Ted's eventual answer set her mind at rest, giving her the address, including the postcode. She transcribed it into the back of the Moleskine notebook she used as a cross between a diary and a place for lists. It was, as she had imagined, on the north side of town; in Dublin Street, a street that ran sharply down the hill from the Scottish National Portrait Gallery. It was just the sort of place that she could see him living in, and from that moment it was invested in her mind with a sort of glow. Of course he would live in Dublin Street because it was ... well, it was just right for him.

The address revealed on which floor of the five-storey tenement building his flat would be: the figure and letters "2FR" meant that James would be on the second floor, in the flat on the right hand side of the landing. Armed with this information, anybody could, in theory, walk up the shared stone stairway and ring the bell – provided, of course, that the lower door onto the street was left unlocked. If it were locked, then there would be a bell system allowing for the remote opening of the door. All you would have to do would be to tug at the appropriate bell-pull and the outer door could be answered from above.

Ted had other things to say in his e-mail. He was now studying Romance languages in Cambridge. "You should come and see me," he wrote. "I have a room in St John's looking out onto a quad – they call them courts here – and if I put on the right music – Tallis or somebody like that – you would think you were back in the sixteenth or seventeenth century. It's the opposite of Cayman, and I am *seriously* happy. I mean, seriously, seriously happy. I have a friend who's an organ scholar here and we're going to go to Italy in the summer. He knows people in Verona and Siena. They say that we can stay with them. Can you imagine it? And you? What about you? You'll see that I've put James's address in at the end of this e-mail. I hope that you get to see him, but ... all right, I may as well be honest and say what I want to say, or what I think I need to say. Don't die of a broken heart. I mean that seriously. It's very easy to break your heart and it may be – it may just be – that our hearts have been broken ever so slightly by the same person. Just a thought. Remember that he doesn't mean to make us unhappy – he's far too kind for that. But you know something? James may be like the sun. It's nice to have the sun out there but you can't look at it directly or get too close to it, can you? End of lecture. Be happy. Come and see me in Cambridge and we'll go out on the river in a punt. If it's summer, that is; if it's winter we'll go to a pub I know where they serve fish and chips and disgusting warm beer. You can sleep on my floor, or rather I'll sleep on my floor and you can have the bed. It's only moderately uncomfortable. Tuo amico, Ted."

She thought about Ted's invitation – it would be good to see him again, and he had proved a loyal friend. Those friends, she thought, were the ones whom one almost did not notice; the ones who were just there in the background, the unglamorous ones, the ones you took for granted and then, quite unexpectedly, might prove their loyalty by coming to your rescue in a moment of crisis. In her mind, Ted had remained, rather curiously, the little boy that he had been when they had first known one another; that was another feature of loyal friends – they were slow to grow up, and often, in your mind at least, failed altogether to get much beyond the age at which you first met them – that was an absurd notion, of course, but it concealed a more prosaic truth about old friends: they did not change. And yet here he was giving her advice, as one contemporary to another – which he was, of course, as they had entered the Cayman Prep on the same day, all those years ago, excited and frightened at the same time by the change that was occurring in their lives: that first step through the school gate is for most of us the biggest step we ever take – the step out of Eden into the world beyond.

She would accept the invitation, she decided, but then she stopped thinking about it because Dublin Street came back into her mind and now she had the address. She would go down there one morning – the following day, perhaps – and just take a look; that was all – just take a look. The timetable of the first year economics course was available online, and she consulted it. The first lecture on a Tuesday was at ten: *Macroeconomic Modelling*. How dull that sounded, and yet it was what James did, and that somehow rescued it. If the lecture were at ten, then he would have to leave his flat by nine-thirty at the latest to give himself enough time to walk up to George Square. Of course it was uphill most of the way, and that meant that he would need to leave somewhat earlier – by nine-fifteen perhaps.

If she were to be in Dublin Street by nine-fifteen, she would see him. He would come out of the door and she would be on the opposite side of the street – not too close – and she would see him. She could then walk behind him – sufficiently far off not to be seen – she could follow ... She stopped herself. It was not *following*. She was not the sort of person to *follow* somebody. All she was doing, she told herself, was taking the opportunity to see somebody, and there was nothing sinister about that. It was entirely natural to want to see friends in that way when you felt too shy, too proud, perhaps, to make the first move. And pride did play a part here; she acknowledged that; pride mixed with an element of tactics. Now that she had his address it would have been simple for her to go to see him, but she did not want to do that because he would think her pushy and she knew that men did not like being pursued – a woman who chases a man puts him right off, everybody knew that. Bide your time; wait for him to come to you. If she were to seem indifferent to James then there was a chance that he would come round to seeing her in the light in which she saw him; it might occur to him that she might be right for him. But if she made the running, it could spoil it all. He would back off ... not, she reflected with a smile, that he had ever backed on. The realisation made her sad – that was the only word she could find for her feelings; James did not love her, or, if he did, he loved her as a brother, or as one friend of childhood may love another, platonically, fondly, and in no other way.

Of course there was Padraig. This, though, had nothing to do with him. This was her private business, and it was not as if she were being unfaithful to him. She would never have a love affair with somebody while seeing another person; her conscience, in that respect, was clear. Padraig did not need to know about James – beyond what she had already told him – because this was a private domain within her life, like a private enthusiasm, a self-indulgence that one did not discuss with other people because it was simply that – a private passion. You did not have to tell others you liked to listen to a particular piece of music and would play it again and again, or that you liked Rembrandt or Hockney and that you could spend hours poring over their paintings, experiencing the thrill that something entirely beautiful can impart; you did not have to share these things. You did not have to tell others that you loved a boy who you understood would never love you back but who was your secret treat, like a concealed box of chocolates. Nobody was harmed by such things.

"Why so early?" asked Ella.

She had made herself a slice of toast and a cup of coffee and was having these in the kitchen by herself when Ella came in, eyes still filled with sleep – Ella never got out of bed until ten unless absolutely obliged to do so.

"Seven-thirty isn't early. Not for me."

"It's virtually last night as far as I'm concerned," said Ella, making her way to the coffee pot. "May I pinch some?"

"Yes."

"So why so early? Are you going somewhere?"

"I thought I'd get some work done. I'm behind with an essay."

She thought: *this is what it is like to lie about a small thing; and there are people whose whole lives are built around lies, whose every move must be something like this.* For a moment she felt appalled at herself, and could have abandoned her plan, could have gone back to bed; but it was more powerful than she was – whoever the *she* was.

Ella poured herself coffee, cupping the mug in her hands, as if to warm them. "But the library doesn't open till nine."

"There's a departmental library. The Fine Art Library. That's open much earlier. It's a great place to work." This was half-true. The departmental library was sometimes open at eight-thirty, but not always; and she had never worked there.

Ella shrugged. "I've got a hangover. I don't deserve it. I had two glasses of wine – max – I swear it."

"Go back to bed."

"I will."

Clover left the flat ten minutes later and began the walk across town to Dublin Street. The streets were quiet at that hour, and barely light. It was technically late autumn, but there was a hint of winter in the air – a sharpness that was a harbinger of what was to come. Yet the sky was clear and when the sun rose properly it would be one of those sunny, exhilarating days that a northern city like Edinburgh can sometimes pull out of the hat – a day in which the senses are rendered more acute by the cold in the air; a day in which distances are foreshortened by clarity. The sunlight would not be warm, but it would still be felt, like the breath of an unseen creature upon the skin, a soft, slight touch.

She arrived at the top of Dublin Street a good half hour early. Broughton Street was not far away, and she thought that she might find a coffee bar there that would be open. There was one, a small room decorated with out-of-date posters advertising plays from the Festival Fringe. Even at this hour it was busy with people dropping in on their way to work; the people who were too busy to eat breakfast at home, or found they had no coffee in the flat, or simply wanted a few minutes to themselves before work started. She sat at a table with her steaming cappuccino and looked at the people about her. They were part of a world that seemed parallel to hers; a working world that she knew nothing about. What did people *do* in Edinburgh? She looked at the woman sitting at the table nearest hers; she was wearing a woman's business suit – a dark skirt and top under a neatly cut jacket. At her feet was a briefcase and on the table in front of her an open organiser-type diary. She was studying the diary, annotating it here and there; her days mapped out, thought Clover – her expensive time sold in little packages. She must be a lawyer. Or a financial adviser perhaps; telling people how to parcel out their own lives, how to move things about, how to move their money from one place to another.

Sooner or later, she would have to join them: everybody did. She would find herself in an office somewhere, working with people, doing the things that she currently had no idea about, living with one eye fixed on some goal or other – some promotion, some opportunity to do better than the next person, some inducement dangled before her. But for the time being she was spared all that and could sit and listen to people talking about art because … She hesitated, and then admitted it: because somebody else, somewhere else – her father – was doing exactly what this woman was doing. He went off to his office in George Town and sifted through papers and wrote figures on documents and looked out through air-conditioned air into the glare of the unremitting light until he went home and cooled off in the pool and was too tired to read or think very much. And he did all that not so much for himself – because he never seemed that interested in acquiring anything – but because of her and Billy and her mother, to enable them to do the things they did.

The woman at the next-door table glanced at her watch. Then, snapping her diary closed, she took a last sip of coffee and stood up. As she did so, she looked across at Clover and smiled. Clover, embarrassed at being caught staring, returned the smile guiltily.

The woman picked up her briefcase. "So, have a good day."

It was said in a friendly tone.

"I will. And you."

There could have been a barb to the exchange: the woman could hardly have missed the fact, from dress, from pace, from a number of other clues, that Clover had no job to go to, that she was a student and that none of this business of getting to work affected her yet. That might have produced a wry resentment, but had not.

Clover looked at her watch. Something had happened to her, and she thought that it was probably to do with having a brush with normality. The woman with her business suit and her diary had something real to do, as did all the others in the coffee bar. Their daily lives were real in a way in which the world she was creating for herself – a world of dreams – was not. She shook her head, as if to rid herself of an unwelcome idea. She did not have to go through with this; she could go back to the flat and forget that she had ever entertained the thought of coming down to Dublin Street.

She made her decision; she would do that, and immediately felt a sense of relief. She looked up. She was no longer a ridiculous love-struck girl on a pointless mission, not much more than one of those air-headed young teenage girls – as she thought of them – who swooned outside the hotels where boy bands stay on tour, ready to squeal with excitement when their heroes ran the gauntlet of their fans.

She finished her remaining coffee, savouring it though it was now lukewarm. Her thoughts turned to the day ahead. She had a tutorial at eleven and she would now have the time to finish the prescribed reading for it. She would throw herself into her work. She would lead a normal life. She would have one boyfriend, whom she would appreciate, and she would stop thinking of James.

And then, suddenly, he was there. She had not seen him come in because she was facing away from the entrance, and now, he was at the end of her table, half-turned away from the counter where he had been about to place his order, distracted because he had seen her.

His surprise seemed as great as hers. For a moment he was silent, but then he laughed and said, "Well, of all the people …"

She made an effort to recover her composure. She had half-risen to her feet but now sat down again. She thought it possible that if she tried to stand again her feet would buckle under her.

"James …"

The assistant waited patiently behind the counter. James turned to him and placed his order. Then he turned back to address Clover. "You're not in a hurry, are you? You looked as if you were about to go." He gestured to the other chair at her table. "Do you mind?"

"Of course not. I was about to go but I ..."

He interrupted her. "But you could do with another cup of coffee? Come on. My treat."

She acceded, and he called out to the assistant, "One more, Anton."

He sat down, casually resting his elbows on the table. "I've never seen you here before."

"No," she said. She was searching for an explanation, for an excuse for her presence, but her mind, for the moment, was blank.

"Somebody told me you live over on the south side. You do, don't you?"

She nodded. "A friend ..." she began. She wondered who had talked to him about her. And why?

He cut her off. "Yes, of course." He looked away, and changed the subject. "They make great coffee. The best in this part of town, I think, and it's just round the corner from me. I live on Dublin Street."

She almost said, "Yes, I know," but did not, and simply nodded at the information.

"You're lucky," she said. "New Town flats are nicer, I think."

"It depends. There are some that aren't. The rent's higher too."

It then dawned on her what he was thinking, and why he had dropped his enquiry as to what she was doing first thing in the morning on the other side of the city.

She felt herself blushing. "I don't usually come over ..."

He cut her short. "It's not the other side of the world," he said, and grinned. 'I sometimes go to that pub in Marchmont. You know the one?"

She nodded. She wanted to correct his mistaken impression, but could not see how to do it. She could hardly say *I came over here to see you walk out of your front door.*

Their coffee was brought over to the table. "I need this," he said. "A lecture at ten."

She spoke impulsively. "Something boring? Like macroeconomic modelling?"

He laughed. He did not think it odd that she should know. "Right. Actually, it's not all that bad. It sounds it, but it isn't." He paused. "But ... well, I'm on the wrong course. It hasn't taken me long to discover."

"You're going to change? I thought you liked economics."

"Universities."

She caught her breath. "You're going to leave Edinburgh?"

"Yes, next semester. I can transfer the credit on the courses I'm doing this semester. Glasgow has exactly the right course for me. It'll fit what I'm going to be – an accountant." He smiled. "Like your dad. I should have chosen it first time round, but I wanted to come to Edinburgh. And I've really enjoyed Edinburgh – it's just that the subjects I want to do are right there in the Glasgow course."

She was silent.

"Are you all right?"

She nodded.

He was staring at her intently. "You don't seem happy, Clover. Are you homesick, do you think?" He gestured towards the street outside. "This place is very different from Cayman. Obviously." He paused. "I miss it too, sometimes. And will even more in the future, I think."

She wondered what he meant. "Why the future?"

"You haven't heard? Sorry, I thought you knew. My folks have left Cayman. Two months ago."

She felt her world slip further away.

"Where to?" Her voice sounded strained.

"Australia. My mother's from there originally, you know. She wanted to go back, and I think my dad was a bit fed up with Cayman. He wanted something new. He's got a job in a medical practice in a place called Ballarat. It's not all that far from Melbourne. I'll be going to see them over Christmas."

Clover struggled to keep herself under control. This was the end. It was what she had decided she wanted, but it was still an end.

James was still looking at her. "I don't think you're happy," he said quietly. "Boyfriend trouble?"

She shook her head vigorously.

He reached over and placed his hand on hers. "Are you still with the same guy? The Irishman ... what's his name?"

"Padraig."

He took his hand away. "I hope he makes you happy." And then, after a brief pause, "That's what I want, you know."

She thought: I have to tell him now. If I don't, I'm going to have the rest of my life to regret it. There's a chance – just a chance. I have to tell him.

But instead it was he who spoke. "You see, I never had a sister and I suppose you're the closest thing I have to a sister."

She struggled with the words. "But I don't want to be your sister ..."

He drew back, in mock apology. "Sorry! I don't mean to burden you."

"It's not that …"

But he interrupted her. He had remembered something and looked down at his watch. "Oh God, I've forgotten."

"Forgotten what?"

"I have to get a book back to the library by nine. And it's still in the flat. I'm going to have to run."

She could not say anything.

He wiped the foam off his lips. "I'll see you sometime," he said, and added, "Are you going home for Christmas?"

She nodded.

"I envy you."

She stared at the surface of the table, at the crumbs of something – a croissant, perhaps – that had lodged in a crack in the wood. She did not want her misery to show, but the thought struck her then – the strange, unexpected thought – that misery was not just in ourselves – it was in the things about us in the world.

"Then you'll see Ted," he continued. "Tell him to come up to Scotland and see us both. Either Edinburgh or Glasgow."

"I will."

"Good."

He waved to the assistant behind the counter, who waved back. Then, as if it were an afterthought, he blew a kiss to Clover. She blew the kiss back.

27

She went home for the full three weeks of the university's Christmas vacation. Amanda met her at the airport, accompanied by Billy, who was himself at boarding school now but had come home earlier. He was full of news of his soccer team, and regaled her for the whole journey home with his accounts of their last match. His goal, in the final minutes, had saved the match, he said, and had been mentioned at school assembly – enough to turn any head.

Her room was just as she had left it, but, and she found this curious, it was no longer her room: the things it contained were hers, but seemed like relics – exhibits in a museum of what had once been but was no longer. And it seemed strange, too, that her parents were leading the lives that they were: everything seemed so small, so limited; even people's conversation seemed to be stuck in a groove from which there was no escape. Her father still talked about the office; her mother about the tennis club; Billy about soccer and the doings of his friends; and Margaret about the people she knew at church, who, like everybody else, were doing, as far as Clover could work out, much the same things that they had always been doing.

A Christmas party had been planned, to take place a week before Christmas itself, and Amanda suggested that Clover could invite her friends too, or such of them as were on the island. "Ted's here," she said. "You'll know that."

Clover had yet to see Ted, although she had spoken to him on the phone. She would invite him, she said; he did not always like parties, but she would invite him.

"I thought everybody of your age liked parties," said Amanda.

"I did."

"Ted's different. Not everybody's the same, you know.""

"Ted's a nice boy, though."

She nodded. They were sitting together on the patio, on the edge of the pool. The water was cool and inviting, although neither had swum that morning.

Her mother glanced at her, and then looked away. "It's a pity that James isn't here," she said.

Clover reached down for a leaf beside her chair and twisted it in her hand. "Yes, it is."

"Because he'd be company for you. I'm worried that you're going to be bored, with all your friends in the UK now and nobody left here. Except for Ted, of course. And that Edwards girl – the one whose name I always forget. Her mother, by the way, has put on an immense amount of weight. She's as large as a house now. As large as a hotel, actually."

"That's a bit unkind. And she's called Wendy."

Amanda smiled. "Maybe. But if you're too worried about being kind to people, you end up saying nothing about anything."

"Possibly. But still …"

"People lose control of themselves," Amanda continued. "They see food and they eat it. They lose their capacity for self-control. Look at the cruise ships."

"What about them?"

Amanda took off her dark glasses and polished them with the hem of her blouse. "The cruise ships that call in here … the ones that come over from Florida. Look at the people."

"What about them?"

"They eat too much. Those boats are vast floating kitchens."

Clover shrugged. "It's the food manufacturers. It's the people who put the corn syrup or whatever it is in the food. They've made people into addicts, haven't they? It's not the fault of people themselves."

"So nothing's our fault? Is that what you're saying?"

"No, I'm not saying that."

They lapsed into silence.

Then Amanda said, "You have to make your own life, darling. You don't just accept what you're given ..." She left the sentence unfinished.

Clover waited, but when her mother did not continue, she asked, "Given by whom?"

"By life, I suppose. The cards we're dealt. Call it what you will."

Clover dropped the leaf she had been fiddling with. Her fingertips were now stained green by the sap. "Some people may not find it all that easy to do that."

Amanda agreed. "Of course not. Of course it's not easy." She looked at her daughter. "I'd never say it was easy." She closed her eyes. "It can be very hard."

There was a silence between them now that lasted for several minutes. Clover was conscious of the sound of her mother's breathing – and the sound of the water lapping at the edge of the pool. There was a rustle, too, in the undergrowth at the edge of the flower beds – a lizard or a ground bird pursuing its prey. Then Amanda said: "My darling, I know that you live with a big disappointment in your life. I know that because a mother can tell these things. You don't have to tell me that it's there because I know exactly what you must feel. Parents can put two and two together.

"And this disappointment isn't necessarily going to go away. It may get to hurt a little bit less as the years go by, but it may never go away entirely. So what you have to do is to get on with life and try to fill the place that one person once occupied with another. That may not work entirely, but it'll help. It's the only way of getting through life. You stop thinking about the things that haven't happened and think about the things that *are* happening, or might happen."

Clover was staring fixedly at the pool as her mother spoke. But she heard every word. "That's what I'm trying to do," she whispered.

"Good. I'm glad." And then, "Me too."

Clover turned to her mother. "You too?"

There was a moment of hesitation, but it was brief; the admission may not have been intended, but now it was made, and it could not be left where it was. "You must have wondered why Daddy and I spent that time apart. I know you never asked, and we gave you a very vague explanation about people not always getting on – that sort of thing. But you must have wondered."

Clover gave no confirmation.

"There was fault on both sides," her mother went on. "Your father seemed to lose interest in our marriage because he worked so hard. Men do that. It's nothing unusual. And then I discovered that I was becoming fond of somebody else. People do that too. Men and women. Everybody. It's terribly easy to do – particularly in a place like this."

She studied the effect of her words on her daughter. Clover was paying attention; she was not looking at her mother, but she was listening intently.

"I don't know what to say about what happened," Amanda continued, "and I've often thought about it since then and I've tried to be rational about it." She laughed. "It's the one thing, though – the one thing – that you just can't be rational about. And I think that's because love is fundamentally irrational – so how can you be rational about something that doesn't make sense?"

She paused, as if expecting Clover to answer, but she remained silent.

"It was as if a whole lot of colour had suddenly been injected into my life," Amanda went on. "You know those films where black and white suddenly becomes colour? The mood changes – everything lifts. Well, that's what it was for me. I found somebody I wanted to talk to, somebody who made the world about me seem different. I thought at the time that it was something special – that feeling – but of course it's the commonest thing in the world. It's what everybody feels when they fall in love. They just do.

"But it wasn't to be. Sometimes love simply isn't to be. It's as straightforward as that."

Clover spoke quietly. "So you had an affair anyway? Even if it didn't work out?"

"I wouldn't call it that."

"But that's what it sounds like to me."

"Well it wasn't – at least it wasn't in the way in which most people would use the word affair."

Clover felt relieved – but puzzled too. Did her mother mean that she fell for somebody but failed to take it any further? That must be it. In which case ...

Amanda provided the answer. "It was maybe a bit like what happened to you. I became fond of somebody from a distance. It never went further than that."

Clover made a face; she could not help herself. But suddenly aware of what she was doing, she stopped. Amanda, though, had noticed. "I suppose it disgusts you. And I can understand that. Parents aren't really flesh and blood, are they? They're never quite the same as we are ourselves."

She rushed to apologise. "I'm sorry, Mum. I didn't mean it like that."

"I shouldn't have talked to you about this. It's my fault."

"No," insisted Clover. "It's mine."

They exchanged glances, tentatively, but feeling, rather to the surprise of both of them, fonder now of one another than at any time before, now that the transition to an adult relationship had been made. It had not taken much: just the admission of defeat, of disappointment, of human failing.

"Are you going to be all right?" asked Clover.

Her mother reached over and touched her arm gently. "Of course."

"Though it must be sad for you."

Amanda looked thoughtful. "Yes. I suppose it is." She hesitated. "But don't you think that sadness like that has ... well, I suppose, a special quality to it."

"I'm not sure."

"Well, I think it does. You're studying art history. You look at paintings, don't you? Some of them must have that in them – the sadness that goes with something being just out of your reach. Something unattainable."

"Maybe. I hadn't thought about it."

"Well, think about it now."

She had a question to ask her mother, and she was debating with herself as to whether she should ask it.

"There's something on your mind," said Amanda.

"Yes, there is. This person …"

Amanda looked away. The easy intimacy of the previous few minutes was suddenly no longer there. "I don't think I should talk about him. I hope you don't mind."

"You know about … about me and James."

"Yes, I know that. But I'm your mother. It's not surprising I should know."

"And shouldn't a daughter know about her mother's …" She was on the point of saying lover, but Amanda said it for her.

"Her mother's lover? That depends. In this case, there wasn't one. I told you: he never became my lover." She started to get out of her chair. "I think we should have a swim. Then we can go over to the tennis club. I know you say your tennis is rusty, but I'll play with one hand behind my back."

"You'll still win."

Amanda laughed as she reached down to give Clover a hand up. "Mothers have to win something. They lose a lot as it is, you might as well allow them to win at tennis."

Their party, planned to be held at the poolside, was threatened by rain. Heavy thunderclouds, towering cumulonimbus stacked high into the sky, built up in the afternoon, and by early evening were discharging sheets of rain. The tables, already laid out with linen – the bar, wheeled out on a trolley – were all quickly moved under cover by Margaret and her helpers. But then, their burden discharged, the clouds disappeared, and everything was moved outside again in time for the guests to arrive at seven.

Clover knew just about everybody, although there was a sprinkling of new friends that her parents had made amongst the shifting expatriate community. The old friends she had known all her life – her father's colleagues from the office, the same as they always were but slightly more worn-down; the dentist and his wife with their flashing smiles, walking advertisements for the benefits of cosmetic dentistry; the American dermatologist from over the road and his Colombian wife, smothered in gold jewellery; the Jamaican accountant, with his air of sad acceptance, and his stories of the times they had in Port Antonio before – and this with a shake of the head –"it all went wrong".

Ted was her guest, and she sat with him by the pool after they had filled their plates at the buffet.

She said to him, "You're going to come and see me in Edinburgh – remember?"

He nodded. "After you come to see me in Cambridge. I asked you first."

"Maybe."

She looked at him. His hair seemed a bit different, but it could have been ten years ago, and they could have been sitting in the tree-house.

Ted looked over at the knot of guests around the buffet table. "Look at them," he said.

"What about them?"

"Don't you find it hard to believe that they're … that they're still here?"

She laughed. "Yes, I do. Just like when I arrived at the airport and saw that it was still there. And when I think of other airports where there are thousands of people and you walk through tunnels and so on and there's no sky, nothing, and here you can pick flowers when you get off the plane and walk over to the building."

"Yes," he said. "Yes."

"And then there's everybody doing the same thing – and saying the same thing."

He had noticed too, he said. "I don't think I could ever live here again. Not permanently. Visits, maybe, but that would be all." He looked at her enquiringly. "What about you?"

"Probably the same."

He looked thoughtful. "Do you think that it's odd that here we are at our stage in life – we aren't exactly ancient – and we're already thinking about our past with a sort of nostalgia? Do you find that odd?"

She did – to an extent. "It's probably because we spent the earlier part of our lives in this rather peculiar place. It's like being … well, it's like being born in a garden, I suppose. And then you get a bit older …"

"And you step out of the garden," he interjected. "Yes, that's absolutely right. That's what it is."

"But we find a life on the outside," she said. "And we like it. It's more exciting. There's more of everything, not just the same old, same old."

"Yes," he said. "That's exactly what I feel."

She smiled. "We always agreed – you and I."

"Yes, we did."

She thought: *we were made for one another – except for one thing. For that reason, and then because I can't get over James. James. James.*

She looked at Ted. "Are you happy?"

He nodded vigorously. "Seriously happy. I think I told you that."

"You did. You sent me a nice e-mail. Just reading it, I felt really happy for you."

"I love Cambridge," he said. "I love the buildings. I love the sense of history. I love the gentleness of it all."

"Gentleness?"

"Yes, it's very … very civilised. People treat one another in a way that's very different from here. It's money here, isn't it? That's what really counts. Money."

She happened to see her father as Ted said this. "My father counts money," she said. "So do most of the people at this party. Or they do things for people who count money."

Ted laughed. "Very funny."

"That's the way it is."

She raised the subject gently. "And you've met somebody?"

He was slow to answer, and she wondered whether she had intruded. But he had told her about it first and so he must be ready to talk about it.

"I have," he said. "And I'm pretty pleased about it."

"Just pleased? That doesn't sound very enthusiastic."

"No, I am enthusiastic. Very. Yes, I've found somebody whose company I really enjoy. And I think he likes me too."

"That's important."

"Yes, it is."

"He's a really good musician. In fact, he can do most things really well. He's a keen skier too. I've never learned, but he's good enough to be in the university team. But he doesn't have time to do it – he's an organ scholar and they have to spend all that time in chapel."

"It sounds great."

"It is. I know it is. I think I mentioned we were going to go to Italy. He knows these people. His dad is pretty grand, actually, and they have all these wealthy friends with villas in Italy and so on. He's been invited, and he says I can come too. We're going to go in the summer."

"You must be very happy."

"Of course I am. But I know it's not going to last."

She looked at him with concern. "You shouldn't say that. How do you know?"

"Because these things don't. I'm being realistic. They don't last all that well in the straight world, let alone if you're gay. It's more difficult, I think. It just is. People don't meet at university and stay together. They get bored with one another."

"I thought that was changing."

He sighed. "A bit, maybe. But not all that much."

"I hope that it will for you."

"Thank you." He paused. "And you? What about you?"

She looked beyond the guests. The two helpers Margaret had brought – a Jamaican couple from her church – were laying out more plates. They both wore white, as Margaret did when she went to church.

"Me?" she said. "I'm fine. I suppose I'm fine. Yes, I'm all right. Yes …"

He reached out to her.

"Because of …"

"Because of him. Yes."

"You can't."

"I know I can't. I know what I should do. People keep telling me. My mother. You. Everybody. Although you told me once not to give up – remember? Then, when you wrote to me, you said something different. You said what everybody else says." She made an effort now, and composed herself. "I'm going to be fine.

I'm going to live my life, and I'll try to get as much as I can out
of it, but all the time I know I'm going to think of him. Sad, isn't
it?"

"I don't think so. Not sad in the sense of being pathetic. Sad
for you otherwise, I suppose."

"It's forever," she said quietly. "Whoever is up there in the sky
looked down on me and said – 'It's forever for you.'"

The tension was defused. "You sound like Margaret."

"Maybe. But she believes it. I don't."

"You don't believe there's somebody up there ... allocating
things for us?"

She shook her head. "I believe there may be something – I
don't know why, but I just think there is – but it's not a man with
a white beard."

"Or a woman?"

"No. If it were a woman, she wouldn't make things so hard
for women."

They laughed, but she thought: *would it be less embarrassing to
talk about a goddess than a god?*

"When I was a boy," he said, "I thought I would get struck by
lightning if I said things like that."

"I saw some lightning today," she said. "In that storm."

"I wonder who was struck."

"I didn't see. But I bet they deserved it."

They looked at each other and smiled. She wanted to kiss him
at that moment, and she wondered whether he would object. A
chaste kiss, to the cheek; a kiss that would say everything about
everything; about the value of old friends; about how she wanted
him to be happy forever, in spite of his belief that happiness, for
him, in his own view of his situation, was likely to be temporary.

But surely all happiness was temporary, she thought – or most of it. That was what made us aware of it – the fact that it was a salience, something that stood out from our normal emotional state. She would not describe herself as unhappy, and yet she knew that she could be happier than she was at present. She would be happy if James were with her, which he was not; and, she thought, he never would be. She heard a snatch of song on the radio – a line from a folk tune – that resonated and somehow seemed right for her. The singer reflected on things that could never be, or at least would never come about "until apples should grow on an orange tree". Until then, she thought; until then. The song finished and was gone, and she had not heard its title or the name of the singer. The plaintive line, however, remained in her mind. *Until apples should grow on an orange tree.*

28

James went to Glasgow at the end of the semester. He sent her an
e-mail a few months later, but it did not say very much. She read
it and re-read it, and then, resolving that she would treat it as
nothing special, deleted it. Ted gave her news of him from time
to time, and when Ted eventually paid his visit to Edinburgh she
invited James to join them for a meal. The distance between the
cities was not great – forty-five minutes by train – but they were
different worlds, it seemed, and he rarely made the journey. On
that occasion he was away – he played rugby for a university team
and they had a match that weekend in Inverness. Ted seemed
relieved that James would not be there.

"It is nice to have you to myself," she said. "And besides …"

He looked at her quizzically.

"I'm over him," she muttered.

"Are you? Really?"

She shook her head.

"You see," he reproached her. "You should listen to me."

"I will. Eventually."

He looked doubtful. "Try harder." And then added, "I like
Padraig. What's wrong with him? I don't see anything. Mind,
you get a bit closer to him than I do …"

"Padraig's fine," she said. "He's considerate and witty and I
like him a lot."

"Like?"

"Like."

Ted shrugged. "That's the problem, isn't it? Liking and loving
really are different. But I'm not here to lecture you."

The visit was a success, and he came back to Edinburgh later that year. She went to Cambridge, and Ted put on a picnic for her by the river. He took her to Grantchester and recited Rupert Brooke's "The Old Vicarage" by heart, learned, he told her, specially for the occasion.

"You're very clever," she said teasingly. "How many boys can recite Rupert Brooke and understand about art and everything? And be good-looking at the same time. How many?"

"I'm not good-looking."

"Yes, you are. You're everything a girl could want."

He laughed. "Except for …"

"Who cares about that?"

He affected surprise. "Are you asking me to marry you? Really, Clover, you're rather *forward*, aren't you?"

She said that she would be happy to be married to him. "We could have a pact. If nobody else ever asked us, then we could settle down together."

"I'd love that," he said. "No, I really would. I could promise that I wouldn't ever look at men and you could promise to look the other way." He became serious. "Does Padraig mind? Does he mind your going off to see another man like this? Some men would be jealous."

He said this with a smile, and then winked at her.

"He's not the jealous type."

"Good." Then after a pause, he asked, "Are you going to stay with him forever?"

She did not reply immediately. She had not really thought about it, but now that she did, she realised that this was not what she intended. And the fact that she had not thought about the question itself provided the answer.

"No." The word slipped out.

"I thought you wouldn't."

"Things are all right at the moment. We enjoy being together. It's ..."

"Comfortable? Is that the word?"

"Maybe. But what's wrong with being comfortable?'

He thought that nothing was wrong with it. But he pointed out that one could go to sleep if one became too comfortable.

"And what's wrong with going to sleep?"

What was wrong with being asleep, he said, was that sleep amounted to nothing, and that the more you slept the shorter your life – your real life – became.

"Oh well," she said.

"Yes," he said. "Oh well. So how long are you going to keep Padraig? Until you finish at Edinburgh?"

"I'm not that calculating."

"But that's what's probably going to happen."

It was, she conceded, and he was proved right. Over the three years that followed, she stayed with Padraig. They did not live together, but they spent much of their spare time in each other's company. In those three years, she saw James four times – twice at parties in Edinburgh when they happened both to know the host, once in a pub in Edinburgh after a rugby match between Scotland and Wales, and once, by chance, in the street. Although brief, each of these meetings seemed to open a wound that she had thought closed. James was kind to her – as he always was – and treated her as an old friend whom he saw very occasionally but was always pleased to meet again. But that was all. She did not see him with a girl, and hesitated to ask, even if he asked after Padraig. Ted had hinted that James had met somebody in Glasgow but he had been tactful and had not said much. She had closed her ears to the information; she did not want to hear it.

The meeting in the pub was the most difficult one for her. She was there with Padraig who had gone to the game at Murrayfield Stadium and had arranged to meet her for a drink before going out to dinner. Padraig was at the bar, ordering the drinks, and she was standing in a crush of people, looking for somewhere to sit. James had appeared beside her, and had leaned over and kissed her on the cheek. He was with several male friends, whom he introduced to her, but she did not get the names.

"You're here with Padraig?" he asked.

She glanced towards the bar. It was taking time for Padraig to be served. "Yes, I am. And you ..."

"Pity."

The word was muttered, and she thought she had misheard him. But it had sounded like it; it had sounded like *pity*. She caught her breath. *Pity*. Did that mean that he hoped that Padraig was over – that she was free to go out with him? She closed her eyes momentarily, feeling dizzy.

The moment passed, and she thought: *he did not say it. It was what I wanted him to say – that's all.*

He spoke about the rugby. "I've been at the game," he said. "Scotland played okay – not brilliantly, but okay enough."

"They try," said one of his friends. "They try but in rugby it's not a question of trying, but scoring tries."

She looked at James. I'm standing next to him, she thought. I could easily say to him, James, I've wanted to say something to you for years now and here we are standing in this bar and I have the chance and ...

The moment passed. Padraig returned with drinks and James went off with his friends. She could not stay.

"I don't want to stay here," she said to Padraig. "I'm really sorry. I'm not feeling well."

He was solicitous – he always was – but she turned down his offer to accompany her home and left by herself. The street outside was filled with rugby supporters. Some of the Scottish fans, draped in tartan, were singing a song about ancient wrongs; she avoided them and went down a quieter side street. She stopped and looked in a shop window – the first shop window she came to. There was camping gear on display, and outdoor clothing too. There was a large picture of a young man and woman standing on top of a Scottish mountain, a cairn of stones by their side. She looked at them, and at their smiles. She turned away and began to walk down the street again. She felt the tears in her eyes, and within her a bleak emptiness – a feeling of utter, inconsolable sorrow over what she did not have. For all the time that had passed – for all her efforts – he could still do that to her. It was her sentence, she decided, and it seemed that it was for life.

When the time came for her to graduate, Padraig, who was about to embark on a master's course, was awarded a six-month travelling scholarship. He chose to spend his time in Florence and Paris, with three months in each city. He told her of the award and shyly, and rather hesitantly, invited her to come with him. She sensed, though, that the invitation was less than whole-hearted, an impression strengthened by the fact that he seemed relieved when she said that she had other plans. These plans were barely laid – her parents had offered her a gap year, which she had decided to take, but beyond that she was uncertain as to what to do. She had thought of going to Nepal with a friend who had taken a job as a teacher of English, but nothing definite had been arranged.

"I think we need to split up," she said. "I don't think you really want me to come to Italy and France with you."

"But I do," he protested. "I wouldn't have asked you if I didn't."

"I'll just get in your way."

He seemed hurt. "What do you mean by that?"

She spoke gently. "Things come to a natural end, Padraig. It's nothing to get upset about. We've had three years – more actually – and now …"

He looked resigned. "Your problem, Clover, is that all the time you've been with me, you've been in love with somebody else."

She was unable to answer him. Had it been that obvious?

They sat and stared at one another in silence. She felt empty, but she could not rekindle something that she knew now, just as he did, had run its course.

Eventually Padraig spoke. "I suppose you can't help it. I don't hold it against you for exactly that reason. It's your … how should I put it? It's your burden. But I must admit I feel sorry for you. You're in love with somebody who isn't there. He just isn't in your life. I'm sorry, Clover, but I think that's really … really pathetic. Sad."

His words struck home. *He just isn't in your life.* But he was. He had been a friend to her over all these years. She rarely saw him – that was true – but he was always so nice to her when she did see him. He smiled at her. He clearly liked her. He was kind and showed an interest in what she said to him. He was in her life. He was. And as for Padraig's pity – she did not want to be pitied, and told him so.

"All right, I'm sure you don't – and I'll try not to. But for

God's sake, don't let it completely ruin your life. You only have one life, you know. One. And you shouldn't try to live it around somebody who isn't living his life around yours. Do you see that? Do you get that?"

She wept, and he comforted her. They would always be friends, he said, and she nodded her assent.

"Don't wreck your gap year, Clovie," he whispered. He rarely called her that; only in moments of tenderness. "People fritter them away. Do something with it. Promise?"

She promised.

"And don't spend it thinking about him. Promise?"

She promised that too, and he kissed her, gently, and with fondness, in spite of what he had said – and what he had thought – setting in this way, with dignity, the seal on an ended relationship.

29

Nepal proved easy to arrange, being simply a question of money, which her father, having agreed to fund a gap year, provided without demur. The organisers of *Constructive Year Abroad*, though, were unable to fit her in to their programme until six months after her graduation. They had other suggestions to fill the time – a three-month engagement as an assistant (unpaid) in a Bulgarian orphanage? She would be working for part of the time in an orphanage in Nepal – the rest of her time would be on a school building programme – and she was not sure whether she wanted to spend too much time on that. They understood, of course, and suggested a conservation programme in Indonesia. That, though, was unduly costly and she decided to save her father the expense. To stay in Edinburgh until she left for Nepal would be cheaper, she felt, and she could get a casual job for a few months to cover her expenses.

She wrote to Ted, who had arranged to spend a year teaching English in Lyons: "I feel vaguely guilty about the whole thing. The Nepal thing costs serious money and surely it would be better if we were simply to give them the money to do whatever it is I'm meant to be doing there. I can't get it out of my mind that this is all about people whose families have got money – you and me, Ted, let's be honest – pretending to do something useful but really having an extended holiday. A year off; just *off*. That's what it is, isn't it?"

He wrote back: "Yes, of course. They don't really need you in Nepal. But, okay, you won't be doing any actual harm, will you? I suppose if they sent gap year people to build schools that actually *fell down* then there'd be a case for not doing it at all, but you're not going to do that, I take it. There'll be people – *real people* – out there who will make sure that whatever you build is going to be done properly, or at least not dangerously. So don't feel guilty. Sure, don't feel heroic, either, but not guilty. And as for having money, well, we don't really have it, do we? Our folks are admittedly not on the breadline, and they do happen to live in a tax haven, but they're not going to support us forever and we're going to have to earn our living. On which subject, any suggestions? You know what I'm thinking of being after I finish teaching English to the French? A marketing trainee. There's a firm near Cambridge that has actually offered me a job one year from now, unless the economy takes a nose-dive. How about that for glamour? Would you like to join me? We could do marketing together; just think of it."

The job she got in Edinburgh was at a delicatessen that also served coffee. She was to be in charge of the coffee, which she found that she enjoyed doing. The owners, a middle-aged couple who had taken on the business only a few months previously, were still learning and were good-natured. She was happy in her work and made a number of new friends. She had remained in Ella's flat, which was not far from the delicatessen, and it occurred to her that it would be simpler not to go to Nepal at all. But if she felt guilt about her expensive gap year, how much more guilty, she decided, would she feel if she did nothing with the year. She remembered Padraig's advice – his exhortation – that she should not fritter the year away. Padraig had approved of Nepal when she had told him about it.

"Good," he had said. "That's exactly the sort of thing you should be doing – something useful."

She had heard from James, who had called her unannounced

shortly before her graduation and told her that he might be coming to Edinburgh a few days later and suggesting that they should see one another. She had agreed, and they had met in the same pub where they had met after the rugby match. This time it was worse. She had gone into the pub, looked around, and seen him sitting at a table with a girl. She had stopped and had been on the point of retreating when he saw her and waved. It was too late then, and she had to join them.

The girl was from Glasgow, and had accompanied him to Edinburgh. Clover had been able to tell immediately that the meeting in the pub had not been the main aim of the trip, and James confirmed this.

"We've got some friends over here," he said. "They've bought a flat and are having a flat-warming party."

Her heart sank at the word *we*, the most devastating word for the lonely. "I see."

"Yes. I thought it would be good to take the chance to catch up with you. I realised that I hadn't seen you for ages."

He was being his usual friendly self, she thought. He has always been nice to me – always.

James turned to the girl beside him. "Clover and I go back a long time. One of my first friends, aren't you, Clove?"

The girl looked at her and smiled. But the smile, Clover could tell, was forced.

"There's nothing like old friends," James continued. "There was Clover, me, and a guy called Ted." He paused. "Ted says he's going to France."

She nodded. "Yes. To teach English."

"Everybody does that," said James. "Except me, I suppose. You know I'm going to Australia in two weeks' time. Did I tell you?"

Clover absorbed the news in silence. She felt quite empty within. There was nothing.

"My folks are in a place called Ballarat – I think I mentioned that to you."

She nodded.

"Anyway, I've decided that since I can get a work permit because my mother's Australian and I'm going to be eligible for an Australian passport, I might as well do my training out there. I was going to one of the large international accountancy firms anyway, and they said they had no objection to my transferring my training contract to Australia. They have a branch in Melbourne. That's where I'm going to do it."

Clover glanced at the girl. "What are you doing?"

The girl shifted in her seat. "I've got a job in Glasgow. I work for the Clydesdale Bank."

"Shelley's doing a banking traineeship," said James.

"So you're not going to Australia," said Clover.

The question seemed to annoy Shelley. "No," she said tersely. "I'll go to visit James, though, won't I, James?"

It sounded to Clover like a territorial claim. "That'll be nice," she said.

"Yes," said James. "And you should come and see me there sometime too, Clover."

Shelley looked at her, and then looked quickly away.

"Maybe I will," said Clover.

"I mean it," said James. "You've got my e-mail address. Just let me know."

Shelley glanced at her watch. Clover noticed; she herself did not want to stay now.

"I have to go soon," she said.

James seemed disappointed. "But you've just arrived."

"We have to keep an eye on the time too," interjected Shelley. "Maddy and Steve said ..."

"Of course," said James. He turned to Clover and smiled. "I wish we'd seen more of each other. I suppose that my being in Glasgow and you being here – well, somehow I hardly ever seemed to get that train."

She felt a wrench at her heart. It had been a mistake to see him, she felt. And now she was to say goodbye, which would be for the last time, she thought, as Australia was a long way away. She said to herself: I am about to say goodbye to the person I have loved all my life. I shall never see him again.

She stood up.

"Don't go," he said.

"I have to," she said. "Sorry."

She felt the tears well in her eyes; she did not want them to see – neither of them. She turned away. James stood up. "Clover ..."

She reached the door without turning back, and only gave a glance then, and a quick one. Shelley was saying something to James, and then she looked at her. Their eyes met across the floor of the pub, across the void.

Her job became busier as the city filled with festival visitors. The streets around the delicatessen were lined with Victorian tenements, many of which during university term-time were occupied by students. During the summer months the tenants covered their rent by sub-letting to the waves of hopeful performers who came to Edinburgh for the Fringe, the rambunctious add-on to the official festival, bringing with them shows that for the most part would be lost in the programme of several thousand events. Optimism sustained them; the hope of a review, of being spotted by somebody who counted, of being heard in the cacophony of a festival that opened its doors without audition and sent nobody away unheard – even if it was by audiences that sometimes numbered no more than one.

She noticed the groups of Fringe performers drifting into the delicatessen, and spoke to some of those who chose to stay for coffee. The cast of a student *Midsummer Night's Dream*, brought from a college in Indiana, came in each morning shortly before their ten o'clock rehearsals, to rub shoulders with a group of *a capella* singers from Iceland and a dance ensemble from Nicaragua. Their regular customers, those whose normal lives continued over the festival month, were accustomed to the annual invasion, and calmly purchased their cheese and cold meats against this polyglot backdrop. For Clover it meant long hours, but it was what she wanted. Ella was still in the flat, and so she had some company to go back to, but she now found herself slightly irritated by her flatmate's laziness and failure to do her fair share of cleaning. For the first time since she had moved into the flat, she found herself wanting to move out, to get on with the next stage of her life.

With most of her university friends away, she struggled with loneliness. She missed Padraig more than she imagined she would, and she wondered whether he would be feeling the same. Probably not, she decided. He had now taken up his scholarship and was in Florence. He sent her a photograph of himself standing beside the Arno – *Me by the Arno*, he wrote – and he sent her a copy of a piece he had written for the *Irish Times* on a minor Italian artist of the nineteen-twenties who had met James Joyce in Paris and disappeared the next day. "Some people get depressed by contact with greatness," he wrote to Clover. "Some people get disheartened."

She was not sure whether the reference to being disheartened was personal. She did not think that he would miss her; not, she thought, when one could go and stand by the Arno. She toyed with the idea of writing to him and confessing that she missed him and wondered whether they had done the right thing in splitting up, but she decided that she would not. That would be going backwards, trying to prolong something that had come to a natural and not-too-upsetting end. She would meet somebody else, she decided. It was time. There were plenty of young men in Edinburgh; the Fringe seemed to bring them in their hundreds and surely one of them would be looking for somebody like her.

"How do you get a new man?" she asked Ella one evening when she was cleaning up the breakfast plates that Ella had left unwashed.

Ella laughed. "You joking?"

"No, I'm not."

Ella shrugged. "How did you meet the last one?"

"He came up to me and told me his name," she said. "It was at a party."

"There you are. Parties."

"If you get invited to them. What if you don't?"

"Internet dating," said Ella. "Haven't you seen the figures? Apparently that's where everybody meets these days. You go on an internet dating site and you say something such as 'likes eating out' or 'into jazz' or whatever, and then you get your replies. You take it from there."

Clover frowned. "I couldn't. I just couldn't."

"Then you'll have to go to a pub or a coffee bar and sit around.

Somebody will come and talk to you if you're there long enough. It's easy. All you have to do is look as if you're looking for a man. Then they come to you. That's the way it works."

"I couldn't."

"Then you're not going to get a new man, Clover." She paused. "Do you really think you *need* one? Men can be overrated, you know. Okay, they may be useful for one or two things – sometimes – but not for the whole weekend."

They both laughed. Then Ella said, "But isn't there one in the background? I thought there was some guy somewhere you were keen on. Didn't you tell me once?"

"There was," said Clover. "Not any more."

"Is he with somebody else?"

"Probably. Yes, I think he is."

Ella looked up at the ceiling. "Frankly I don't think that's always an obstacle – know what I mean?"

"You mean: detach him?"

"Exactly. Prise him away. Steal him."

"I couldn't," said Clover.

"Then you're never going to get a man, Clover. We'll be old maids together. How about it? We can stay here until we're fifty, bickering. We can go to the cinema and pilates classes together. We can talk about the men we knew a long time ago and about what happened to them."

"No thanks."

"Then you're going to have to be more proactive. Steal him – the one you always liked." She grinned. "Trap him. Or …"

"Or what?"

"Or spend the rest of your life regretting what you didn't do. That's how life is for lots of people, you know – it's made up of things they failed to do because they were too ..." And here she gave Clover a searching look. "They were too timid."

"Is that my problem?"

"Could be. I'm going to say it once more: steal him, this ... what's his name?"

"James."

"Sounds sexy," said Ella. "Steal him."

She wrote to her father: "I know that you said I could use the money for anything – and I really appreciate that. But I thought I'd just check up with you, in case you thought that I was throwing your money around. Everything is sorted out for Nepal, but it's not going to happen for a while yet – not until February, which still seems like a long way away – I'm counting the days. I've been working, as you know, in a delicatessen. It's been quite busy recently but I'm enjoying it. They're paying me just above minimum wage, which is not meanness on their part but because they've just started the business and they don't have much money themselves. I don't mind. What I earn there more than covers the rent for my room in the flat.

"What I wanted to tell you is that I want to spend some of the money on a ticket to Australia. I want to go to Melbourne for a few weeks – maybe three, I think. I've met a girl here who's with a drama company doing something on the Fringe – it seems like the whole world is here at the moment. She's a member of a group called Two-Handed Theatre and they're putting on a couple of plays at the Fringe. She's invited me to come to see her in Melbourne when they go back there in a couple of weeks and I thought: I don't get many invitations to Australia. So I thought I'd go. I can get a ticket through Singapore for under a thousand,

and since you've been so generous I can afford it. But I didn't want you to think I was being … what's the word – profligate? Yes, profligate. Is that okay with you?"

It was. David wrote back: "The whole point of a gap year is that you can do things you can't do at any other stage in your life. Of course you should go to Australia. Going there has been on my list for years but I've never done it. And that's another point to a gap year – it gives you the chance to do things that your parents would have liked to do but have never had the time to fit in. Like visiting Australia. Or Nepal. Or anywhere, really."

The invitation from Frieda, the Australian actress, had been repeated more than once and so Clover knew that it was not one of those casual "you must come and see me" invitations that nobody really intends to be taken seriously. Frieda had been coming in for morning coffee since Two-Handed Theatre had first arrived for their run on the Fringe, and Clover had engaged her in conversation. Frieda was seven or eight years older than she was, but she liked the Australian's easy manner and enthusiasm; Edinburgh, said Frieda, was a box of chocolates that she intended to consume entirely before returning to Melbourne. Her attitude to her show also intrigued Clover; while most Fringe performers had about them an earnest intensity, founded, perhaps, on their conviction that their contribution to the Fringe was on the cusp of artistic greatness, Frieda was realistic. "We're enjoying ourselves," she said. "I'm not sure if the audience is, but we are." And on her own ability: "I can't really act, you know. I sort of play myself all the time but since the audience has never met me before they think I'm acting. It seems to work."

After the second invitation, Clover said, "I could come to Melbourne, you know."

"Great. Come."

"For a few weeks? If I came for a few weeks? Just to see the place."

This would have been the time for Frieda to claim to be too busy, to say that she was going to be elsewhere, but she did not. Instead, she suggested that Clover could stay in the converted fire station that she shared with five of her friends. "Contribute something to the rent, and you're in. You get one shelf in a fridge. Not to sleep in, you know; you get a sort of cupboard for that, but it's not bad. It's quite a big cupboard. You don't exactly get a bed – you get what used to be a bed and is now a sort of mattress on the floor of the cupboard. But as fire stations go, it's not all that uncomfortable."

"It sounds irresistible. I'll come."

Frieda seemed genuinely pleased. "I'll show you round Melbourne. We may have a show on – you can help with front of house if you like." She paused, looking around the delicatessen. "What about this job? Will they hold it for you?"

Clover explained that it was not an issue, as she thought that the owners could manage without her or could easily enough find somebody else. And that proved to be the case.

"It's a relief," the husband said.

"It's not that we don't appreciate what you do," the wife explained. "We do, but paying you is difficult. We just can't manage any more. We'll get somebody more part time."

She confirmed the ticket with the travel agent, arranging to arrive a couple of days after Frieda would have returned home.

"One thing interests me," said Frieda. "Why are you coming? Sorry to sound rude – and I'm really pleased that you're doing it – it's just that I wondered why." She gestured to the street outside. "This place is so exciting. It's like living on an opera set. Why Melbourne?"

Clover hesitated. She had not admitted it to herself yet, and now she was being asked directly. If she found it easy enough to deceive herself, it was not so easy to deceive this new friend of hers, with her trusting openness.

"There's somebody I'd like to see there. I suppose that's why."

Frieda smiled. "A boy?"

Clover nodded.

"I guessed as much," said Frieda. "I thought there was something."

"But people can want to go to Melbourne for plenty of reasons."

"Oh yes," said Frieda. "That's true enough. But it wasn't just the fact that you wanted to go to Melbourne. It's something about you. There was something in your manner that made me think …"

Clover waited for her to complete her sentence. She found the observation rather unsettling.

"A certain – how shall I put it? Sadness. Yes, I think that's it. You know, when I saw you first – here in this place, operating that coffee thing over there with all that steam and hissing and so on, I thought: that girl's sad about something."

Clover looked away.

"I'm sorry if this embarrasses you," said Frieda. "I'll shut up, if you like. We don't like to hear about ourselves. Or at least most of us don't. It disturbs our self-image because how other people see us is often wildly different from how we see ourselves." She shuddered. "The truth can be a bit creepy, I think."

"I don't know …"

"Oh yes, it can be. Most of us have a persona we project to the outside world – it's the part of us they see. And then there's the bit behind that, which is the bit that remains with us when we turn the lights out. You know what it is? It's what people used to call the soul. But now, we're not meant to have souls." She smiled. "It's *really* old-fashioned to have a soul, Clover. But there's this … this *thing* inside us that's the core of what we are – what we are individually, that is. And in your case …"

Clover waited. "In my case …"

"In your case, that bit is sad. It's sad because it's incomplete. It's seen something that it wants more than anything else in the world, and it can't get it." She paused. "Okay, I sound like a New Age freak going on about auras and so on. But it *is* there, you know. That sadness. I'm sorry, but it's there."

"Maybe."

"Good. You're admitting it. Plenty of people won't."

"I don't want to conceal anything from you."

"That's good to hear. But listen Clover – this boy, tell me about him."

The owners were looking at her. Conversations with the customers were not discouraged, but there was work to be done.

"I can't now," said Clover. "But there's this boy I loved, you see. I've loved him ever since I was six, I think – or thereabouts."

Frieda beamed. "That's really romantic. I just love that sort of story. Eternal love. Enduring love. It's great. We need more of that. Roll it on. Roll it on." Her smile faded. "But he …"

Clover nodded.

"He's in love with somebody else?" Frieda probed.

"I don't know."

This brought surprise. "You don't know? How come? Haven't

you asked him?"

"No. Not really."

Frieda looked incredulous. "What's wrong with you people? Are you so uptight? Is this something to do with being English?"

"I'm not English," said Clover. "My father's from here originally and my mother's American."

"Then you've no excuse for being so English," retorted Frieda. "Listen, so this guy's in Melbourne?"

"Yes. He moved there quite recently. His parents live in Australia now – his mother's Australian."

"But he's in Melbourne, right? This … what do you call him?"

"James."

"This James is in Melbourne. Well … well, that's where you need to be, Clover. Welcome to the Old Fire Station." She fixed Clover with an intent look. "Do you need some help with this? I think you might."

"Thanks, but I don't see how you could help me."

"You don't? Well, you'll see."

The following morning, Frieda showed her a picture of the Old Fire Station. "Friendly building, isn't it?"

Clover said that she liked the look of it.

"That's where the fire engines came out," said Frieda, pointing to a large window. "It used to be a door. And we've still got the pole inside, you know, that the firemen used to slide down to get to the engines, but nobody slides any more. Somebody did when he was drunk, though. He forgot to hold on. You have to grip the pole quite tightly as you go down, or you go down too fast. He broke his ankle." She paused. "I can't believe you're coming, Clover. It's going to be great."

'Thank you."

"And that little problem with that boy. We'll deal with that. We'll get it sorted."

She swallowed. I've made a mistake, she thought. She wanted to say: *You can't sort things out just like that,* but there was something about her new friend that made her feel almost helpless.

Frieda reached out and patted Clover's arm affectionately. "Still sad?"

Clover shook her head – an automatic response to an intrusive question.

"I think you are," said Frieda. "But we can sort that out."

She noticed Clover's expression. "You don't believe me?" she said, smiling. "You don't believe I can sort boys out?"

30

"Did you think it would be like this?" asked Frieda. "Is this how you saw the fire station? Of course, I showed you that picture, didn't I – when we were in Edinburgh. But reality's always a bit different, isn't it?" She made a face. "Thank God for that too. When I look at a photograph of myself I think: reality's different, so no worries."

Somebody had created a door as well as a window within the large double door at the front of the building. This led into the hall in which Clover now found herself standing.

"Is this where the fire engines …" she began.

Frieda lifted Clover's backpack from the concrete floor. "Yes. That wall over there blocks off the main garage – and it's all changed, of course. But this is where they parked them. Actual red fire engines – as advertised. Big hoses. Bells – the works." She was an actress, and it seemed she could not resist. "The calls came through. *Big blaze over at the Convent of the Good Shepherd.*" She imitated the nasal tones of a telephone voice. "Nuns on fire! Come quick! Girls escaping left right and centre!"

Clover stared at her.

"Only joking, Clover."

"Of course."

"We did a play about those nuns, you see. They took in girls thought to be in moral danger. That was the expression. Girls in moral danger, and I played one of them on stage. Most of them weren't in real moral danger – whatever that is. Having affairs with boys, perhaps – off to the convent with you. I'd love a bit more moral danger in my own life."

Frieda gestured to the stairway behind them. "This way." They began their ascent of the stairway, which was badly in need of a coat of paint. "This place was converted for fashionable people," she said. "But the fashionable people went away, as fashionable people are prone to do. It was allowed to go bush and they started to let it out to students. Then they went one worse and let it out to actors. That's us. Some of us are real pigs – purely in the domestic department, of course. And only the men. They're the ones who never wash up. Or clean. They spend a lot of time in the shower, though. No problem there. It's just the kitchen where they show themselves to be a bit flaky. Poor boys – they try, I suppose. Do you think men try, Clover?"

Clover felt dizzy from the lengthy flight. She shook her head. "I can't think very much at the moment."

Frieda was solicitous. "Of course. You're jet-lagged. I slept for twenty hours when I came back from Scotland, you know. I was knocked out. I'm still waking up at odd hours."

There was a dark corridor that somebody had tried to brighten by sticking colourful posters for long-dead concerts on the walls; at the end of it, an open door. "That won't stay shut," said Frieda. "You have to tie it with a bit of string. The string is your key, so to speak."

"I see."

They reached the door.

"I warned you it was a cupboard," said Frieda. "But you can actually lie down – I promise. I tested it myself. I lay down in your cupboard, and it felt perfectly roomy. This is officially a one-person cupboard."

She needed to sleep and Frieda left her with the promise that she would be somewhere in the house when she woke up. The cupboard was really a room, Clover thought, as it contained not only a bed but a small wardrobe and chest of drawers as well. There was a window looking out over a yard outside, and beyond that to the backs of neighbouring houses. She gazed out of this window for a moment, taking in the details – the red Victorian brick, the corrugated iron of the roofs, the shabby guttering with its blistered paint; and above it a cloudless sky, washed of colour as the sky can be in the brief transition between day and night. She was struck by the thought that this was Australia; that in spite of its distance from where she had started her trip, the things about her, the brick, the earth, the sky were of the same substance that she had left behind her in Scotland, but were at the same time so different.

The following morning Frieda said to her, "I am that great cliché – the resting actress. I'm resting today and tomorrow, and working the day after that. So let me show you Melbourne – or at least let me show you our local coffee bar and the supermarket at the end of the road. There are other things – arts centres, museums et cetera – but you know how it is."

In the coffee bar, Frieda looked at her with mild curiosity and asked her what she wanted to do in Melbourne. "I'm not sure you can find two weeks' worth of things to see," she said. "You could look at the river, I suppose. There's something called the Yarra. You could look at it for hours, I imagine, but I'm not sure what conclusions you'd reach. It's a great place just to be, though. There's a difference between seeing and being, I think. This is a great place to be – not to do anything in particular – just to be." She paused. "But you've got your friend to see, haven't you? Have you made any arrangements?"

Clover shook her head. "No. He doesn't know I'm here. Not yet."

Frieda sipped at her coffee thoughtfully and then put down her cup. "You should have told him," she said.

"I didn't want to. I wanted it to ... to look natural, I suppose."

Frieda's eyes widened. "To look natural? Oh, hello, I just happen to have dropped in from the other side of the world! That sort of natural?"

Clover did not answer. Frieda was right, of course.

They sat in silence for a few moments, and then Frieda said, "Invite him round. Tell him you're here, visiting friends, and then invite him round. Simple." She paused. "I take it you've got his e-mail address?"

"Of course."

"Then invite him round for tomorrow. Dinner. Seven o'clock. There'll be five of us altogether. You, me, him. Two of the other inmates are in residence, I think. Three are out for good behaviour."

Clover agreed.

"Tell me a bit about him," said Frieda. "Good-looking?"

"Seriously."

"I see. That's good. But it's also bad, isn't it? Good-looking boys often know it. They take advantage of it."

"He doesn't know it. Or he doesn't act as if he does."

Frieda said this was perfect. But she needed to know more. "Funny? Does he make you laugh?"

"Yes."

"It gets better. Tall?"

"Yes."

"Oh my God, this is Adonis we're talking about. So what's the problem? Likes girls?"

"Yes. He's had girlfriends." It caused her pain to say it.

"But not you?" said Frieda. "You and James haven't been a number?"

She looked down at her hands. "He refers to me as a sister."

Frieda was silent for a moment as she absorbed the admission. "Oh, my God, that's terrible," she muttered, reaching out to Clover in instinctive sympathy. "What a terrible thing to say. His sister!"

Suddenly, and at the same time, they saw the humour in the situation.

"My sister," said Frieda, with exaggerated concern, "my poor sister, to be his … his sister!"

"I'm making a fool of myself," said Clover. "I know it."

Now Frieda became serious again. "Send him that e-mail," she said. " I can't wait to see him. And then I'll be able to advise you, as long as …"

She left the condition hanging in the air.

"As long as what?"

"As long as you don't behave like a sister when he comes round here. You see, that might be the problem. He's been treating you like a sister because that's how you've been behaving towards him."

"But …"

"But nothing. But nothing. Think sex, Clover. Act – don't think about reasons for not acting." She smiled. "That's the way some people go through life. They sit about and think about the consequences. Make the consequences happen. Embrace consequences." She drew back. "Do you know something? I've just said something really profound. I think I'm going to write it down before I forget it. *Make consequences happen.* How's that for a really … a really important aphorism? *Make consequences happen.*"

You're talking about my life, thought Clover. You're not on the stage.

"What?"

Clover shook her head. "I didn't say anything."

"Well, don't think it, then. Act. Do you want me to dictate the e-mail for you? No? Yes?"

"I can write my own e-mails."

"You sure?" But there was a quick retraction. "I'm sorry – of course you can. God, I'm pushy! But go ahead and do it – because you're never going to be happy, Clover, until you take control of your destiny. That's another aphorism, by the way. I'm so full of them today I'm going to make myself sick."

James replied almost immediately. He was surprised, he said, but "really, really pleased" to hear that she was in Melbourne and yes, he would love to come round the following evening. He was going to play squash but he had been looking for an excuse to get out of it because the particular squash partner with whom he was due to play was a bad sport. "He's a mathematician," he wrote. "Not that that has anything to do with it, but he seems to want everything to work out neatly in his favour. That's the way his mind works. I don't like playing with him any more, but it's hard to get rid of him. I find myself wanting to lose so that he doesn't get into one of his bad moods. And that's not the point of squash, I think. Anyway, that's my problem – not yours. I'll be there tomorrow. And is it really a disused fire station? I'll find out tomorrow, I suppose. And Clover … thanks for coming all this way to see me!"

She dwelt on his last sentence. When she first read it, she had been aghast at the thought that he must somehow have guessed that her purpose in coming to Australia had been to see him. She felt the nakedness of one whose secret motives are suddenly laid bare; the shock that one has been *seen through*. But then she realised that he was joking; nobody would travel to Australia just to see a friend with whom contact had more or less been lost – nobody in her right mind, that is.

But at least he had accepted the invitation, and the general tone of his message was welcoming. Of course he had always been like that – apart from one or two moments when they had been much younger and for a short time he had seemed to lose interest in her company. For the rest, he had been friendly and interested in what she had to say. And that brought her back, as it inevitably did, to the thought of his kindness. It was like love, really – a kindness that grew from love; it must have, because things cannot come from nowhere – but it was not actual love, not love of the sort that she wanted him to feel and that he had given to others, but never to her. Could you make do with kindness rather than love? What if you were to lead a life in which you were never given the love that you craved, but found friendship and the kindness and consideration that went with that? She could not imagine that this would be enough, although she knew that there were people who had to make do with just that.

She offered to make the meal the following day and Frieda was quick to accept. "I was hoping you'd offer," she said. "We *love* our guests to do the cooking. It's why we have them. No, I'm not serious about that. We have them to defray the rent. No, I'm not serious about that either. We have them because we like them."

She went to the Victorian market and wandered about the stalls, returning with fish, fennel and wild rice. She realised that she did not know whether James had a favourite dish, and this led her to reflect that although she had known him for years, she still did not know all that much about him – the details of his life, the likes and dislikes, the music he liked to listen to, the books he read, what he liked to drink. Those things she thought, were the context against which a life was led, not the life itself. The person himself was something quite different from the surroundings of his life: he was a disposition, an attitude, a way of looking at other people, and as far as all that was concerned, she felt that she must know James better than any of his more recent acquaintances. It did not matter that she did not even know whether he liked fish.

She spent the afternoon worrying. It now occurred to her that although she wanted to see him, she did not want to hear about his life in Melbourne. She had only been in Australia for a couple of days but already she understood the attractions: the warmth, the spaciousness – even in a city; the high, empty sky; the sense of being on the edge of something that was just beginning. Surely this would be just as seductive for James as she suspected it would be for her, and he would be creating for himself a whole new life in which she would have no part. I am his past, she thought; I am not even his present, let alone his future.

Frieda was auditioning that afternoon and was not back until six. She thought she had not been successful. "They hate you if you look a day over eighteen," she said. "Let me warn you about casting directors."

Clover said, "But I'm not an actress. I don't know any."

"Look out anyway," said Frieda. She picked at an olive from the bowl that Clover had just prepared. "Nice. Olives are so … I don't know. How would you describe an olive?"

"Small and round."

"Exactly. Small and round." She popped the olive into her mouth and looked at Clover thoughtfully. "A small round man is probably the answer, you know. He'd never stray. He'd be so appreciative of everything you did for him because small and round people usually are." She paused. "Small, round and maybe a bit rich."

Clover laughed.

"It's no laughing matter," said Frieda, reaching for another olive. "I can't even find a small and round man. Not in the theatre." She looked at her watch. "This man ..."

"James."

"Yes, James. Leave it to me."

Clover felt a surge of alarm. "Listen, Frieda, it's not that I'm ungrateful, but I thought ..."

Frieda affected hurt. "You think I'm going to be tactless? Do you really think I'd say something unhelpful?"

"I didn't say that."

"You *looked* it. There are some things you don't need to say; you just *look* them."

Clover made a soothing gesture. "I'm sure you understand how I feel."

"Nervous?"

"Yes."

Frieda put an arm about her shoulder. "No need. We're pretty relaxed round here. It'll be a really easy evening. And you know what? I've had an idea. I'll suggest we go out to this bar round the corner – have you seen it? The Atrium. Then I'll suddenly remember that I have to be somewhere else so that the two of you can go together. It'll be very natural."

"Very."

Frieda made a face. "Don't be so pessimistic. That's the trouble with you people – you just give up."

Clover was unsure what people Frieda was talking about: the British? Everybody who happened not to be Australian? People who weren't actors? People like her, who could be said to have given up because they allowed boys to think of them as sisters?

They were both in the kitchen when the doorbell rang.

"That's him," said Frieda. "Go and let him in. And Clover ..."

"Yes?"

"When you see him there on the step, kiss him. Okay? Kiss him."

She looked away, resentful of the advice. She felt her heart thumping within her; a shortness of breath. Her palms would be moist, she decided, and she wiped them against the side of her jeans. Frieda saw her and smiled.

"I know what it's like. I sometimes feel like that when I go on stage. Some people use talc, so that when the romantic lead takes their hand he doesn't think *Oh my God: dripping with sweat!*"

She left the kitchen and made her way towards the front door. This was the reason she had made this journey, and now those thousands of miles were culminating in a few short steps.

He stood there, smiling at her, and then stepped forward to embrace her. She closed her eyes, and felt the dryness of his cheek against hers. She was suddenly afraid that she might cry; afraid that the pent-up emotion within her would break its bounds. But those bounds had been long in place, and well founded, as are the defences behind which any concealed love must shelter. Lifetimes might be spent in tending such ramparts; and have been.

Later, she could not recall what he had said to her and she to him in those first few minutes. There had been an enquiry about her journey, and remarks about Melbourne. He had just seen something in the street outside, but she paid no attention to what he told her about it: a poster that amused him, or triggered some memory that he thought she might share. All that she was aware of was that she was in his presence; that he was real, he was there in the flesh, and that she had not been mistaken in her feelings about him.

She introduced him to Frieda, who looked at him from under her eyelids, her head slightly lowered, in that rather unusual and disconcerting manner that she had noticed before. But if he was taken aback by this scrutiny, he did not show it, and the two of them moved immediately into the relaxed, good-natured banter that the Australians excel at; an assumption of good will, a default position based on the understanding that there was enough for everybody – enough of whatever it was that people needed: space, food, the chance to make something of life.

She could tell that James liked Frieda, and for a moment she felt a twinge of jealousy as he quizzed her about her acting. He had seen her, he said, on television a few weeks ago in an episode of a serial to which his flatmate was addicted, and the recognition pleased her. It had been a small part, she said, but had paid well, as banal roles could do.

"If you're going to be boring," she said, "you might as well be well paid for it."

James turned to Clover and asked her about her plans.

"You should stay longer out here," he said. "You'd like it."

"Yes," said Frieda. "Stay longer."

Automatically – and foolishly, she later decided – Clover

explained that it was a brief trip and that she had to get to the next stage in her journey. She said this as part of the pretence that she had not come to see James.

"Where?" he asked.

Again she spoke without thinking; her return journey would be through Singapore, but it was only for a change of plane.

"Singapore," she said.

James looked puzzled. "Why there?"

"There's a friend," she said. "I knew her in Cayman, ages ago; and in Edinburgh too. Judy. She has an apartment in Singapore and I thought I'd spend a bit of time with her. She said that she might be able to get me a job doing something or other. Just for a few months."

"Difficult," said James. "You can't just pick up a work permit there."

Clover was vague. "She didn't say …"

They were joined by Frieda's two flatmates who had been invited to the dinner. Like Frieda, they were both actors, although one, Chris, was about to give up in despair after his last television role, his first for three months, had been as a parking attendant with one thing to say, which was *thank you*.

"I did it so expressively," he said. "I put my soul into it."

Frieda shrugged. "The theatre – what can one say?"

Chris said, "Thank you – which is what I said."

The two flatmates did not stay beyond the end of the meal. Frieda cleared up. "So James," she said as she took his empty plate. "You're pleased to see your friend?"

If he was surprised by the question, he did not reveal it. "Of course."

Clover squirmed.

Frieda seemed impervious. "And you, Clover?"

Her response was muttered. "Yes."

Frieda continued breezily. "You two go back a long way, don't you?"

Clover winced.

"Well you do, don't you?" persisted Frieda.

"To six, or thereabouts," said James. "Don't we, Clove?"

"Yes."

Frieda smiled. "Destiny," she muttered. "Childhood sweethearts."

James laughed. "Not really. More like friends."

Frieda waved a hand in the air. "Friends make the best sweethearts."

Clover glared at her, but Frieda was looking at James. He seemed to hesitate, and then, looking at his watch, said that since he had to be at work early the next morning, he would have to think of getting home. "I'm going down to Adelaide for the next four weeks," he said. "An audit. It's really dull." He looked at Clover apologetically. "It's bad timing, I'm afraid. Next time, I hope I'll be able to show you the town. And why not bring Padraig?"

She felt empty.

"Padraig's in Italy," she said. "And we ..."

She would have gone on to say that she was no longer seeing Padraig, but James had risen to his feet and had begun to thank Frieda for the meal. Then he bent and kissed Clover on the cheek.

"Write to me," he said. "I like getting e-mails from you."

Frieda saw him to the door and when she returned to the kitchen she found Clover in tears.

"I did my best, Clover. But what more can I do? I gave you every chance in the book."

Clover looked away. "I don't care. Just leave me alone please."

Frieda sought to defend herself. "You can hardly blame me. You should have told him about Padraig, and what did you say? Just something about Italy. How pathetic!" She shook her head. "I despair of you, you know. I completely despair. You say that you want him, but you know what I think? You don't. Not really."

31

She left the Old Fire Station two days later, in spite of Frieda's apologies, that came the next day: *I always, always, always put my feet in things; I'm really sorry, Clover; you have every right to be cross with me, my God, I know that.* She made light of these, and told Frieda how grateful she was for giving her somewhere to stay, but she felt restless, and her restlessness was not helped by the irritation she felt over her older friend's ways – her over-statements and her extravagant way of speaking. The cupboard itself seemed less attractive now, and following up an advertisement in a give-away newspaper she found a room in a flat that the other tenants were happy to let her take for a few weeks. With James away, she had no real reason to be in Melbourne, but she somehow lacked the will to do the obvious thing and leave for a backpacking trip. She found herself brooding over her evening with James and how, before it had begun to go wrong, it seemed to be going so well. He had looked at her with fondness in his eyes – she was sure of that – and her recollection of what he had said – in so far as it went – was encouraging. If only she had been by herself, without Frieda, and her obvious, ham-fisted hints, she might have been able to convey to him what she had so long wanted to tell him but had found impossible.

There were moments of complete clarity when her situation presented itself to her realistically, just as she knew it to be. At such times – moments that came without warning when she was sitting in a coffee bar, browsing in a bookshop, or simply lying in bed looking at the ceiling – she understood exactly what she was: a young woman of twenty-two, who had been given every advantage, who had everything she needed in a material sense, who had parents who loved and supported her, who had never been obliged to struggle for anything or work against the odds. All of that she knew – and did not take for granted – but she was more than that young woman; she was also somebody who did not have the one thing she wanted in life and now, in such moments, understood and accepted that she might never get it.

At such moments, along with this self-understanding, there came an awareness – and acceptance – of what she had to do next. She had to wait out her remaining few days in Melbourne and then return to Scotland. She had to try to get her old job back – or something like it – and then in due course go off for the rest of her gap year. There was Nepal, and that school somewhere that she would help to build. Then she had to find a proper job, support herself, meet somebody else, and start leading the life that everybody else seemed to be prepared to lead without constantly hankering after something that was not to be. That was the plan, and as she marked time in Melbourne, it even began to have an aura of desirability about it. The rest of my life, she thought. The rest of my life.

But then James came to her in her dreams – not once or even occasionally, but every night, or so it seemed. He was just there – entering a room in which she found herself – a room that was somewhere geographically vague: not quite in Scotland, nor in Cayman, but somewhere in between. One night, in that dream that precedes wakefulness – the one that remains, if only for a few seconds, in memory – she was in Australia, because that was how it felt, and she was with James outside a house with a silver tin roof, and there were swaying eucalyptus trees behind the house, and he gestured to her that they should go in. She took his hand, and he let her place it against her cheek, and she

kissed it, and he said: *Of course, Clover; of course,* and then was
suddenly not there any more and she felt a great sense of having
seen something that she had never seen before, of having been
vouchsafed a vision of sorts, as a religious person might see an
angel in the garden, or a child an imaginary friend. The house
with its silver roof, of course, was love; she had read enough pop
psychology to understand that.

She woke up and stared at the still darkened ceiling, and it
seemed to her that James had really been in the room with her
and had somehow sanctified it by his presence. Which is what
he does, she thought. James makes everything whole for me.
She thought that, and allowed the words to echo in her head,
luxuriating in them; then she turned and closed her eyes for sleep
again, if it would come, so that she might return to the dream
in which he had been present. She hugged herself, imagining
that her hands were his, but then let go, almost guiltily, struck
by sheer embarrassment at the thought that she was one of those
people who must rely on the embrace of an imaginary lover. She
thought of Padraig, again with guilt, and asked herself whether
he had meant anything to her. Had she treated him badly by
allowing him to think that she loved him when all along she had
only ever loved one person, and it was not him? Or had they
both been a temporary solution for each other – an equal bargain
between adults, a perfectly adequate way of filling an absence; in
her case for the boy she remembered and in his case for the girl he
hoped might one day come into his life. She had always known
that he had such an idea; she had seen him glance on occasion
at some girl and had said to herself, with the satisfaction of one
who detects a clue to some mystery or conundrum, *So that's his
type*; so different from her – self-possessed types, with hair swept

back, and the confident poise that went with their education at
south of England boarding schools. Their cool Englishness was
the polar opposite of Irishness, and yet he obviously liked them.
Yes, for all his advice to her not to live in thrall to an impossible
love, Padraig had been doing exactly the same thing himself.

The thought occurred to her that perhaps most of us were like
that; perhaps it was common to live with an image in our minds
of what might be, of what we truly deserved if only the world
were differently organised – in a way that gave proper recognition
to our claims. So the lowest paid imagined the sumptuous life of
the banker, the lame envisaged what it must be like to be athletic,
the lonely closed their eyes and saw themselves surrounded by
friends. We might all cope with a dissonance between real and
unreal simply by making do, simply by admitting to ourselves
that dreams are just that – dreams. Perhaps the real danger was
to think that the thing you felt you deserved could really be
achieved. And yet it was also possible that you could get what
you really wanted, if you simply took it when it presented itself.
She had come across a poem by Robert Graves that put it rather
well; a poem called "A Pinch of Salt" about the bird of love, who
came sudden and unbidden, who had to be clutched by the hand
in which he landed, clutched and held tight lest he fly away. That
had struck her as being true, and yet she had not done what
the poet said you should do, and so the warning implicit in the
poem, the warning of loss, applied to her.

She got on well with her temporary flatmates whose
uncomplicated ambition, as far as she could ascertain, was to
have fun. They were two young women and one young man.
One of the women was an architectural student, and the other
was marking time before going off on a working holiday to

London. The young man, Greg, who was loosely connected with one of the women in a way which Clover could not quite understand – he was an ex-boyfriend, she thought – worked as a copywriter in an advertising agency and had ambitions to be a novelist. The social life of these three consisted in endless outings to bars and restaurants, and they were happy for Clover to tag along with them. She did so, and met their friends, who were doing much the same thing as them, and accepted her with the same readiness that they seemed to accept everybody else. "Success," pronounced one of these friends, "is being able to eat out every night. Every night. 7/7." She thought he might believe it, even if he said it with a smile.

Greg flirted with her – mildly and with a certain wry humour – and she responded. But when he came to her room one evening after they had been in a bar together and said pointedly how lonely he found Melbourne and the worst thing was loneliness at night, she could not bring herself to an involvement that she knew would be short-lived and mechanical.

"I'm in love with somebody else, Greg," she said. "It's not that I don't like you. I do. It's just that I've loved somebody else for a long time and I can't ..."

"It's just sex," he said. "That's all."

She laughed at this, partly to defuse a potentially awkward situation, but also partly because what he had said struck her as being so completely wrong – not wrong in any moral sense, but in the sense of being psychologically reductive. Sex was not *just sex*; it was everything. It was ... She faltered. It was James.

"I'm sorry, Greg."

"No need to apologise. Should we watch a DVD instead?"

"It's just a movie," she said. "That's all."

He nodded his agreement. "DVDs are better than sex. Everybody knows that. Or at least everybody who's not getting any sex."

They watched together, and at the end she took his hand in a friendly, unthreatening way, and patted it. He grinned at her. "I'm glad you said no," he said. "I'm glad you're faithful."

She smiled at his tribute. *More faithful than you can imagine,* she thought.

"I'm going to miss you when you go next week," he said. "I've enjoyed having you around."

"Would you mind if I stayed a bit longer?"

She had not thought it through, but suddenly she did not want to go. James was in Melbourne – or would be – and she did not want to leave the place where he was; it was as simple as that.

"No, of course we wouldn't mind. Aly and Joy will be fine. They like having you here too."

Now the rest of her inchoate idea came to her. She would change her ticket for a later departure – her particular fare would allow for one change – and she would stay in Australia without telling James. She did not want him to know. She would allow herself a final … she struggled with the period, and decided it would be a month. She would have a final month and then she would begin to do what she knew she should have done all along: she would begin to forget. And in that final month she would allow herself just a few glimpses of him. That was all. She had his address now, and could see him on the street. She could watch him coming out of his flat. It would be saying goodbye from a distance, slowly, as goodbye used to be said when you could actually see people leaving; when they left by trains that moved slowly out of stations, or by ships that were nudged gently away from piers still linked by paper streamers; or when people simply walked away and you could see them going down paths until they were a dot in the distance before being swallowed up by a world that was then so much larger. It was only watching; that was all. It was definitely *not* stalking. Stalking was something quite different; that was watching somebody else with hostile intent or with an ulterior motive. She had no such thing; she loved James, and that was what made it different; she was not going to make any demands of him. How could she?

James, of course, would think that she had gone on to Singapore to stay with Judy, and it would complicate matters to have him think differently; more than that, it would be impossible to explain what she was doing. She would write to him as if from Singapore, and in this way she could keep some contact; again, there was no harm done in *writing* to somebody. There was e-mail. You can't tell where e-mails come from, she thought; in a sense they conferred a limitless freedom, for they came from somewhere that could just as easily be Singapore as it could be Melbourne.

She told Greg. She had not planned to, but at the time it seemed right, and it helped her too. They were in the kitchen together and had shared half a bottle of wine. She felt mellow, and in a mood for confession. The disclosure made her feel less anxious, less burdened.

Once she had stopped speaking he looked at her in astonishment, and she wondered whether she would regret what she had just said. Her story, she knew, must sound absurd to others, and it *was* absurd. But then *we* are absurd when you come to think of it, she thought; we are absurd, every one of us, with our hopes and struggles and our tiny human lives that we thought mattered so much but were of such little real consequence. *Think of yourself in space, as a tiny dot of consciousness in the Milky Way,* one of the teachers at Strathearn had said. *It puts you in perspective, doesn't it?*

Greg's look of astonishment changed to one of puzzlement.

"You actually told him that you had gone to Singapore?"

"Yes. I know it sounds stupid, but I did. I suppose …"

He waited.

"I suppose I wanted him to think that I had a life of my own… I suppose I hoped it would somehow make me more interesting." She looked ashamed. "Does that sound odd to you?"

He looked as if he was making an effort to understand. "What do you expect me to say? No, it's quite normal to tell somebody you're in Singapore when you aren't? Is that what you expect?"

She did not answer.

"I suppose," Greg continued, "that people try to impress others in strange ways. Maybe being in Singapore would impress him – I don't know. But what bothers me is the point of it all. Why? I mean, most people would just tell him the truth, don't you think? They'd go up to him and say something like *I've always had the hots for you.*"

"Would they?"

He grinned. "I would, if I were a woman and there was this guy I wanted."

"That's what Frieda said. That's what everybody's said all along."

He shrugged. "Well, there you are. I think that's about it."

She wanted to explain – as much to herself as to him. "But the problem is this: I know how he feels about me. He doesn't think of me in that way. I'm just a friend to him – somebody he's known since he was six or whatever. That's all." She paused before the hardest admission. "And there's somebody else. He's seeing this girl."

Greg sighed. "Another girl? Oh well, that's not so good, is it? If somebody has somebody else, there's not much you can do."

"He'll never love me," Clover said. "I know that. And I know that if I were to go up to him and tell him how I felt that would probably end our friendship. He'd feel sorry for me and ... and that's the last thing I want. I'm a little bit of his life right now, but I'd be less if he decided that he had to keep me ... keep me at arm's length because I had gone and fallen in love with him and spoiled everything." She stared at Greg, hoping he would understand. "Do you see what I mean? If somebody falls in love with you and you don't fall in love with them, then they're just a nuisance. You're embarrassed. You want them to go away." She willed him to react. "Do you get what I'm trying to say?"

He tried. "Maybe. A bit." Now he looked intrigued. "So let me get this straight: you've told him that you've gone on to Singapore?"

"Yes. I know that sounds ..."

"Weird."

She said nothing, and he continued: "So now he's back from Adelaide and he thinks you're in Singapore staying with this girl ..."

"Judy."

He looked at her dubiously. "Who exists?"

"Of course she exists."

"I just wanted to make sure how big the fantasy is. That's all." He looked thoughtful. "It's peculiar, but you know what? I suppose it's harmless – and fun too. You're inventing a life for yourself there?"

She nodded. "It sort of grew. I sent him an e-mail telling him I'd gone and he sent one back. He asked me about Singapore and what it was like and I was so pleased that he had actually answered me that I wrote back."

"Telling him about it?"

She looked down at the floor. "It was an excuse to be in touch with him. I bought a book – a guide book. And one of those coffee table books with pictures."

He suddenly gave a whoop of delight. "Oh, Clover, you crack me up! You're serious fun – in a vaguely worrying sort of way."

"He wrote back … again."

"And you continued with the story?"

"Yes."

"All of it invented? Made up?"

"I told you: Judy exists. And I was going to stay with her for a few days on the way back. So it's true – in a way. All I've done is to bring it forward by a few weeks."

They had been talking in the kitchen of the flat, and now he got up from his chair and walked over to the window. "You know what? Let's make one up. Could I try? Get your computer and write it down."

"Do you …"

"Yes, come on. *Clover's day in Singapore.* You go shopping. That's what people do in Singapore. Big shopping place. And you buy …" He broke off to consider. "You buy a T-shirt. Big deal. But that sounds just right because people do that sort of thing, don't they? They go out shopping and they come back with a tee-shirt. Yours says … You know what it says? It says *Foreign Girl,* but you can't resist it because you think it says it all. You *are* a foreign girl, and here's this T-shirt that admits it. It's a very honest T-shirt."

He warmed to his theme. "And on the way back to the flat somebody steals your purse. You don't know how it happened, but it goes. Maybe there was this guy – yes, there was, I remember now – this guy brushes past you and he says how sorry he is but he's actually taken your purse and he goes off in the crowd."

"There's no crime in Singapore. My book said that. Or they have a very low rate of crime."

He laughed. "That's what they say. And maybe it's true. But even if it is, there's bound to be some crime. So you go to the police station and ... and it's really clean. Clean policemen, clean desks, clean criminals – not very many of them, of course – and this sergeant ... It was a sergeant, wasn't it?"

She entered into the spirit of it. "Yes. He was Sergeant Foo. He had one of those name badges on and it said *Sergeant Foo*."

He said, "Oh, I like that guy. I wouldn't cross him, but I like him. Sergeant Foo takes your statement and then he says, *This is very regrettable. Rest assured, lady, that we will catch this ... this malefactor. He will be severely punished.* And then you went home. And Judy had invited these people over for dinner and she didn't have any ..."

"Arborio rice. She was going to do Italian and she needed some Arborio rice."

"So you went out to this shop round the corner," he said. "And there was this whole stack of Arborio rice because there were some Italians living nearby and they were always wanting Arborio rice. All the time."

They laughed together. "Silly girl," said Greg, gazing at her fondly.

She avoided his gaze. She did not feel silly. Nothing about her feelings for James was silly.

She had imagined that there would be one or two e-mails from Singapore, but she was to be proved wrong. James replied to each, often almost immediately, and began to include, in his responses, news of his own. There was a different tone to his e-mails now – something that she had not noticed in his earlier messages. He had been almost business-like before and had said little about himself and what he was doing; now he seemed more open, more inclined to chat. He told her about Adelaide and the hotel that he was staying in. "It's one of those old Australian hotels that were always built on street corners," he wrote. "There's a pub in it called the Happy Wallaby – I'm not inventing this; it really is – and this fills with rather rowdy locals each evening and it depresses me, I'm sorry to say, and I wish I were back in Melbourne. I like this country, and I know that I'm half Australian – just like you're half American, aren't you? – but there are little corners of it that seem … I don't know the word. Is it *lost*? Is that what I'm trying to say? There are places where somehow everything is *lost* in the vastness of it all. The buildings stand there against a backdrop of emptiness, or mountains, or whatever it is and they seem adrift. It's like being on the sea. And if there's a wind, you find yourself thinking, *Where's this wind come from?*"

She wrote back to him: "I know what you mean about Australia. I liked it too – not that I saw very much of it. And I liked the people – I liked them a lot, but you could very easily feel lonely there, couldn't you?"

'Yes," he replied. "You could feel lonely."

She stopped saying very much about Singapore. This was not because she had no ideas as to what she was doing in her

Singaporean life – she and Greg spent hours imagining it, and his suggestions, although occasionally preposterous, would have made up a quite credible daily life – but she felt increasingly guilty about the fact that what she was saying amounted to lies. She was deceiving James, and she did not like doing it. And yet she had started it; the whole conception had been hers.

In due course she would tell him, she decided. She would make light of it – as if it were a long-drawn-out joke, and as harmless as a joke might be. He might be surprised, but surely he would not be hurt by what she would portray as innocent imaginative play.

"I'm going back early," he wrote. "The audit took less time than they thought we'd need and so it's back to Melbourne for all three of us. But not for long. Listen to this: Singapore. The firm has a big client there – it's an Australian engineering firm that does a lot of South-East Asian work and they're looked after by our office in Singapore. But one of their staff is in London for a month and another has been poached by an American firm. So ... Singapore for two of us from the Melbourne office – for five weeks – quite a big deal for a first year trainee but that's par for the course with this firm, apparently. Right, then ... dinner next week? I love Chinese food and somebody told me you can get it cooked on wood fires in Singapore. And there are these big food markets where you can eat – have you been? I leave here on Wednesday, which gives me three days to get ready after I get back to Melbourne. Tuesday or Wednesday suit you?"

She read the message twice, and then sat still, appalled by what she had done. She had known that there was a risk that her deception would be exposed, but she had not imagined that it would happen so soon. She went to Greg, who read the e-mail and then raised an eyebrow. "Exposure, Clove. It happens. So what are you going to do? Come clean?"

She shook her head. "I can't."

"I don't blame you."

"I'm going to tell him eventually. But I can't do it now. I can't face it."

He was silent.

She reached her decision. "I'm going there. As soon as I can."

"Singapore?"

"Yes. I was going to see Judy anyway."

He made a face. "Money?"

She explained about her father's gift. "I can afford it. I'll have to pay to change the ticket again, but I can do that."

He shook his head in disbelief. "I can't believe this, you know. You'll do anything it seems for this guy – anything. Except tell him the truth about how you feel."

"How can I?"

"Open your mouth and speak. It's that simple. Give him a call. Ask him. Say: *Are you still going out with that other girl?* And if he says yes, then end of story. If he says no, then you could say what everybody's been telling you to say. Get it sorted out one way or another."

"No."

"That's all you can say? No?

"Yes. I mean, no."

"I give up," he said harshly, and then, almost immediately, relented. "Sorry. I wish I could be positive, but how can you be positive about something that has disaster written all over it?" He repeated the word to underline his warning. "Disaster."

32

Judy gave her an enthusiastic welcome.

"I can't tell you how pleased I am that you're here," she said. "I've asked *tons* of people to visit me and not one has taken me up on the invitation. Not a single one – apart from you."

They were standing at the window of the spare room in her flat. This flat was in a building that was not high by Singaporean standards – four storeys, arranged around a courtyard dominated by an inviting blue swimming pool. Two young children, brother and sister, frolicked in the water at the shallow end of the pool, watched by a uniformed nurse. The nurse spoke constantly on her phone, occasionally getting up, mid-conversation, to admonish the boy for splashing his sister too enthusiastically.

"Those children," said Judy, "belong to some people on the floor below. You never see the parents with them – just one of the Filipina nurses. There are two of them – the Filipinas – and I've got to know one of them quite well, but not this one. They spend their lives working for other people, although they have children of their own back home. The other woman's sister works in the Middle East. She looks after the children of some ruling family over there. She says the children never even learn to tie their own shoe-laces because they have a Filipina to do it for them. Can you imagine that?"

Clover watched the children. She had grown up with that sort of thing in the Caymans, where the Jamaicans did the work of the Filipinas.

Judy looked at her and smiled. "The truth is – I'm bored stiff. I don't know what to do. I'm only here because my parents want me to be. I'm going to have to talk to them about leading my own life."

"Do another degree," said Clover.

"That's what I'm planning to do. That's what master's degrees are for, aren't they? To keep graduates out of the unemployment statistics." She paused. "How long do you want to stay?"

Clover suggested two weeks and Judy gave a cry of delight. "Oh my God, that's fantastic. I thought you were going to say two days. That's what most people do – they come here on their way to Australia or Bali or somewhere sexy like that and then they go. Or, in my case, they don't come in the first place."

Clover took a deep breath. She knew that she would have no alternative but to tell Judy about her deception, and now she did so. Hearing her own account of what happened only served to deepen her disquiet. "I know it sounds stupid," she said at the end. "But that's what I did."

Judy's reaction took her by surprise. "Totally reasonable," she said.

"So you don't disapprove?"

"Why should I disapprove? Nobody's died."

Clover said that she felt that she had involved Judy in her dishonesty.

"No," said Judy. "You didn't. It's entirely up to me as to whether I play along with this – and I'm cool with it. Absolutely. Men mislead women all the time – they're such liars – this is just a return match."

"You'll back me up? You'll go along with what I said happened?"

"Of course. Just give me the details."

She gave her the broad details of the imaginary life that she had created for herself. Judy listened with growing amusement. "We had a terrific time together," she said. "Our virtual life was much more interesting than real life."

"We're going out for dinner on Tuesday," Clover said.

"Tuesday? Good. I'm free."

Clover was silent for a few moments. She had invited herself to Singapore and she could hardly tell her friend that she was not welcome at dinner. Judy, though, picked up her hesitation.

"Sorry, it was going to be just the two of you. I shouldn't have …"

"No, I'd like you to come. You'll have the chance to catch up with him."

Judy did not protest. "All right. Thank you. I haven't seen him for ages. Not since Cayman, really – we didn't connect in Edinburgh."

"I'm sure he'll be keen to see you."

Judy smiled. "I know this really great place where everybody wants to go these days. My father knows the owner – we'll get in no matter what time we arrive."

She made a list of the places that she had mentioned to James in her e-mails to him, and asked Judy about these, reading out what she had written – the fiction of her created life.

Judy seemed bemused. "You wrote that about me?" she said. "You told him that we went out for a meal and saw that movie and so on? All of that?"

Clover nodded ruefully. What had started with so little thought, what had seemed so innocent and inoffensive at the time, had now taken on the appearance of a monstrous deception. "I don't know why I did it," she said. "Well, I do, I suppose … I suppose I wanted to be involved with him. I wanted him to pay attention to me and what I was doing. Does that make sense to you?"

"It does. In a way – as a form of attention seeking."

"I feel such a fraud," said Clover.

Judy laughed. "But you are," although she rapidly added, "No offence, of course."

And soon, rather sooner than she might have wished, James arrived in Singapore and telephoned from his hotel. She took the call with trepidation, signalling to Judy across the room. "Him?" mouthed Judy.

She nodded, and Judy gave the thumbs up signal.

After the call, Clover said, "He never phoned me before, you know. Or hardly ever. It was always me."

Judy was encouraging. "I've got a good feeling about this," she said. "I think that something's changed. I think it's over between him and …"

"Shelley."

"Yes. He wants to see you, I think."

"You really think so?"

Judy grinned. "Well, why else would he bother?"

"Maybe he just wants somebody to show him round Singapore."

Judy shook her head. "People don't need to be shown round Singapore," she said. "You get a map and places are where they're meant to be. It's very well organised. No, I think at long last he's come round."

"I feel as if I know this place," he said.

Judy had poured him a beer and was sitting opposite James in the flat. Clover was on the sofa next to him.

"You've been to Singapore?" Judy said.

"No. Not Singapore. This flat. Clover wrote to me and told me what she was doing. What *you* were doing."

Judy caught Clover's eye, and smiled. "Chick lit," she said.

"*Two Single Girls in Singapore*. How about that for a title? Fiction section, of course."

James seemed amused. "It wasn't very steamy," he said.

"The whole place is steamy," retorted Judy. "You've probably been in air conditioning since you arrived. Open the window. Let in the steam."

Clover felt uncomfortable about this exchange and tried to change the subject. "Judy knows this place for dinner," she said. "What's it called, Judy?"

The answer was addressed to James, and not to her. "Billy Lee's. It's mostly seafood, but you can get other things. He has this incredibly ancient chef – he's ninety or something like that, and he comes out and speaks to everybody and asks them whether they'd like to come and help in the kitchen. And when they say yes, as they tend to do, he says that it's the washing-up he was thinking of, and everybody laughs."

"That's where we're going?" asked James.

Again the conversation was between James and Judy. "We thought you'd like it," Clover interjected.

James turned to her. "But of course I will."

"I didn't know whether you liked Chinese food."

He smiled. "But don't you remember? We went for that Chinese meal in Cayman – a hundred years ago. Remember? It was Ted's birthday party – we were about twelve or something, and Ted's mother took us all to that Chinese restaurant near the airport and they had made a massive cake for Ted. Don't you remember?"

It came back to her. She remembered wanting to sit next to him, but he had been with other friends and she had watched him over the table. He had been her hero, the object of her admiration, her longing. It was well before she had an inkling of what love was like, but it was there, already planted, its first tender shoots about to take root; which would take over her life, she now thought.

For a moment she was back there. "I wanted to sit next to you," she said. The remark came unbidden.

James looked surprised. "To me? At Ted's party?"

Judy was watchful.

"Yes," said Clover. "I wanted to sit next to you, but you always seemed too busy for me. You wanted to be with other people." She stopped herself. She had not intended to say any of this.

James was abashed. "I'm sorry. I didn't mean to … to ignore you, or whatever it was I was doing."

Judy now entered the conversation. "Boys don't like girls at that age. They want to be with other boys. Look at groups of kids. The boys all talk together and so do the girls."

"Oh, I know," said Clover. "But they can still be friends, can't they? And lots of people are. Lots of people have best friends of the opposite sex when they're young."

Judy looked doubtful. "I don't think so. What do you think, James? Did you have a best friend?"

He picked up his glass. Clover noticed the pattern in the condensation where he had held it. His hand. James's hand. "I had a friend called Ted," he said. "I don't know whether you'd remember him from Cayman."

Judy shook her head. "No, I don't. We left so long ago."

"He's a friend of Clover's too. I suppose that Ted was my best friend for a long time. We went to different places, though, when we were sent off to boarding school."

"Ted's gay," said Clover. She felt a moment of doubt, and

wondered whether she had unwittingly betrayed a confidence: had Ted talked to James about that? She thought that he made no secret of it, but was not sure now that he had mentioned it.

James did not react. "Yes," he said. "Of course he is."

Clover thought she knew what Judy was thinking. Judy would be imagining that this was the thing that she – Clover – had failed to spot all along. James was not interested in her because of a very simple reason, and you, Clover, didn't pick up on it because you were too obsessed by him to see the glaringly obvious truth. Talk about naïveté!

But it was not true – it simply was not true. Ted and James had never been boyfriends because … She hesitated. Ted had confessed to her that he saw James in that way but had never hinted that his feelings were reciprocated. And James had had various girlfriends, which pointed the other way, except, of course, if he were repressing something.

"Women," said Judy, "like to have a best gay friend. He's no threat. You can talk to him."

"Of course," said James. "Whereas you can't talk to straight men, can you?"

There was a sardonic note to his remark, and Clover watched its effect on Judy. The other woman had to think quickly. "You can," she said, adding, "If they allow you. Straight men have barriers."

"Oh?" said James. "Do we?"

Do we, thought Clover. And she wanted to say to Judy, "That settles that." But then it occurred to her that it did not. It depended on the sincerity of the *we*. Or the possible irony.

Judy looked at her watch. "I reserved for about twenty minutes from now and we need to go." She turned to Clover.

"How should we get there, Clover? What do you think?"

She was taken aback by the question, and it occurred to her that in entrusting Judy with the story of her subterfuge she had created a hostage. She did not think that Judy was about to reveal her secret to James; rather, she thought that she was playing with her here – taunting her with the possibility of exposure.

"It's up to you," she said evenly. "I forget how we did it last time. Taxi?"

Judy grinned, acknowledging that Clover had batted back the verbal grenade.

"Taxi, then," she said.

They made their way to the restaurant. James was clearly excited to be in Singapore and asked Judy a series of questions as they made the taxi journey. Judy seemed to enjoy the attention; she knew the city well and he listened attentively to what she had to say about it. Clover sat back and stared out of the window. Everything was going wrong, and it was all Judy's fault. Somebody on their course in Edinburgh had once described Judy as selfish, and Clover had defended her; but the criticism must have been justified, as she was selfish here; an unselfish friend would never have suggested accompanying her as Judy had done.

In the restaurant, Judy paraded her knowledge of the menu and her few, mispronounced words of Chinese, patiently received by the staff.

"I'm trying to remember what we ate when we came here," said Judy, picking up the menu. "Do you remember, Clover?"

Clover looked at the selection. "You had far too much," she said dryly. "You felt sick. Remember?"

This brought a sharp glance, and Clover bit her lip. She would have to tolerate Judy, because a word from her could spoil everything. She did not trust her.

After the dinner, they picked up a taxi directly outside the restaurant. Judy asked James the name of his hotel and then said, "It'll make sense to drop you first. It's on our way."

James accepted. And then to Clover, "I'll call you. Are you free on Friday evening?" That was three days away.

Clover noticed Judy staring at her, and wondered whether she assumed she would be included in the invitation. "Fine," she said quickly. "I'm free." She stressed the *I*.

"I ..." began Judy, but James cut her off.

"Maybe you should come round to the hotel," he said. "We could go out somewhere from there."

She noticed that the remark was very clearly addressed to her and that it excluded Judy.

James turned to Judy, and said, apologetically, "School reunion time."

Judy made a carefree gesture. "Of course. Clover will know where to take you, won't you, Clover?"

"Yes," said Clover. "No problem there."

They dropped James off at his hotel and continued their taxi journey home. The tension in the atmosphere was palpable, although the niceties were observed.

"A good evening," said Clover. "Thanks for the recommendation of the restaurant."

"You're very welcome," said Judy icily.

"What did you think of him?" asked Clover.

"He's okay," said Judy. "Average. I can't see why you're so keen, frankly, but *chacun à son goût*, as they say."

Clover chose her words carefully. "I thought you took quite a shine to him."

"Did you?"

"Yes, I did."

"Well you were wrong," said Judy. "I like them a little bit more mature. But I suppose one has to take what one gets."

They reverted to silence.

Their dinner together had been on a Tuesday. That Wednesday, Judy had to attend a family lunch party with Singaporean relatives on her stepmother's side. It was the birthday of an aged uncle, and she explained that although she would have liked to invite Clover she would not inflict the extended family on her. "They'd give you no peace," she said. "They love asking questions. And you'd have to eat and eat in order not to appear rude."

Clover did not mind. She wanted to visit the Asian Civilisations Museum.

"Sure," said Judy. "You can go there."

"And I could take us for dinner tonight. Somewhere … Maybe you could choose."

Judy looked doubtful. "Our lunch will merge into dinner," she said. "Sorry."

"Oh well …"

"We could do something tomorrow," said Judy. "I have to meet some people, but we could go and have tea in Raffles. Everyone's ancient, but it's the thing to do in this place."

The suggestions were made without enthusiasm, and Clover decided that there might be a good reason for Judy's having received so few visitors. Judy was bored, she decided, and any visitor, she felt, would be sucked into her vortex of boredom. It was a state that Clover recognised from people she had known in Cayman: the boredom that comes with having money.

They both spent Thursday afternoon in the flat. The weather seemed particularly sultry, and they cooled down with a swim after lunch. There was a group of Russians staying in one of the flats, and they were in the pool too, shouting exuberantly. One of the men made a remark in Russian that was clearly directed against Judy, and was censured by one of the Russian women, who wagged a disapproving finger at him.

"These people are ghastly," said Judy in a loud voice. "Don't worry: their English isn't good enough to know what ghastly means. They're disgusting."

They went inside to escape the Russians and the heat. The air in the flat was chilled and Clover felt her skin tingling to its touch. Judy said that she was going to go to her room to read. "We can meet some people for a drink tonight," she said, "since your friend seems to be too busy."

"He said he has to work in the evenings," said Clover. "He won't be free until tomorrow."

"Of course," said Judy. "I forgot. Work." She sounded as if she didn't believe it.

"He does," said Clover. "They work all hours. They just do."

"Yes," said Judy. "Okay. They work."

Clover went to her own room and lay down on the bed. She picked up the magazine she had been reading and began to page through it. She dozed off.

She awoke twenty minutes later. She was thirsty – the effect of the dehumidified air. She sat up on the bed. There was a telephone in the kitchen and it was ringing insistently. She heard Judy open the kitchen door to answer the phone. The door closed behind her. She heard her talking, but could not make out what she was saying. There was laughter.

The conversation seemed to last about ten minutes. Then she heard Judy come out again.

"I'm going out to get some stuff for the kitchen," Judy called out. "I'll be about an hour or so. If you want to go down to the pool again, remember to take your key."

Clover replied that she would remember. The front door was opened and then clicked shut again.

Clover left her room and went into the kitchen. There was a large bottle of Badoit water in the fridge, and she poured herself a glass. She finished the glass and poured herself another half glass.

The telephone rang again. She hesitated. She could let it ring because it would be for Judy and not for her, but she was a guest, and guests had certain responsibilities.

She picked up the receiver.

"I'm sorry to call back," said a voice. "I forgot to give you the address to pass on."

It was James.

"James?"

There was a silence at the other end of the line. "Is that you, Clover?"

"Yes."

He sounded surprised. "But Judy said you were out. I called a couple of minutes ago and she said you would be out all day."

Clover said nothing.

"You still there, Clove?"

"Yes, I'm here. I'm surprised she said that. I was here all the time. In my room."

"Oh well, I called – the first time – to tell you about a change of plan. I've found a fantastic place for tomorrow. I gave her the name of the place but not the address. That's what I phoned back about."

"I see."

"It's just that I thought it would be easiest for us to meet there because I'm going to be near the restaurant. We have a meeting a couple of blocks away and it would save me going back to the hotel." He paused. "Would that be all right with you?"

"Of course."

"I suppose she thought you were out."

"I suppose so."

She wrote down the details and he rang off. She returned to her room and waited for Judy to come back.

"Did James call?" she asked.

Judy did not flinch. "I don't think so," she said. She had several shopping bags with her and she placed these on the kitchen table. "Were you expecting him? I thought he was working."

Clover shook her head. "No," she said. "I just wondered."

She decided to go for a swim in the pool by herself. She slipped into the water and swam slowly across to the other side.

They went out that evening with Judy's friends – two young men of about their age – both Australian – and a slightly older woman from Hong Kong, a barrister who had just started her practice. Clover enjoyed their company, but could not get out of her mind her distrust of Judy. One of the Australians whispered to her during the evening that he found Judy difficult. "How well do you know your friend?" he said.

"Not all that well."

He grinned. "Careful," he said.

"Oh yes?"

He winked. "Yes. Very careful."

"What do you mean?" she asked.

"Men," he said. "She likes men."

Clover smiled. "So?"

"Other women's," he whispered.

That night, Clover dreamed of her mother. It was a very clear dream, in which she was sitting with Amanda in the garden in the Caymans. Her mother was wearing her tennis outfit and a blue headband.

"Darling," said her mother, and then stopped.

Clover said, "I know what happened. I know who you loved and how hard it's been for you."

Her mother stared at her. "Do you really?"

And then she woke up. She thought of her mother, and the insight that she had had in the dream came to her, as knowledge now. *Her mother loved her father.* Suddenly she wanted to speak to her; to give her the forgiveness that a child may feel he or she must give to a parent – a forgiveness that usually comes only much later, when we come to understand that our lives have at heart been much the same life led by our parents, even if led differently in their externals.

She closed her eyes. The air conditioning was humming and a clock beside her bed ticked loudly. It was clear to her now. Her mother had survived it, and she would too. You can love and not be loved in return. You can live without the thing that you want above all else; you can be free of it. We all have to do that; we all have to make a compromise. She would let James go, as people everywhere gave up on the unattainable. And in giving up, there was a certain freedom, for herself as much as for him.

The pursuer abandons the pursuit and the quarry gets away; both are free, for the moment. Let some other girl – anybody ... but maybe not Judy – have him. He did not want her, and it was foolish, and ultimately self-defeating to carry on thinking that things could be otherwise.

She steeled herself to say goodbye. She would not say it in so many words, of course, but she would say it nonetheless, in any of the other ways in which goodbye could be said.

The restaurant was busy, and they were asked to spend some time waiting for their table in the small bar. It was an intimate place, and they had to sit close to one another on an upholstered bench.

"Your friend, Judy," said James.

"Yes," said Clover.

He shook his head in amusement. "At that restaurant – you know when you went out to the Ladies?"

"Yes?"

"She turned up the flirting. Full blast."

Clover said that she was not surprised. "But you didn't respond?" she said.

"Of course not," said James.

"She's not your type?" asked Clover.

James shook his head. "It's not that. It's because ..."

She waited.

"It's because I've always loved you," he said.

33

Amanda had suggested it.

"Picnics should be spontaneous," she said.

Clover thought about this. "Everything should be spontaneous
– sometimes. Kissing people. Eating chocolate. Dancing."

That reminded Amanda of a newspaper headline that she
had read about: *Dancing breaks out*. Dancing, like peace, could
break out – could overturn what was there before – when people
decided that they had had enough. "Yes," she said. "Yes."

They went to the place they always went to. Amanda parked
the car in the shade of a tree, as it was mid-day, and if she did not,
the car would be a furnace on their return. The heat pressed down
like an invisible hand, seeming to hold down even the surface of
the sea, dark blue and sluggish. There was the shriek of insects
in the air, an ever-present tinnitus, that Clover now realised she
had missed. In Australia it had been birdsong; in Scotland it had
been the sound of the wind; here it was the chorus of insects that
had always been there, a background sound to her childhood.

They did not bring much with them – a plastic sheet that
they had always used for picnics and had never replaced in spite
of the scars it bore; a thermos flask of iced water; a couple of
bread rolls into which Amanda had tucked a slice of ham and
the mayonnaise that she knew her daughter liked. It was too hot
to eat, but she thought a picnic required at least a nod in the
direction of food.

They looked at the sea.

"I'll swim a bit later," said Amanda. "I have to summon up
the energy."

"The sea's going nowhere."

Amanda smiled. "That's very profound, darling."

Clover lay back and closed her eyes. She had never thought about it before, but the only time that she would close her eyes in the open, outside, was when she was with her mother. She thought about this. Trust. Protection. It was something to do with that.

"Where do you think you and James are going to live?"

"We'll see. He has another year in Australia."

Amanda nodded. "I suppose we're always going to live apart. The family, I mean. Us."

Clover opened her eyes and looked at her mother. "It's because of this place, isn't it? It's because everybody here is from somewhere else."

"Yes, it is. But that's what the world is like. That's what it's becoming. Everybody comes from somewhere else. Living apart from the people you grew up with is nothing unusual."

"I'm not complaining," said Clover suddenly.

"I didn't think you were. But thank you for saying that."

"I mean it."

Amanda looked at her. It was a whole separate life that she had created; that was the miracle of parenthood, and it never seemed to be anything less of a miracle; you made a whole world; several worlds – one for each child. And then you let go of those worlds, as a creator might do of a world he has created; you let go and watched. "Why did he never say anything to you?" she asked.

Seeing her daughter's hesitation, Amanda was on the point of changing the subject, anxious not to intrude. "Sorry, I shouldn't pry."

"I don't mind. I don't mind at all."

Amanda waited. A small child had appeared out of nowhere,

it seemed, and was making her way on unsteady feet to the edge of the water. The mother followed, wrapped in a towel. They exchanged brief glances – acknowledgements of sharing the tiny beach – and then a hand raised in passing greeting.

"He thought I wasn't interested in him."

"Really?"

"Yes."

Amanda smiled. "Well, he was wrong."

Clover shook her head. "Maybe it was my fault. Maybe I should have told him, rather than letting him think that. And he said that he thought I was with somebody else."

"And you were."

"Yes, but only because I couldn't be with him."

Amanda pointed out that James was not to know that. "We all make that mistake, don't we? All the time. We imagine that people know what we're thinking, and they don't. We misunderstand one another."

They were silent as they watched the mother lift her child and dangle her toes in the water. The sea could not be bothered to respond. The child gave a squeal of delight and struggled to escape her mother's grip.

"We used to do that with you," said Amanda. "We used to swing you over the edge of the water. You loved it. I suppose you thought that we would let you go and you might end up in the sea."

"But you never did."

"No."

Clover looked away. "Thanks for all of that. All of it."

"For what?"

"For making the sacrifices you did. In your life …"

Amanda weighed each word carefully. "I didn't make any sacrifices. I found out that I didn't need to."

"I thought that," said Clover. "Or rather, I found it out. It came to me – sort of."

"That your father and I ..."

"Loved each other. After all."

"Yes, after all."

Amanda brushed sand off the edge of the plastic sheet, but stopped herself. You could not keep sand off you on a beach picnic. You had to give in. "People believe that love lasts forever. Or theirs will. That's what they believe." She glanced at her daughter. "I think that you've been ... well, just amazingly lucky. The two of you. Sometimes you find that. People meet one another when they're very young and they stay together for their whole lives, which is as close as we get to forever."

"Yes, maybe we've been lucky. I love him so much, Ma ..."

"Of course you do. Of course you do."

"I love him so much I could cry."

"Well, you mustn't. Not on a picnic ..."

They were distracted at that moment. The child had slipped from her mother's arms and fallen into the water. But she did not seem to mind. She was buoyant.